In this contemporary reimagining of Flaubert's classic, Sophie Divry makes painfully vivid the conflict between freedom and comfort that marks women's lives in a materialistic world.

It is the story of a woman's life, from cradle to grave, somewhere in provincial France, from the 1950s to just shy of 2025.

She has doting parents, does well at school, finds a loving husband after one abortive attempt at passion, buys a big house with a moonlit terrace, makes decent money, has children. All in the comfort that the middle-classes have grown accustomed to.

But she's bored.

No matter
what she does,
nothing truly satisfies her.

Will it take a ruinous affair to shake her sense of overwhelming ennui?

Also by Sophie Divry in English translation
The Library of Unrequited Love

Sophie Divry

MADAME BOVARY
OF THE SUBURBS

Translated from the French by
Alison Anderson

MACLEHOSE PRESS
QUERCUS · LONDON

First published in French as *La Condition Pavillionnaire*
by Les Editions Noir sur Blanc, Lausanne, 2014
First published in Great Britain by MacLehose Press
This paperback edition published in 2018 by

MacLehose Press
an imprint of Quercus
Carmelite House
50 Victoria Embankment
London EC4Y 0DZ

An Hachette UK Company

This book is supported by the Institute Français (Royaume Uni)
as part of the Burgess programme.

A CIP catalogue record for this book is available
from the British Library

ISBN (MMP) 978 0 85705 470 8
ISBN (Ebook) 9780 8 5705 469 2

10 9 8 7 6 5 4 3 2 1

Designed and typeset in Albertina by Libanus Press Ltd
Printed and bound in Great Britain by Clays Ltd, Elcograf S.p.A.

We cannot change our lives on our own and being free in our
    dreams means nothing.
The problem of freedom concerns the entire herd.
Either all the herd will be free, or not a single beast will be.

JEAN GUÉHENNO

PART ONE

It is a story that began before our time, that will continue for as long as we keep records, hold conversations, erect walls, dig with bulldozers, grow vegetable gardens, raise children, afford surveyors and engineers and workmen; for as long as it remains possible to meet in an air-conditioned room at the solicitor's to print out a deed of sale in four copies. It's a story that will carry on after we are gone, as long as there are couples to live there, to love and clean and do the place up and have people over – to live, in other words; for as long as they are fertile enough to reproduce, to give birth to a family with several members, and in this family there is you, the woman, M.A.

You are sitting at the kitchen table. Your gaze is absently deciphering the label on a jar of stewed apples that is standing on the plastic tablecloth. And in the early afternoon silence, the refrigerator compressor starts up.

It's a built-in model, one metre thirty high by forty-five centimetres wide, consisting of a white door with a little plaque on it which says BREUND CONFORT; a green light is shining; to the left of the diode a knob in the shape of a stylised snowflake reads SUPER COOL. If you press it, you will hear a little rumbling noise to indicate the passage to a lower temperature. The door is

9

covered with postcards and a dozen or so magnets; some are the size of a drawing pin – white, gold, silver, or black; there are larger ones: a square magnet with the drawing of a cat that says GATTO DI ROMA, and which must be a souvenir from Italy; a little wooden heart decorated with a flower and some sprigs of raffia; another magnet the shape of a camel; one an ostrich, and the last one, which must be from an African country, depicts a woman pounding grain. Several postcards are held in place by these magnets. On the uppermost one there is a sunset, with the inscription EL PORT DE LA SELVA, COSTA BRAVA; beneath it there is one featuring a landscape that says LES CLOCHES DES PYRÉNÉES, another one with the Moroccan desert, one from Greece, one from Petra in Jordan. There is a postcard with a dolphin peering out of a translucent sea, and the creature looks as if it's laughing; a second photograph is set into this first one, showing a beach full of bathers, and above the dolphin is written BONJOUR, and beneath it, DE CARNAC. On the fridge door there is also a photograph of three children and on it is written, "Happy Birthday, Mamie". Further down there is an older, yellowed photograph of a child squatting in a paddling pool; the boy must be four years old or so, he's having his bath, and he's smiling, squinting in the bright light; to the right of the basin a toy has been abandoned in the grass; to the left of the photograph is the aluminium handle which opens the fridge.

We now know that these magnets were presents from family members; we know that these postcards have been here for months, even years; we know that they will be moved as soon as new postcards arrive in your letterbox; we know that the children on the photographs have grown up, become mothers, fathers, and homeowners, they are travellers long returned to tell of their holidays, in another kitchen.

Whereas you, in moments like this, you are on your own, and you remember.

I

When you were little you often got bored.

You had to walk for ten minutes to get home from school. Your parents lived in a house in a neighbourhood that people in the village of Terneyre referred to as "the housing estate". The closest town was called Valvoisin, and the town council later renamed it Valvoisin-sur-Isère, but you didn't go there often.

Occasionally on a Sunday your mother would put some lamb's brains in a glass to soak; you were disgusted; you would turn your head to one side as you made your way through the kitchen.

"Oh, my . . . Such a sensitive child!"

On your papa's lap: "A farmer went trotting upon his grey mare, bumpity-bumpity-bump . . ."

You remember the motor oil in your father's garage. Six days a week he would hammer away on the cars, and you were proud as could be, because the family name was there on the sign.

When you stopped in to see him after school, you could smell that acrid mixture of oil, chains and tyres, and nothing seemed more beautiful to you than your papa in his overalls all smudged with black. He would take you in his arms and lift you up in the sky.

"Well, then, my little queen?"

"Come and give us a little kiss."

"Go on, one more spoon and then we can have dessert."

You were sitting on the schoolbench, rocking with laughter.

The taste of pencil lead between your lips. Your mother: "Stop chewing that, it's poison!" That word, *poison*, how it just made you want to suck on the pencil even more.

Things your schoolmates said:

"Open your mouth and close your eyes."

"I'm going to tell you something, but it's a secret."

"Liar, liar! She's in love!"

The metallic toothpaste tube that your mother was carefully rolling against the edge of the sink:

"Mustn't waste."

"Mind you keep clean!"

"Be careful!"

Suddenly a spark flew out of the fire and burned you. Your father quickly cut open a potato and placed it against your skin; the accident allowed for a different order of things, usually all you heard was "Don't play with your food."

*

You counted the days until your birthday. The big candle for when you turned ten.

You got a fever. An adult's hand on your brow.

On the kitchen table in Terneyre, vegetables brought home in the net of the string bag.

You remember the red-and-green-checked apron your mother used to wear over her skirt while she was cooking.

Her woollen dressing gown, how you liked to snuggle up against it.

Your pride when you overheard the adults talking about you. When they said, for example, "She's working hard at school", or "What a temper she's got!"

How excited you were, those first evenings your parents left you at home alone. You went and searched their room, you put on one of your mother's skirts, tried her lipstick. You pranced around in front of the mirror dressed like that, and lifted your hair up on your head. Suddenly the front door opened; quick, you hurried to take everything off. But even your fear was a pleasure.

Things your grandparents would say:
    "He's been poaching, one day he'll get into serious trouble!"
    "If we all keep to ourselves everything will be fine."
    "Poor woman, her husband drinks."

*

Your bedroom window overlooked a very narrow, very green garden.

The vegetables down at the end, a swing that no-one used anymore, a few hens that had disappeared by the time you reached your teens.

"They're too much work."

"And besides, they're filthy creatures."

Drawing flowers on blank pages, always the same drawing.

"She's a regular little woman."

"You'll end up making her depressed."

"Sometimes she answers back," said the French teacher to your mother, and they told you you were insolent. You asked what you were supposed to do after someone asked you a question, was it so bad to *answer*?

"Do you think we're stupid?"

"Go to your room."

"Don't you speak to me like that."

The magazines you bought in secret with your pocket money.

You listened to the radio in your room, your heart pounded as you watched the films on television.

You collected pictures of horses.

You were bored.

*

Then you left for the city to study. You ate sandwiches that cost ten francs, you got to know the names of the classrooms and lecture theatres, you smoked cigarettes, you could not sleep the night before an exam, you waited for buses and metros, you learned to order a pint and to join in the conversation when you were sitting around a table with a dozen friends or more, you read books in tiny print, you drew charts, you came to realise how expensive life was, for the first time you fell ill and your mother was not there by your side, on Friday evenings you'd go home with your load of washing, your parents seemed to be moving more slowly, their faces had aged, you couldn't wait to leave again, you took part in a general meeting calling for a strike, you went to a strange party, you gave sanitary towels to your girlfriends, you thought you were poor, since no-one was watching you ate your noodles straight from the pan, and then one day you got your degree.

But – before that, you had to *settle on your future*.

Your teenage self had neither the soul of an artist nor the vocation *to help others*, according to the careers adviser at the lycée in Valvoisin-sur-Isère. She suggested you study economics at a faculty in Lyon: as a rule, thought the civil servant, this went down rather well in your sort of family. "I think I've settled on a profession," you said, very excited when you went back to Terneyre that evening, and no-one found any reason to protest. A new world was opening up to you, a world where you would no longer have to listen to your father slurping his soup.

You would never go on what are called *business trips*, but your degree in economics meant you would be hired by the Bédani

Company in 1978, then by Coead in 1995. Thanks to this degree – quite sought-after back then – you would find your place in a market economy, and in those days, that meant a job that was done thoroughly and meant to last. So your life as a student was only a stage; difficult mornings after "the wild party last night"; shopping at the Prisunic; your first joint; losing your virginity; arguments with the neighbours, everything you would go through; just a necessary stage before you were hired to work in furniture manufacturing at Bédani, and later you were hired to monitor I.T. suppliers.

(We might note here that with that sort of university background you could easily have found yourself working in:

> baby food,
> egg noodles,
> telephone cables,
> industrial stationery,
> luxury lingerie,
> or atomic reactors.)

Because she was good at her studies, that little girl who only yesterday found all those forms her parents were filling out so mysterious; forms for their retirement plan, for the Sécurité Sociale, for credit; the little girl who had asked one day whether there was "a school for becoming an adult" would in the space of only a few years become a tenant, a student, an intern, an employee. You would move into a two-room flat and do what you had to do to have running water and a hook-up to the city gas line, since all it took was a few trips to the counter to obtain access to all the mod cons, you would make the most of them; without ever pausing to wonder how the pipes that warmed you in your flat had actually made their way from the lower echelons of some societal public works.

But for the time being: you were still an adolescent in your room with yellow walls in Terneyre. Everything around you seemed mediocre – your father's pleasantries with the neighbour, his arm across the hedge as he handed over half a kilo of green beans.

"We had a bumper crop this year. I've never seen the likes in ten years or more."

"Well, when you think of all the rain we've had!"

Getting the baccalaureate was what it would take to get away from there. You studied every night. But you were already having trouble concentrating; you stretched out on the bed. You were seventeen and melancholy and you stared at the ceiling. Outside the window, a car drove by. You took out some purple paper and began a letter to Catherine, a girl you had met in the first year of lycée who became your friend, until her father was transferred to Paris. Writing to each other had added another dimension to your friendship, something which elevated you above the common herd. You were not the only girl in the neighbourhood who found relief from boredom through this type of correspondence, but your letters were particularly touching. The lycée, the composition you had to hand in on Monday, and the latest argument with your mother featured large, but a few paragraphs further down you would go into the description of your ideal life: you would live at night and sleep during the day, you would go around the world and marry a dark handsome man you would travel a long way to be with; then; with a little ginger dog yapping by your side, you would run naked along the beach, rolling in the sand, returning at twilight to an immense house overlooking the ocean, and you "would be happy, infinitely happy" – you ended your letter with a joking aside to say that you were no fool.

Catherine's letters were laden with the particular mystery of her home in Paris. You watched and waited for the postman. Just the sight of the postmark PARIS-MASSY allowed you to envisage the Métro, the crowds, Brigitte Bardot . . . With the envelope in your hand you would rush upstairs, lock your door and, lying on your stomach on the bed, you would greedily decipher her handwriting. Catherine thanked you for your letter, she told you about her move to the capital, her new lycée, she told you she'd been to see the Eiffel Tower, the Trocadéro, Notre-Dame, the place de la Concorde, that she'd wandered around the Latin Quarter; you could hear all sorts of different languages spoken; this amazing city never slept. She swore to you that despite the distance you would be friends for life, "sisters of the heart". Your mutual pledges gushed forth in a burst of sincerity which you took for emotional depth, for love; because during adolescence one believes it's enough to cloak friendship with grandiloquent promises for it to exist in that form, and to endure in that form, and never become misshapen, consumed or eventually broken by life. You entrusted Catherine with your desire to escape your *bloody bedroom*, she scoffed at her old parents, told you that she wanted to run away "for real" . . . and your letters filled your hearts with dreams of freedom that echoed identically from Paris to Terneyre: after the baccalaureate, life will be ours!

The country was booming, it was a time for pleasure, and there was work to be had for anyone prepared to do their bit, as your young physics teacher enthusiastically informed you; but, above all, Lyon was only seventy kilometres from Valvoisin. What a joy it would be to get to know this great industrious city, to wander alone through the streets, to go to the cinema and then have a yoghurt for dinner if that was what you felt like. Ah, you wrote on the purple paper, you couldn't wait for the day when you could finally leave *this rotten hole* where the neighbours were always asking you about your latest marks at school. Worst of all were the ones who would call out to you as you walked home from school:

"Tell your papa that I'll come for the motor on Tuesday. Hey, you won't forget to pass it on?"

In the kitchen, more and more often, dinner ended in an argument.

"You're never happy!"

"Nothing is good enough for you!"

The door slammed, and there you were in tears, in your room. Major strikes all over France; in moments like that, your isolation seemed all the crueller, you would have liked to be with them – not the workers with their glum expressions, but the gang of long-haired Parisians, the very ones your father insulted in front of the telly; you went on sobbing with rage in your room, and now you pictured yourself as some *poète maudit* heading off down a dusty road with your pack on your back . . . Anything rather than stay here, engulfed by conversations about engines to repair and other things such as:

"Could you tell Renée to come and fetch her soup tureen."

"Hand me those socks so that I can darn them."

Sometimes it was so suffocating that you were haunted by the thought of suicide. You hurled yourself from the balcony and then came the terrible moment when your body was found, your parents' sorrow and remorse, the funeral and everything that people would say about you, how your destiny had been exceptional, misunderstood . . . These imaginings absorbed you, and you forgot about the pain that had caused them and which overwhelmed you again the moment you came to the end of your funeral. You curled up in a ball on your bed. If only you'd had brothers and sisters! Together you could have dressed your dolls, and played cowboys and Indians, and climbed trees, and at bedtime you would have read them fairy tales . . . Oh, it must be wonderful to be pregnant, you wrote to Catherine, it must be so sweet to touch your belly and feel a little thing moving. You would have several children, four at least, you would hold them tight so they would never be cold, you would all go for a walk in the wind, then have a delicious meal in the white house with their papa, the same one by the vast ocean, with the little ginger dog.

Otherwise, there was always reading: it alleviated the boredom. A schoolfriend had given you *L'Astragale*, you pictured yourself as a delinquent, chasing anything in trousers, but after an hour you'd grown bored and you went back down to the living room. You watched soaps on telly in which rich Americans made babies with women who had long cascades of blonde hair, then they married them in a convertible. In the kitchen your mother was mending a pair of overalls. She shouted at you, said you'd do better to do your homework than watch that rubbish.

You replied, surly as could be, that you'd already done your homework, and anyway, what did they know.

The next day you got up at seven. Your father had already left for the garage. Your mother couldn't help it:

"Sure you've got everything? Have you put it all in your schoolbag?"

"Maman, I'm not eight years old."

"I can never say anything to you!"

"Have to go, the bus is coming . . ."

Your first romance, at the sports complex in Valvoisin. Your mother had signed you up for gym class, because she was of the opinion that physical exercise was part and parcel of a decent upbringing (and because it was cheaper than her other idea, piano lessons), and your class was under the influence of girls who had lost their virginity quite early on, and who tried to outdo one another with snide remarks that were terrifyingly precise. You remember the oldest one, a regional balance beam champion whose breasts bobbed abundantly during the exercises; in the evening her boyfriend used to wait for her on his scooter outside the stadium; he had long hair and wore a leather jacket and the girl would swing one long leg over the seat to straddle it before clinging to his back. The other schoolgirls like yourself watched them ride off, and quivered.

You started watching what you ate. You hid a lacy bra in a drawer, you shaved your legs over the bidet; you would have your first kiss with a boy called Antoine, a member of the regional athletics team. You liked his smile, the way he walked, the way he carried his backpack. He stood there with you at the stop for the number 6 bus, a little stretch of pavement that became as romantic to your fifteen-year-old self as any Shakespearean balcony. You stayed there and let the buses go by as you embraced, and held hands, sharing the silly secrets of people of your age; and it was there that for the first time you would know the sensation of a tongue that wasn't your own inside your mouth, and that, for the first time, you felt a warm tide spread beneath your skin, delicious, paralysing.

Back in your room, you wrote page after page to Catherine; how eager you were to see Antoine again the following Wednesday, what he had said to you last Wednesday and, above all: was he in love with you? From the ground floor, your mother shouting:

"Dinner!"

That first love: scenes in your memory.

The day Antoine asked you whether he could be "more than a friend to you".

The day you went together in secret to the cinema.

The day he invited you to his house to "show you something, you won't regret it". He took you up to his brother's bedroom. You followed, a little afraid to be alone in a strange house, and then you saw a basket with a cat and her four kittens.

"Oh, they're so sweet!"

"They were born ten days ago."

The cat purred among her litter. You held your hand out to her.

"Can you pick one of them up for me?"

The boy crouched down and handed you one of the kittens. The warm, delightful feel of it on your skin. You caressed its little head, its tiny ears, and with a stiff neck the creature lifted its pink head, as if its blind eyes were hunting for your hand again.

"He's so funny!"

You were on your knees on the tiled floor, Antoine next to you. You could feel his arm against your shoulder, you could smell his breath and other scents emanating from his torso; then the delicious tide returned, with a violent rush, flooding your face, your legs, your entire body. So this was desire! And you thought only men could feel it so strongly. In a panic, you got to your feet:

"So, are we going to the cinema?"

Your little romance lasted a few weeks. Antoine wrote passionate letters. You still have them, to this day, in your room. All you have to do is open a shoebox and there they are, overflowing with words like:

> My love. I can't help but curse this pen and paper because all they do is remind me, so painfully, of the distance between us. I would like to take you in my arms and look at the stars. If you only knew how much I miss you: your face, your hands, the smell of your clothes. That was a good talk we had the other day. After I saw you at the stadium I danced all over my room, jumping up and down, I was that happy. How can I forget the sweetness of your skin? I've almost never had the chance to meet someone so gentle and beautiful at the same time. I can't wait to see you again. I just wanted to tell you that I miss

you a lot and grow fonder of you every day. Lots of
kisses, more and more, and then some more.

One day Antoine caressed your breasts. You let him.

One day he said, "Have you ever made love?"

You were speechless. Then he hurried to add, "I haven't, ever.
But my brother has."

"Your brother is seventeen. It's not the same."

You thought you had to justify yourself.

"I think you can make love only if you're really, really in
love."

In the end; the terrible sorrow that left you crying for an
entire afternoon, because you thought that Antoine had been
unfaithful to you with another girl from the gym; a young girl's
sorrow . . . But very soon you would have other boyfriends. It
was like a new game: walking on the beam and attracting boys.
Until the day you met with rejection. That same evening you
looked at yourself naked in your bedroom mirror, running your
hands through your hair and lifting it from your neck, putting a
hair slide in the mass of curls, only to have it fall down again. You
gazed at yourself and tried to determine whether you absolutely
were pretty (everyone said you were) and why that student from
the final year didn't want to *go out with you*. You were no longer
looking for one boy in particular, but for the warm wave that
expanded your chest and made you so powerful.

From downstairs, insistently:

"Dinner, I said!"

You put on your sullen face, the face of a princess who is
about to refuse to eat buttered noodles.

"You criticise everything! We'll see how you get on the day you have to cook for yourself."

Dixit the mother.

"Not to mention the fact that it may be you catch a man with what's below his belt, but you keep him with what's behind it."

Dixit the father.

Soon you would be sheltered from all this vulgarity. You had just obtained your baccalaureate. With very good marks. So you had surpassed your parents, and you'd be setting off down a path they hadn't been able to take when they were young; all they ever did was secretarial or low-level management work, putting their money aside for you, conceiving an only child in memory of their poverty: this child would be going up a rung. They could see it in your expression, that trace of scorn linked to your ambition. They talked about it in their room at night, they were proud of the way you were setting out to be successful at what you did; even if it meant they must be fearful for your sake; just as later on you would fear mistakes along the way where your own children were concerned; even if, as the years went by, they gradually stopped asking questions, since they couldn't understand what this job was that you'd been so highly trained for, but they trusted you; just as you wouldn't understand, in later years, when your son tried to explain his job to you, but you would trust him – because a time always comes when the work of raising a child is over.

But for the moment nothing had changed. On the telly there was the Tour de France. Your parents were celebrating your baccalaureate, your mother had cooked a good meal, without "making a fuss" either.

"We mustn't let her get all worked up."

"Now she's got to study hard at university."

To prepare your move to the city, your mother went with you to Lyon and back. It was a special time. You had to enrol at university and find a room. She surprised you by buying you some new clothes; they were almost fashionable.

"Because you're a big girl now, you can't go round wearing just any old thing."

Dinners in Terneyre were spent drawing up lists of all there was to pack, all there was to eat or not eat, say or not say, be polite to the professors, don't stand out . . . You lost your temper again. When it wasn't you they were talking to, it was the neighbours: "My daughter's off to study economics!" you heard, in the midst of the green beans.

You lay on your bed leafing through a magazine, scribbling the same old flowers on one page and thinking about the man who would love you for ever and never smell of sweat. Everything was too small for you here, that was for sure, and as your body sank into the winding folds of the bed you abandoned yourself to dreams of glory; you were silent, relaxed, satisfied, while night fell upon the neighbourhood. The tractors were back from the fields. The next day was a Monday. You gave Catherine your new address. Soon everything would be ready. These were your last nights in the family home, you switched on the radio to the programme where girls talked about their "passionate love affairs". Only a few more weeks and you'd be gone, you thought to yourself with a sigh – when you heard the old box spring bed creaking in the next room. You blocked your ears, disgusted. What?! Those two, who never touched, never shared a tender word, how dare they do something only lovers must do? You were outraged; to think that at their age something sexual could still happen, as demonstrated by the creaking of the old springs; and you turned up the volume on the transistor, trying to forget as quickly as you could the shameful agitation of the parental bedroom.

II

And then one day there you were, in the city. Your father had just bought the latest model Renault, a two-door saloon car with an extraordinarily roomy boot for such a small car, he had paid ten thousand francs, after all, but the dealer had given him a discount – and besides, as you assured him, it made him seem *young*. In those days there were only fourteen million cars in France. You were pretty excited, the three of you, sitting inside. But irrespective of the reason for the removal, and what makes it significant, in this case a child leaving home, in others a couple separating, or the death of a loved one, or the loss or change of one's job, a day like this, in the end, consists in transporting objects from one place to another. Your suitcases were loaded in Terneyre, then unloaded in Lyon.

"It's a very nice flat."

After checking the electricity meter, your father took you both out for a drink, and on the way he spotted other Renault 5s.

"It's true that in the city, it's convenient for parking."

You went into a real Lyon bistro, with checked tablecloths and a grumpy waiter. You looked at everything and spoke a lot. Your parents listened. You explained your university curriculum, they didn't understand, but they smiled, somewhat stiffly;

exactly the way you would smile at your son thirty-five years later when you asked him what "exactly" his job consisted of, and he said:

"Well, in a way, the general coordinator is the one who's the interface between the accountant and the manager, who lines the objectives of management up with the available financial resources, and his role is to ensure maximum rationalisation of the company's efficiency. It's both notification and analysis, in a way. What I like about it is that the general coordinator can even operate as a pilot, or [added Xavier when you looked at him, nonplussed] co-pilot, like on a plane . . ."

But it was already time to say goodbye. The next holidays were not any time soon, and they said you mustn't hesitate to come back for weekends, they'd go and fetch you at the station, because even if you were grown-up now you must never be ashamed of asking your old parents for help. The sound of the engine. Maman and Papa were gone.

You took a few dancing, gymnastic steps. You gazed out of the window – your gaze not yet blunted by habit – as the city began to twinkle with lights, and you felt a joyful urge run all through you, electrifying, irrepressible: a desire to go out and wander through the streets. These streets were cobbled, you'd noticed; the river Saône was beautiful; you would have to go and visit that park over there; come back for a coffee at this pavement café; but it was getting cool . . . Half an hour later, the fatigue of the long day made you turn back. You wanted to be on *your* street, in *your* building, to take the lift and turn the key in the lock. Silent, your flat was waiting for you.

And suddenly on that first evening as you were eating supper alone, rid at last of your father's odours, your mother's curlers, and assorted village gossip, instead of feeling free, suddenly you were afraid.

Solitude: that was your enemy.

Every morning when you got up one of the first things you did was to hold the electric coffee grinder between your thighs and press the red button; the grinder vibrated, making a shrill noise. Years later the slightest shrill sound grating harshly in your ears still reminded you of those mornings, those early days. The water boiled on the gas behind you. You scooped coffee into the filter, placed it over the coffee pot and poured the hot water into the filter, three times. The first time a crater formed inside the grounds, the second time you filled the water up the sides. You were haunted by that smell of coffee and the cold air, the unpleasant noise in your ears, those mornings as you waited for the water to drip, your gaze drifting to the linoleum kitchen floor. The third time you gave a circular twist of your wrist to empty the saucepan from higher up, and the grounds now formed a solid mass at the bottom of the filter. You yawned, thinking nothing, still waiting for the water to run through.

You took your time putting on your make-up; at least your mother wasn't there to watch you. Quick down the stairs, and you trotted elegantly as far as the Rhône and into the university building, your brain ready to be filled with *the major economic stakes of the future*. The air smelled of the refinery at Feyzin.

Mornings passed quickly. At the noon break you had to decide. If you had only an hour, you would eat a snack on a bench, then hang around in the corridors. If you were off for two hours, you would go home; but in that case, as you prepared a makeshift meal, between the fork and the knife as you sat down to eat, you felt a sudden malaise. You ate quickly. In the time that remained before heading back to class you took a nap, of sorts. It was a time of day when the sun shone too brightly on the dirty white surface of the sink, and a knot in your stomach made you listen out for the slightest sound from outside – the neighbour walking about upstairs, a car horn blaring below. You worried that you might be late, so you grabbed your satchel and took the same route as that morning, more sluggishly. A month went by. You knew all the streets in the neighbourhood, your curiosity was waning, you didn't have the courage to embark on long walks through the city centre, the only thing that became a regular temptation was window shopping along the rue de la République, but what was the point on such a tiny budget. You were seen working at the university library; there were some fine-looking boys.

Once you were back in your flat, at six o'clock, the loneliest time began. You could fill it doing the odd bit of shopping, or tidying the flat, or reading your Roneo'd course material. The ideal thing would have been to go to the cinema, but you didn't have the heart to go back out alone. You poured some rice into a pan, it was sure to swell, and every evening you re-enacted the disappointment of dinner. Whether you sat down to eat at seven or at midnight, whether you started with dessert, or didn't eat at all, there was no ritual to respect anymore, and this very vagueness made you lose your appetite. You chewed your grated carrots while staring out at the same urban landscape beyond your single window. Even if you listened to the radio, the absence of another plate beside yours left a shadow over your heart that you could not get used to.

At the entrance to your building there was a wide, tiled corridor, pale green and dark green. The tiles covered the walls to a height of two metres and ended in a scalloped frieze. You went up to a glass door and pushed it open. Beyond it were the building's letterboxes, and yours was on the bottom to the right, you didn't have any post, you walked up to the lift, parted the metal gates and pressed button 4. And then, borne upward by the mechanism, you relaxed. The brightly lit stairwell allowed a faint light into the lift: as it passed through the metallic bars, the light refracted onto the woodwork inside, tracing thin yellow rays, some rising, others falling, as the lift made its way past each consecutive landing. These interwoven rays also lit your face briefly, in the form of broken or continuous lines, and it was like a neutral time; the lift was slow, and you looked at your face in the mirror as it was latticed by these rays of light, and you went past each threshold with the strange impression that you were about to go straight through the ceiling. A few steps left to climb up to your floor, and you were home.

Dinner was eaten, dishes were washed, you curled up in your blankets, switched off the light but could not sleep. You felt better if you'd spoken to someone during the day, anyone. All you needed were a few words for your malaise to fade away: it could be the ticket-puncher on the tram, a lecturer, a fellow student; someone looked at you and your loneliness dissolved. But if, during that autumn when you discovered your own extreme shyness, you spent an entire day without speaking to anyone, your big eyes stayed open wide in the dark – because it is hard to fall asleep in a house where no-one else, in no other room; no child, no friend, no relative; is there to vanish with us into the night.

As you tried to fall asleep in that flat without a past, you remembered those festive meals, as a tiny girl, when you would fall asleep on a chair in the middle of the room where the adults were dancing, and someone – your mother or father or an uncle – would always pick you up in their giant's arms and take you into a room where the other children were already sleeping; the adult would place you delicately on a bed, remove your shoes and tuck you in, and your last image was of that person going out and closing the door, leaving behind a feeling of deep security, a breath of sovereign warm air beneath which you immediately fell asleep again.

You moved. You pulled the blanket up to your chin. The monotonous roar of traffic resonated from the riverbanks. You stared at the dark spot left by a poster on the wall. Then the fatigue, a sort of despair or disappointment, and everything fractured. And you wept in your bed, as sad as a punished child. In the morning the alarm rang. No-one had made you any coffee and no-one had bought you any croissants. The weekends left you at an ever greater loss as to what to do.

So those early weeks in Lyon have been erased from your memory as surely as the dreary ennui of a nameless dentist's waiting room; since these were moments with neither charm nor use nor meaning, moments with which there was nothing to be done, they faded into a sort of cottony substance, to disappear from memory as soon as the day was over. The malaise, the fear remained, and you hid it from your parents whenever you rang them from a telephone box. You told them that everything was fine, that your flat was nice, and the city was "beautiful and misty", but in fact, Chloé would eventually erase those early weeks, Chloé, your fellow student and friend who was suddenly there in your life. And time, at last; what you'd been dreaming of; time at last began to pass more quickly.

The first picture of Chloé was of a girl with long hair sitting high up in the lecture theatre, a girl with a ringing laugh that got her noticed, by the lecturers too. A number of boys gravitated around her, and very quickly they formed a distinct little troupe. At noon they ate tuna sandwiches and discussed social issues. There was something superior about Chloé; you thought she was from Lyon, and for that reason, you didn't dare speak to her. But she had noticed how pretty you were, and how some of the boys from her group were glancing your way. It was she who, one day, complimented you on your skirt, saying it had "an unusual cut". Without thinking, you replied that your mother had made it. Contrary to what you had feared, she was all the more admiring.

"My mother never got any further than the laundry!"

It began with laughter during the breaks between classes, and coffees at the bar, then lunch at the student cafeteria, she came to your place, you went to hers, you became inseparable. The entire city was changed. At last you had someone to walk around with in the evening, someone to wait for you outside room number 6, to talk about the dishiest boys and the meanest lecturers. Chloé had you try on her clothes and gave you advice on how to be "even prettier". You told her about your father and his garage, the gym, Antoine and your first kiss. She listened as she made tea on the electric hot plate, and said "Oh, crumbs", or "That's fabulous". Chloé wasn't from Lyon after all, but from a province even more remote than yours, Savoie. But she had been born in Paris, and it started both of you daydreaming.

"Do you remember anything?"

"We left after they got divorced, my sister was four, I was two: no memories at all."

"If I lived in Paris, I would never leave."

"Absolutely! If you knew what yokels they are, where I live now . . ."

She in turn told you how her father had left her mother, how she had smoked her first cigarettes, how you cannot possibly mess up crêpe batter. You remember; how you talked endlessly, drinking cheap wine, while the slightest rumour, the slightest urge to travel, an upcoming assignment, a wink in the lecture theatre, everything was dissected in that intoxication of speech you had missed so much. When the bottle was empty, you put on a record and sang refrains such as *Tell me you love me, I'll be waiting for you, But what are you doing here?* In those days all you had to do was take an L.P. from its sleeve and put it on the turntable.

You wanted to move in together with the start of the next year. In Terneyre they were afraid of being "ripped off", so they called Chloé's parents. And given that they were more or less from the same social background, it all went well. You had passed your exams, surely your parents could trust you.

"You'll save money."

"If you fail your year, a lot of good our money will do us!"

"It will be fine, I won't fail."

"It's alright for you. You always think everything will be handed to you on a silver platter."

Fortunately October always follows September. And it was time to go back to university, back to Lyon, back to Chloé. In your flat on the avenue Berthelot you furnished the living room with nothing but a low table and pouffes, no doubt you were thinking that chairs were for old people. You cooked, Chloé did the washing-up. Goodbye blues on the rue des Remparts-d'Ainay, you now belonged to a group where names mingled, Gilles, Régis, Juliette, as did flats, you would sleep over at each other's places, you went on camping trips together, you were always prepared to help out in the event of a bicycle puncture or a broken heart, you were always available for a pub crawl, especially to La Renaissance, your local along the avenue. After it closed you would go home to your living room with the pouffes. You made pasta, Gilles would hold the ketchup bottle above your plates and douse them all at the same time, there were splashes and screams, and exclamations like "Isn't this fun?", "Go on, tell us", "No, honestly".

There is one photograph left from that era, a photograph that went everywhere with you for a long time before it was glued into an album no-one looks at anymore except during the random moments of a major cleanout; when we decide to tidy an entire cupboard, because it's springtime, because "I've been meaning to do it for so long", but no sooner do we begin than we stop, the moment we come upon a dusty photograph album, we open it, and we linger over an image, full of emotion;

and when we go back to work later on, our hearts are heavy and yet somehow warmer, as if we were inhabited by the fleeting, happy faces of our youth.

In this photograph there are five of you, in the room with the pouffes, Fabien, Régis, Chloé, Viviane, and yourself. The three girls are sitting on the floor and the two boys are standing. Fabien, on the left, has a pale collar of beard on his face, and he's pointing at the girls; Régis has his arms folded over his guernsey. You are crouching in the middle, your hands in your lap, you're wearing a flowered shirt; you have a splendid smile. What strikes you today is the uniform slimness of your bodies, your long legs mingling with the table legs, your hands waving a cigarette towards the camera lens; your slimness is emphasised by your tight-fitting clothing – you are all wearing denim – and boys and girls alike have the same shoulder-length hair, the same colourful polo-neck jerseys clinging to your torsos caught in an identical position. How young you were then, without children, without commitments, you were constantly talking, and floating over everything, singing, smoking, dancing, laughing loudly.

Your gang went to Spain the following August. What you remember about the trip:

the portraits of Franco; you thought that was just his first name, and you were surprised everyone was on such familiar terms with a head of state;

the smell of the Deux Chevaux, when the back seat heated up in the sun;

the way the shops re-opened so late in the afternoon;

the taste of *horchata*;

but above all the sea, it was the first time you spent that long there.

Your campsite was right by the beach. As soon as you woke up you went swimming. "The water is pure ecstasy," you said when you went back for breakfast. The boys smiled at you when you joined them by the camp stove. Perhaps they sensed how when you went swimming something opened up inside you, you laughed so freely when you came back to them, and the salt clung to your skin. In the evening you swam together, then with your bare hands you ate the grilled sardines you'd bought by the roadside; in the distance, a guitar; at moments like that every-thing was so beautiful; you felt so good that the red sun slipping down into the blue gave you an almost metaphysical sensation.

A young Spaniard who managed to find his way into your bed at the youth hostel left you with an additional memory: the loss of your virginity. When that same Pedro kissed you in the bodega, you played along, you wanted to know what it felt like to desire *all the way*. So why, once you were in the room, did you no longer really feel like it? You did it anyway, as much out of curiosity as politeness; the dominant sensation was not pleas-ure, but rather the embarrassment of being naked with a naked man. Fortunately Chloé let you talk about your experience for hours.

"You might think this is trivial, but I didn't think I'd have to open my thighs so much."

As for the sea, you would miss it. Lying in the sand, you let out a sigh. How unfair it was that the next day, and the day after that, the Spanish sun would go on setting over the waves without you. In France, of course, nothing could be so beautiful. You swam one last time, and there was a great drunken party before you went back to Lyon. Three weeks later you were all together again in your shared flat. Or perhaps the photograph was taken that evening when you all asked each other, "What is your goal in life?" Each of you had answered in turn; you remember what you said; *your goal in life was to be happy*; you all agreed on this point as well: *to be free, travel, find love, have children, be fulfilled by your work*. Today you realise that you thought you would stay friends all your life, whereas only a few years sufficed for your gang to scatter or simply vanish, without animosity, simply because people moved, found a partner, or had babies; you would write a few letters, meet for dinner once a year, then once every two years, then a phone call, a Christmas card, finally just a thought. Chloé would remain, and François, of course: the sea leaves behind a sediment.

Régis had invited him to a party at your place after the ping-pong lessons they were taking together. Since François had come by bike, his face wore that poetical air easily acquired by a reasonably attractive young man when his hair is dishevelled. He stood against the wall, visibly ill at ease in these early hours of a drinking party. You felt almost sorry for him, and went up to talk to him, even asked some questions. François answered at length. He had decided to study mathematics somewhat by chance, even though he didn't understand everything, he liked it, he lived in Villeurbanne, he thought it was very kind of Régis to have invited him, he was afraid of failing his exams. The serious tenor of his conversation set him apart from your friends and their insane laughter, they were already drunk, and the contrast made him interesting. The conversation continued.

"If you fail, you can do something else. It's not uni that makes you smart." (You'd liked saying that ever since you had started university.)

"True. Particularly as I have no trouble adapting, apparently I'm very easy-going."

"It's funny, my parents have always told me just the opposite!"

You immediately felt safe with him. You were both in the kitchen now, he was sitting, you were standing, taking some biscuits out of the cupboard. "I didn't dare ask, but ping-pong really gives you an appetite." He ate. You gave him a glass of water and began telling him how eager you had been to come to Lyon. He in turn described how walking along the river banks gave you such a feeling of freedom. It was absolutely fascinating.

"The Rhône above all. The current is really strong!"

"But the Saône, too; it's smaller, but I like it a lot: you feel like you're in the countryside when you cycle alongside it after days of rain."

He told you about his brothers, whom he missed, and you told him how hard it had been not to have any other children to play with.

"You've no idea how miserable it is to be an only daughter."

He agreed with you. That was why, later, you would have several children.

"It's true that growing up an only child is no fun . . . I don't think we're meant to be alone. I like to see people. For example, I go first thing in the morning to have my coffee in a café, at the bar."

Only a man, a real man, could do that: drink his coffee at the bar.

"But at the same time, if there are too many people in the lecture hall or on the tram, I'm glad when I can find some peace and quiet at the library."

"It's so true, I miss the silence of the countryside. Sometimes you want to find a refuge, hide yourself away . . ."

He stared at you intently as he said these last words. You lowered your eyes. François was wearing corduroy trousers and a cashmere jumper that looked as if it must be as soft as a plush toy. Without thinking, you asked him if you could touch the wool: "I've never seen one like this." François, surprised, tugged on a stretch of jumper for you to touch. But while your fingers were stroking the weave, a delicious awkwardness came over you. François was still looking at you when a noise made him start: the entire gang was leaving, yelling their goodbyes. The electric clock in the kitchen said it was two o'clock in the morning – it was a little round clock with one battery that hung above the gas cooker, just another example of the multiple plastic objects that had invaded French interiors from the 1970s on; the designers meant for it to be extremely simple, as different as possible from the over-elaborate aesthetics of pseudo-antiques. Its two hands, red with round tips against a white background, were like a beacon in the house; you could read the time from the hall by the front door, it warned you when it was time for class, and when a silence fell during a conversation, the clock's ticking carried on. François didn't leave. You told yourself it would be hard to get up the next day, but then you thought of all the times back there in the room where you grew up when you had wondered when you would meet someone; someone who would understand you; and now you were there talking to this stranger, each of you adding to the other's words in a delicious affinity. How you would have liked for that time to last, despite the fact your eyes were closing, lulled by François's monotonous voice as he told you how he used to build cabins in the forest with his brothers.

"You are so lucky! I'm an only child."

You were repeating yourself. There was a silence. François got up.

"I hope I haven't outstayed my welcome."

"'Course not, it's been great."

You kissed him goodbye, clumsily.

François was so deeply affected by this encounter that he went to bed leaving a sink full of dirty dishes, which was not at all his style, as a tidy boy. As for you, you didn't go to class that day, you spent hours talking about him with your girlfriends, reconstructing your conversation, wondering whether you were "in love".

"You can tell right away when you're in love."

"Not necessarily, it can be like a spell, you know, a crystallisation." (Juliette was studying literature.)

"If you're in love, you have to think about him all the time."

Later, to Chloé, you said:

"It could be – remember Pedro in Spain – it could be that it's only desire."

"In any case, François isn't the type who goes to bed with a girl just to have fun. You can tell that right away."

"He does indeed seem much more romantic."

"You have to find out if he has a girlfriend."

"Can you look into it? I don't want him leading me up the garden path."

You were surprised to find yourself using your mother's expressions: lead me up the garden path, let people walk all over you, I wasn't born yesterday . . . You also found yourself remembering tragic lives: all the women who were cheated on, abandoned, kept by depraved men or killed by back-street abortionists. Two years ago, when you arrived in Lyon, you wouldn't have cared. But, after all, perhaps your mothers were right: for all that you admired the sort of woman who didn't wear a bra and took her pick among several lovers with whom to *have it off tonight*, you had been so terrified your period might not come, after Pedro! For ten days you had feared the worst. At the thought of being pregnant, you felt like a slut, then afterwards you were ashamed you had "given in" so easily to a stranger. It did not help that your first penetration, after a considerable amount of chat, had been a disappointment. Pedro left quickly the next morning and because you hadn't slept well, you were tired, you remember; not the tiniest wave in the sea had changed. Love had to be something else. So everything that you had liked about Spain; giving yourself to a near stranger; everything that had made you tremble when Pedro went up to you in the bodega; to learn about physical love, to be possessed by a man with a dark complexion: all of that, in the light of François's tender face, became a counter-example. You secretly disapproved of the way Chloé slept around. You thought that you, on the contrary, were ready for *a real relationship*, in order to build something with the man who would be *the one*.

"I don't want to be taken in anymore."

You said, in the tone of a woman who has a long history of disappointing relationships.

Your thoughts latched easily on to François; you wondered whether he was the one, the man who could love you, reassure you, surprise you, understand you even when you hadn't said anything, protect you yet leave you free, be faithful to you, raise your children, earn a good salary and not come home late. Did he fancy you? Did he want to go out with you? Did he think you were pretty? And you thought again of that unsettling moment when you touched his jumper.

The hands on the kitchen clock turned for ten days before you met outside the Pathé cinema. You had accepted his invitation with joy, but now that you were alone, you both felt awkward: he was silent, you were talkative. When the lights dimmed in the theatre you were sorry your companion did not try to caress you, and he let you have the entire armrest. Then you forgot his presence. It was a good film and afterwards your conversation focused on the plot and the characters. François listened to you.

"That's great! Men don't often listen."

Said Chloé, subsequently.

He took you to a pizzeria and paid the bill.

"That's classy, don't you think?"

He walked you back to the avenue Berthelot. You talked for another hour and still didn't manage to say goodbye. You didn't dare ask him to come up.

"You're such an idiot! I would have asked him up for a nightcap."

But François had already qualified Chloé – in a friendly enough manner – as being slightly "out to lunch", and you had a sense that he liked serious girls. You swore once again you would not give in easily. As soon as he had ridden away on his bicycle, you went up the stairs four at a time; radiant and hysterical, you woke your roommate up to tell her about your evening. François, you told her, among other things, had failed his exams, and didn't know what to say to his parents, so you had been searching for solutions for this very romantic failure, and he suggested another evening at the cinema, "regardless of the film".

"He said that? Then it's in the bag!"

Indeed. On March 12, 1974, while you were waiting for him for the second time in front of the posters at the Pathé, your future husband, after two conventional pecks on the cheeks, without a word, kissed you right on the mouth. You thought that was ever so bold!

"Yes, I'll grant you that, it's not bad."

François then asked you if you wanted to see the film. You sensed he didn't want to, so you said no. He put his arms around you again, and the two of you stayed out in the street for a long time. You walked wherever the wind took you; lost, happy, stopping in a well-lit café, then setting off again; he held your hand and his eyes were gleaming, he kissed you again, then as you moved apart you stood by his side and started walking again; and even today, as in the past, you see lovers walking like this, exhilarated, a little wobbly about the legs yet they are tireless, walking through a city only they can see, a city that has opened its gates to them alone. And that evening it was the two of you, it was actually you, that couple embracing, while cars slipped indifferently by, their yellow beams illuminating your faces; that was you crossing that majestic bridge, and it was he who kissed you against the railing, the lights of the city reflected in the river in a thousand shimmering stars and, high above, the moon: of course.

"It's so beautiful!"

You confided to him in a whisper that as an adolescent you had wanted to commit suicide, not only out of despair, but also to make your life into "something exceptional". François said hotly:

"But you're an exceptional girl!"

You kissed him right on the mouth. He held you close.

"You know, I was afraid just now that you were going to reject me."

"Reject you, me? I'd sooner die!"

And as just then you stumbled on the pavement, you added:

"Well, perhaps not right away!"

And for the first time since you had met you were laughing (in fact, that was the problem with François, and you could have noticed it right away: he was a calm, serious, reliable boy but, with the exception of a few fleeting gestures which over a lifetime could be counted on the fingers of one hand – gestures like that kiss on March 12 which had required a great effort on his part – he rarely displayed any originality or humour.) You could not tear yourselves apart, so you went to his flat. François could sense, by the way you were suddenly, if slightly, more distant, that *you didn't want to*, he didn't try to make you change your mind, no doubt he was secretly relieved by your reserve, because he was not a man to make multiple bold moves in one evening.

He let you have the bed in his little bedroom and he went to sleep on the sofa. Exhausted by all the emotion, he fell asleep very quickly. The next morning you were woken by the sound of the shower.

It all seemed so natural. Like you, François took his coffee with sugar and preferred biscottes to bread. You parted outside his building saying "See you tomorrow", and that was how your life as a couple began. A few days later you were sitting on his bed. He was stroking your breasts, he told you you were beautiful, that he'd been in love with you since the first day (or something like that). What was the point of acting modest anymore since you were sure he liked you? You helped him undress you. He kissed you, you touched him. It was not frightening to sleep with François, it was just another way of continuing your conversation, it was gentle and uncomplicated; you made love and then made love again for most of the day; at last; the warm wave was able to spread all through you; at last that moment where we can hold another person close, a person who desires us.

And then; when you took the train on Sunday evening, after a short break in Terneyre; when your father dropped you with all your suitcases at the station at Valvoisin – the old man had insisted on boarding the train with you to be sure you had a seat – and the words he spoke were tender, a tenderness he did not ordinarily express, but since he was alone with you for a moment without your mother; he squeezed your cheek in his podgy fingers, "Take good care of yourself, pet", and his eyes were not the same colour. But you didn't notice his deep affection, you were waiting for the stationmaster's whistle. When at last the train began to move, your father waved to you one last time, then he walked away, both proud of his student daughter and heavy-hearted to be going back to a house where your presence, even sullen, used to give a different hue to his all too similar days. The old man went to be with your mother. You did not know that that evening would be sad for them, that it was painful for them to come to realise – perhaps individually, perhaps together – that their daughter was slipping away from them, making her own life now, *that's the way things are,* and they didn't know that the moment you were settled in your compartment, you, that very child whom they had cared for and brought up, whose nappies they had changed, now that very girl would tilt her head to one side and with her gaze slipping backwards over the landscape, would wallow in delightful thoughts about the man who loved her. That Sunday spent at your parents was left behind as quickly as the local hills to give way to a broad plain where thoughts of love could spread wildly; and while every time the train stopped at a station it would rouse you briefly from your dreams of love, the way brackets suspend a sentence for a moment, the slight jolt of every new departure plunged you once again into your tender languor. You were thinking of his smile, his hair, his caresses, the first things you would soon say in Lyon; you wondered if he would be waiting for you on the platform, you were drawing up a list of all his qualities; you played back the moments you had already spent together, noticing, as you brought them back to life in the major key of your imagination, how kind a certain gesture of his had been or how burning his gaze could be when he looked at you; you thought about him with the kind of distance a vision from high above can give to a familiar land-scape; and honestly, honestly, you could find no fault in him.

He was Man, he was Love. No-one in the compartment dared disturb your somnolence. Halfway there, your daydreaming, together with the swaying of the train, aroused the desire that had been contained by absence. Through your half-open eyes you saw a cattle farm, a square church tower, the *route nationale*. You gave one last thought to your parents, they were frozen in the last position you had seen them in, as if you alone would be continuing the true flow of life. Your excitement was growing, secreting the most violent thoughts. What if there had been an accident during these few days without him? Did François still love you as much? You pictured his mother dead, his apartment destroyed by flames, another woman come to tear him from you; fear was stifling you, a fear you took a strange pleasure in fuelling. But the multiple jolts over the points informed you of your arrival. You saw the smoke from the refineries, the basilica, the vastness of the city made your heart swell with a warm vanity. You knew that at the heart of this sprawl of roofs, roads, buildings and chimneys, of aerials and smoke, at the heart of this mass of anonymous inhabitants a man was waiting for you; the one who at that very moment was crossing murmuring avenues and boulevards; avenues, boulevards and narrow streets that you would walk down together on your way home; you would hurry through the rain, he would touch your hair and your neck and say "I missed you"; so your feverishness, once they had announced the final station, made you stand waiting in the corridor to be able to rush out onto the platform to look for him, and, as you had agreed, if he wasn't there you would go to your place, if he was there you would go to his place . . . he was there!

Two lovers kissing in the crowd.

III

From the 1960s on, the country began building a network of roads exclusively for cars that within four decades would surpass ten thousand kilometres. At the time it was hoped that these motorways would make it possible for every region to open up and develop, and most of us thought, along with President Pompidou, that the private car was an instrument of liberation that would enable people "to leave when they want, go where they want, and stop where they want"; the people of France would therefore become accustomed to brief pauses at motorway rest areas, to industrial food, and to taxes – supposedly temporary – in the form of motorway tolls. As for the localities cut in two by the asphalt, they would witness the overnight appearance of graffiti proclaiming VILLAGE DESTROYED BY THE A8, denouncing what the engineers in their research consultancies referred to as *noise issues* as they placed their faith in future technologies to eliminate them. The result of all these roadworks was that in 1976 the cars that took the A43 out of Lyon would enter the Épine tunnel forty-five minutes later. At the other end was Chambéry. It was to this city, or more precisely, to a two-room flat in a four-storey building, that you would move that year, with François.

You experienced the move as an important choice in your life, a decision that required you to set aside other choices. At the time you did not know that this flat would only be another transition before you settled down for good, before motherhood would moor you to a well-charted everyday life: the children's bath, the evening meal, Saturday shopping; before your position at Bédani; before the indivisible property, the plot and land in the locality of Empan-sur-Nive, there came François's creation of what you both, all life long, would refer to as "the agency". It was with this in mind that you went to visit the two-room flat.

"It's only a ten-minute walk from my work."

"Rents are cheaper than in Lyon."

"Yes, monsieur. And in this sort of building you have all the mod cons – there will even be a telephone connection within the next three months."

You had a man in your home, who was there for you, who could receive all your effusions of love. On the mirror in the bathroom there were words, written in lipstick, "You are the best", "Courage", "Have a good day, my love"; even the most insignificant discovery – for example that François liked to eat his salad together with the main course – was a source of additional joy. After a day apart (you were looking for work and decorating the flat, François was at the agency), you were together again, and you shared with each other everything you had done right down to the most trivial incident. An hour later you would go out onto the balcony to smoke, and you listened as the traffic grew lighter; you talked again of how you first met, each of you describing for the umpteenth time all the emotions he or she had felt on March 12; even though you concluded that those moments would always retain *an element of mystery*. And when an hour later François dozed off in your arms, you could almost believe that you were not like other couples, that you were unique, undoubtedly more in love than any other couple on the planet.

One thing was certain: François loved you deeply, sincerely, stubbornly, uniformly. He was solid love. Your displays of affection were something he received stammering with happiness, and in return he showered you with kisses, compliments, plans for the future. So many compliments. François praised you in particular for having taken care of the rental of the two-room flat while he was getting his bearings at the agency. He thanked you for having dropped your plan to go on with the internship at Panzani, because you said you would find another job easily, since you were "a skilled graduate".

"You believe in yourself. That's good, that's brave."

"But so you do, darling, and you've been brave, too."

François was all the more impressed in that he had been raised in the shadow of two brilliant older brothers and often lacked self-confidence. That was why you wrote "courage, you're the best" on the bathroom mirror, so that in you he would find not only love but also the fervour of an admirer; for, like most men, François had a childish, narcissistic, vital need to see himself twice his actual size in his wife's gaze.

All these gratifying discoveries, not to mention other more physical sources of satisfaction, had made your presence indispensable to his well-being. You were his "breath of fresh air", and he was your "reassuring support". Words you had come on during the preparation for the wedding. Initially a joke, then endorsed by your parents, *real sticklers for things like this*, the notion of marriage had found its way into your discussions. Besides, it was only normal to get married when you wanted children.

"And not just one child, that would be too sad."

"Life with you is never sad."

"Thank you, my love, it's kind of you to say that."

The preparation for the wedding consisted of three two-hour meetings at the parish of Saint-François.

"It's very enriching."

Or so you said to your old friends, who were also in a pre-matrimonial phase. There were fourteen of you at the recently renovated presbytery. One post-conciliar Catholic couple introduced a topic of discussion which placed the emphasis on the necessity for dialogue and the expression of one's needs, while listening respectfully to the other; each partner then had to spend some time alone to think about a particular issue, then in the next phase you spoke as couples, and finally shared your experiences.

"A breath of fresh air" was what François had written on a sheet of paper during one of those meetings. You had charmed him because you liked to be playful, have fun, run in the rain, go camping, pick flowers, drink until you were tipsy; and there was your unpredictable side; when you went to fetch him at the agency without telling him and then took him to eat chips in town. François loved that, just as he loved seeing you painting the walls in your flat, and celebrating Christmas "just the two of us"; yes, those were happy years in Chambéry; in those days you were not yet clearly fenced in, you loved the novelty of everything, you loved waking up next to him, laughing, making love, opening a bottle, playing cards until late at night. You loved all that. Life with François meant life with the most conciliatory and amiable of men, "a reassuring support", as you put it. François took in your words with a breath of manly pride, and the printer looked on as you picked out your wedding invitation.

"Which one do you like best?"

"I don't know, they're all good. Whatever you like, darling."

"The off-white with the wavy edges is pretty."

"We'll take that one. With the envelope the same colour, please."

While smoking on the balcony, you came up with a formula for the wedding invitations, then you drew up the list of guests and composed the menu. Although you did not want to ruffle anyone's feathers, you did prefer to do something rather modern, so you replaced the traditional wedding cake with a selection of desserts, a *farandole*. François saw this as a sign of your independent spirit. You teased him about his reluctance to take risks: "Good job you're in insurance!" François defended his position by saying that you always wanted things to be surprising, but that the surprises had to organised.

"But that's not true at all, I love everything!"

So you played at provoking and teasing each other, these were your first concessions; all of this long before issues such as buying a second car, or moving again, or taking out a loan, or should the little one go to state school or private. For the time being you were still rather daring in your behaviour: you bought red lingerie, you allowed ginger sweets to melt on your tongues; or what about the Saturday when you had been to a foam party and then went back to the car park, excited, brimming with desire, and made François lie down on the back seat, and he was only too glad to submit, just saying over and over, "Someone will see us, someone will see us . . ."

But it was no foregone conclusion, that happiness of yours. Your last summer in Lyon had been eventful. Your parents had been relieved to learn you'd obtained your master's in "business administration", and glad to know that their daughter was leaving behind that campus with its dubious morals to enter a domain with which they were more familiar, the job market. It was true that the last term had been geared towards *beginning one's profession*: you'd learned about economies of scale, market research, long-term strategies, and that women, too, mesdemoiselles, could become company directors, you pictured yourself giving orders to a bevy of secretaries in an office all of glass where growth curves were made to multiply. That was what you would do, yes, when the time came; for now, you thought you were still in a learning phase.

Press your foot on the middle pedal to slow the vehicle down, brake slightly, look to the left, start heading into the crossroads, turn. With your left index finger lift the lever in order to activate the blinking rear light showing that you are changing direction, rotate the steering wheel, turn to the right. With your palm move the gearstick up, then to the right, then further up again to change gears, press your right foot on the right pedal: accelerate.

"But why not, if it makes us happy!"

You would not listen: you wanted to pay for your driving

licence with your first pay cheque. You were an intern at Panzani (in those days interns were paid). Chloé was also puzzled.

"Why don't you take the test in Lyon, as you're the one who's paying?"

"Oh, no, that would be far too dangerous. They drive like idiots there."

"Right. But it would piss me off to go back to my parents' just for that."

Your father, as a motor mechanic who was well-known throughout the canton, had found you a good rate for classes at a driving school. After a week at Panzani you took the train to Valvoisin. You learned the right moves to be a good driver, in the presence of a kindly female driving instructor. At night you slept at your parents'. As a result, between the to and fro from Lyon to Terneyre, between your parents and your boyfriend, the internship during the day and your evenings in your shared flat, you divided your time among several lives; you would have to choose wisely. For example: should you introduce François to your parents? You did not know how to broach the issue. To say "Guess what, Maman, I'm in love" seemed completely incongruous to you. Particularly as François had failed his first year of law school and now, after switching to the mathematics department, this second failure was downright alarming. Often when you were with him he would remain silent, biting his fingernails all evening. François was terrified at the thought he might not find his place in society; he belonged to that category of young men who desperately wanted to belong to a group, haunted by what Katherine Mansfield termed, in another register, *this terrible desire to establish contact*, young men who are far too fearful of being relegated, socially or emotionally, to indulge in dilettant-ism, marginal behaviour, or rebellion.

But you didn't know any of that. You were having fun at Panzani, you were proud of your job title, "assistant secretary for raw materials". In the evening you tried to entertain your fiancé with office anecdotes, to no avail. You began to have doubts. What would be the point of introducing him to your parents? You could already hear your mother:

"A boy who fails at university is not a good match."

Without saying anything to his family, François had been working for the last few weeks at Réserva, an insurance broker's known for their aggressive policy. He came across as honest, and this inspired trust. François would come back from each of his rounds with new signatures, and he was relieved to be accomplishing something. Those were the only evenings when he stopped biting his fingernails and could go out to the cinema. Until one day his boss called him into the office and offered him the mission of starting up an agency in Chambéry; his job would be to convince the peasants of Savoie and the inhabitants of the Aix region to take out a policy with Réserva – the best on the market, of course. It was as if he were colonising virgin territory.

"But you're young, I'm sure you'll enjoy the challenge."

François told you what his boss had proposed. He was tempted, but he was afraid. In that profession, if you didn't have "a major portfolio of clients" you couldn't make a decent living. Not to mention the fact that his parents would always be cross with him for not obtaining a degree.

"But they'd be proud if you were your own boss!"

By encouraging him to open the agency, you felt you were doing your duty: wasn't a woman supposed to spur on her man's ambitions? François dithered. Maybe he was nervous about the years it would take to build up a clientele, nervous about the days he'd spend waiting for a client to come to the office, or the days he'd spend driving around the countryside and coming home late to a house where the children might already be asleep in their beds. He asked for some time to think it over. You were beginning to get annoyed by his indecisiveness, and he said sadly,

"You deserve better than me."

Then he took the train to Montélimar, where his parents were waiting. You had mixed feelings on parting. He promised to write. It was the end of July, you had finished your internship. You might be signing a contract in September: everyone was very pleased with you at the noodle factory.

"It's a pleasure to work with such a discreet and efficient young woman."

You began your holidays by failing your driving test. You had some cake anyway, your father and mother were happy to have you at home. They cheered you up. For two days you made the most of the peace and quiet, but all too soon you were bored. You felt as if you were seventeen all over again, that stifling sensation, that indolence. Nothing had changed: the vegetable garden, the little yellow room, the Tour de France on the television. What was the point of staying if it was only to run into girls from the *collège* who were pregnant up to their ears? You went back to Lyon. But three days later Chloé left for the Drôme to "replenish her funds" by working at the apricot harvest. So you didn't know what to do with yourself.

*

Lyon was empty during the month of August, and the heat seemed to have engulfed all human activity. Your usual hang-out, the Café de la Renaissance, displayed a sign saying ANNUAL CLOSURE, something you saw on a good number of other businesses. You would put on some skimpy clothing and go out early in the morning or late at night when the temperature had dropped. You walked across the pont de la Guillotière to the place Bellecour, then went back to your old neighbourhood and up to the basilica along the cool narrow streets, then you came back by way of Saint-Paul station. Or you might walk along the Rhône as far as the construction sites for the new railway station and shopping centre, and everything that was being built.

Along the quieter streets old people had brought out their chairs and sat peacefully talking. You were ruminating, your thoughts uneasy, painfully assessing the fact that François had never suggested the possibility of moving to Chambéry together. You were so lost in thought that, with the help of the heat wave, what was merely something unsaid was transformed into a humiliation; this was the sign that he no longer loved you – or that he was hiding something from you, because if he was hesitating about what to do, it was your fault, or in any case had something to do with you, it had to be connected to you. It was a well-known fact that when men felt comfortable with a woman they told her everything, they dared anything; this must mean that François no longer loved you the way he had; maybe his family wanted to separate you, or perhaps for all his gentle manner François had met a virgin at the law faculty, and they had got engaged in that town famous for its nougat, his next letter, for sure, would tell you he was breaking it off with you, how could you have been so naïve? You stopped in a bistro and drank a lemonade. You revived; all around you the tables were filled with workers spending their summers there, just as they did every summer.

In the flat it was so hot that you couldn't sleep until two o'clock in the morning. You smoked and listened to the radio. There were a few drunkards, yelling. The last time you had spoken on the phone you had not found François in a very good mood; perhaps your feelings were weakening: this Love, with a capital L, that had inhabited you for over a year, could it vanish all of a sudden? You wrote an urgent letter to Chloé. She replied that boys were less considerate than girls, to be sure, but that if you thought that François would be happy in Chambéry working as an insurance salesman and living with you, you ought to suggest it to him, quite simply. For couples, communication was super-important; she'd had enough of picking apricots.

It did you good to read those lines, but your overheated imagination was not satisfied. You wondered if fate wasn't hounding you. It really was odd that you'd failed your driving test – you were always such a good student; and strange that your boyfriend was hiding his intentions from you. With the help of your insomnia, you eventually reached the conclusion that there must be *something else*. You liked this thought, it wrapped itself around your mind; there was *something else*, a dense mystery you had to solve . . .

One night you heard a programme on the radio about clairvoyants. The people who were interviewed, voices trembling with gratitude, told how fortune tellers had helped then to make the right decision at a "critical point in their lives". Was it possible, therefore, in exchange for money, to learn new things about yourself? In the big telephone book for the Rhône département, you looked up the names of fortune tellers, astrologers, cartomancers. A certain Maude caught your attention with a little inset advertisement: FIFTEEN YEARS' EXPERIENCE – SERIOUS WORK. No, it was ridiculous. You snapped the phonebook shut. After a half-hearted sigh you thought you could see, out of the corner of your eye, the pages still moving as they came together.

The Yellow Pages were the direct descendant of the *Almanac of Business and Industry* created by Sebastian Bottin at the end of the eighteenth century. In 1973, the business directory was indispensable to anyone who had a telephone. It owed its name to the fact it was printed on yellowish bible paper of inferior quality; it contained the addresses and telephone numbers of every business and service in the département; it could be obtained for free at the post office; as you went through it, pencil in hand, it occasionally gave you an impression of industrious activity, and you could no longer ignore the profusion of various businesses that sprouted up in the neighbourhood.

The directory had a nice inky smell and the pages, as your thumb riffled through them, clumped together, tickling you. You lit a cigarette and tried to reason with yourself. Clairvoyance was something for superstitious housewives. But your curiosity was piqued. You dialled Maude's number and muttered something; a very kind voice replied that you were overcome by emotion; that sometimes it prevents us from expressing ourselves outwardly the way we might hope to inwardly. Maude agreed to see you in two days' time.

You had expected to find an old building, and an old woman, her eyes lined with kohl, in a cramped room full of cats. You were surprised to come upon a recent building. Maude opened the door in the corridor just as you were coming out of the lift. She was a woman in her forties, rather large, with short hair that was not particularly clean. In her office two armchairs faced each other, and between them was a table covered with a woollen cloth. Only a candle on the right-hand side gave the room an esoteric touch. The psychic talked to you about the traffic, you told her you were in the process of getting your driving licence. She replied (was this a prediction or mere politeness?):

"You're doing the right thing. It's difficult to find work without a car."

The woman shuffled a deck of cards. You understood that the conversation had no other purpose than to put you at ease. You took out the photograph of François, the one which Maude had asked you on the telephone to bring. You reminded her that you had come with a "relationship question". Maude didn't seem to be listening to you. She placed the photograph on the table and lined up four tarot cards; the rest of the deck she spread in a semicircle and told you to choose four cards and place them next to each of the four cards already displayed. Silence reigned in the room now. You trembled slightly as you made your choice, the clairvoyant took a deep breath, her gaze seemed to cloud over. She said:

"You are a very proud person. On the verge of arrogant."

A pause. She made a face as if to indicate it was not necessarily a flaw.

"You are also capable of giving a great deal, and you like to advise other people."

A pause.

"You need company, you need to have a lot of people around you. You are very sociable, and solitude is not your thing."

You could not take your eyes off her. She was actually talking about you! What a delight!

"I see you as a woman who can be influenced quite easily, in spite of your pride. There are many different influences in your life."

Maude focused her gaze on you and asked if this description matched who you were. Everything matched perfectly, you felt a rush of childlike joy. You had forgotten about François and wanted Maude to go on talking about you, on and on. But she picked up the photograph and narrowed her eyes.

"I see a great deal of emotion on his part, a great deal of love, and honesty. He is an upright person."

She broke off in order to grope for words, then continued:

"He is someone you can count on. I also see a great deal of stability, a base, something material, he likes security, something stable. I don't know how else to put it."

Your voice sounded too lively, too shrill, in the room:

"Yes, exactly, it's because he works in insurance!"

Another silence fell.

"He's very much in love, I sense there is a good bond between you. There is a natural meeting of the minds."

And then:

"I also see a question, a question between you, that has not been asked. Something that has not been said, but not in a negative sense, am I right? Something that is still unresolved on his side. A personal or professional commitment."

You were holding your breath. Maude looked at the cards. At the photograph. And back at the cards. She ran her hand through her greasy hair.

"I see children, several children with him."

Your heart was pounding. You were afraid you might have misheard.

"With him?"

"Yes."

"So I'm going to marry him?"

Maude smiled before she continued:

"That, I cannot say. But, well, I feel fairly confident. I see a couple, in any case, the two of you are in a couple. There is something lasting, solid, something that's just beginning. I also see a move, something that will happen over time, but it won't always be easy, either, O.K.?"

Then the clairvoyant added, her tone more motherly:

"You know, mademoiselle, love is not a fairy tale."

Maude slumped back against her chair as if she had made a huge effort. You told her about your fear that François was becoming distant, and how you would like him to commit, and accept the job offer, but that he was very shy. Raising your eyebrows, you told her, too, that you were gobsmacked (as you put it to your girlfriends as well, later), absolutely gobsmacked that she had come out with so many things about you without knowing you.

Maude scooped up the cards. Time was up. It has not lasted more than twenty minutes altogether. You immediately wanted to know if there were good clairvoyants in "towns smaller than Lyon". Maude's voice became sharper, as if you had touched a sore point. She began to lament the closure of individual offices because of practitioners that did readings by telephone. Times were hard, to practise this profession with proper concentration one had to limit the number of clients, and that was why she could not go away on holiday in August, she paid far too much in the way of social contributions and she had no paid leave. Oh, it made her laugh, these young people who thought they'd become millionaires once they set up shop, when in fact they were more like social workers. You wanted to catch your bus now, but Maude kept you there, launched into her diatribe against those dishonest practitioners that dangled the prospect of miracles before people's eyes, thanks to an abundance of enticing advertising.

"It's unfair competition, but no-one talks about it. No-one comes to the defence of small tradespeople like us!"

You finally got away, one hundred and fifty francs poorer. That very evening you wrote to François: you wanted to go and live with him in Chambéry. Three days later he arrived by train, held you very close in his arms and talked for an hour without stopping. You had never heard him come out with such a flow of words in succession. François shared all his fears with you, told you how hateful his parents had been, saying yet again that he was "worthless", he said he didn't dare take you off into a life "with no security, because you deserve the best", but he was sad at the thought of leaving Lyon on his own, he didn't want to lose you, and so on.

This was your first major discussion as a couple. You decided to move to Chambéry in September – François would ditch his studies, you would ditch Panzani – so that he could set up the agency. Later you lay on the bed. Later still, lifting your head from the pillow you said,

"Do you think I am easily influenced, my darling?"

And you remember that as you gradually accumulated your meetings at the Presbytery, your estimates from caterers and your discussions on the balcony, a date for the wedding was set, and the invitations were sent out; so that just like 350,000 other heterosexual couples that year, 1978, you could experience that exceptional day. The death of your grandfather the previous week did, however, cast a pall over the event. The old man had fallen from a ladder while picking fruit in the village where he had spent his entire life.

When you saw the motionless body at the mortuary, you understood that never again would you see your grandfather coughing softly, putting logs on the fire, emptying or filling his pipe then falling asleep in his armchair; never again would he wake up and say, "Well my treasure, what mischief have you been up to?" Cruelly yet typically, his death strengthened your tender feelings towards him, and to the shock of his death this added the frustration of having to keep those exacerbated feelings to yourself. At the church the mayor delivered a speech to the glory of your grandfather, summarising his seventy years on the planet in a few words. Since the old man had been a widower for a long time, your mother decided to get rid of the furniture and sell the house – it was impossible to heat – and this would allow you and François to "have a little capital to get started in life". After the wedding you went back to help her sort through all the little things that are so precious to us when we are alive, and which are quickly forgotten as they are packed away in cardboard boxes by our descendants; a pipe; a pouch of tobacco on a varnished table; a pair of corduroy trousers draped over an armchair and which, given the shiny patches on the knees and the trace of creases in the cloth, seemed not only to be waiting for the deceased man, but even to bring him back to life.

After the long intimate conversation that had followed your visit to Maude's office, you had informed your parents that you would be moving to Chambéry, and that you were in a relationship with François. They mentioned marriage almost immediately, because it was out of the question not to *make your situation official*. But on the whole they took your news well, they would be pleased to have a son-in-law, which meant almost a son; and they hoped he would give them grandchildren; they were already jealous of his parents, because it was the groom's parents who would provide all the little maids of honour. All François's family had made the trip. The night before, you yourself had arranged the flowers in the church aisle, and all night long, preoccupied by everything you had to do, you thought of that magical moment when, to the strains of the wedding march, you would enter the nave, and everyone's gaze would be upon you.

There is one official photograph from the wedding that stood on the dresser in your bedroom for a long time, like a little emotional radiator warming up your everyday life. Later it would be joined by photographs of your children and grandchildren, their baptisms and their own weddings, and eventually you would come to mix up all those ceremonies. On the wedding photograph François has one hand on your hip and his cheek against your brow; he is wearing an elegant petrol-blue suit, standing slightly turned away, apparently relaxed; only a slight balding on his crown indicates any difference from the young man you met in Lyon four years earlier. You are wearing the traditional white gown with a train, a voile rose pinned to your chignon, and a light veil falling to your waist. Your smile is more open, with a hint of malice in your eyes for the photographer who must have made some sort of joke; your shoulder is bare, your skin is golden, and your eyes seem lighter than usual. You are holding the wedding bouquet chest high, and thanks to the photographer's instructions the flowers are spot on in the middle of the photograph.

There was the meal: you had gone to so much trouble over it, refusing your mother's charitable interference. The *farandole de desserts* was a success. Towards the end, the older guests wanted to hear you sing a little song. They stopped the music, and you went along with it with astonishing good grace. If you close your eyes today to recall the scene more precisely, you can still hear the ambient noise; feel the warmth; smell the cigarette smoke; you can sense the commotion of the children at the far end of the room; the laughter. A guest came up to speak to you. Everyone wanted to kiss you, to touch your gown, admire it, even for just a moment; as if your wedding dress emanated a magical, ritual power, and it was good to rub against it, and pay homage to it.

Was this the finest day of your life? Today, you wonder. Although you immediately understood the ineluctable nature of your grandfather's death, it took you years to realise what it meant to get married, to be married, to be the spouse of, to be the other partner in the conjugal home, to be officially bound by this legal and moral relationship that began the evening of the day the wedding party ended. You did not regain possession of yourself until around midnight; everyone listened to your little song the way everyone had listened to the mayor's speech, wondering whether they might be next on the list in that village, or recalling an episode from their own wedding party, the eldest among us aware of what awaits the newlyweds once everyone has left, once the tables have been cleared, the last goodbyes are said, and we find ourselves alone in front of a refrigerator.

PART TWO

Deep in her soul, however, she was waiting for an event.

GUSTAVE FLAUBERT

I

Then there was the time you wanted to buy a new television.

Although François seemed likeable enough in his little Fiat to the peasants, to be credible to the big landowners around the lake of Aix, he had to have a vehicle with a more powerful engine. To those who complained about their insurance, word had spread in the canton: "There is a good, reliable guy over on the avenue Jean-Jaurès, go and see him." As his monthly commission had begun to bring in a comfortable amount, reinvested in new purchases, it was easy enough to convince him that the living room required a colour set. And as all the adjustments had already been made at the shop, the first evening you settled down in front of the small screen was truly satisfying.

These were tender scenes, lit by the glow of the lamp; your spouse waiting for you to join him on the sofa once you had tidied up in the kitchen; you planted a kiss on his neck, and together you watched a film, or some sort of entertainment; in this restful moment with the day's work behind you, your husband placed his head on your lap, closed his eyes, felt your belly vibrate when you spoke, or reached up to touch a curl of your hair and inhaled the scent; you leaned forward to kiss his lips, turning down the volume with the button on the remote control. A few years later, your children in their pyjamas, fed and scrubbed, their cheeks pink after a walk in the fresh air, would look at the same screen and thanks to video they could watch cartoons of Cinderella or Tom and Jerry. On the left-hand side of the sofa, little Nathalie with her thumb in her mouth; to the right, little Xavier snuggled against his father, the four of you cocooned in the tender relaxation of a winter's evening, your husband home from work, the kitchen cleaned, the beds made. You would sit between the two little creatures and watch television. Three decades later and you could still be seen on the same sofa with your grandchildren; the television was bigger and flatter, but the films were virtually the same, D.V.D.s you had bought at shopping malls. François would not be as tired as in the previous scene, you would be more relaxed, because the next day Nathalie would be coming to fetch her brood, it didn't matter if they went to bed late, and you even enjoyed viewing these little stories of cat and mouse in hot pursuit in a fairy-tale house.

The bulb beneath the lampshade on the right bathed these scenes in its yellow light, mingled with the rays the television projected, a bluish glow flashing sporadically over your faces. Pairs of eyes staring at the screen; an adult's hand stroking a child's cheek; the sound from the cartoon with its caricatured voices and persistent refrain; someone was speaking. It was François, saying that the programme was better than last night's cartoons; his voice was interrupted by the cat on the screen yowling with vexation; you said yes, then added a comment about the D.V.D. that had just finished, and said it was time to go to bed. This is the way one becomes a grandparent.

*

But long before, there was one obvious thing you must do, a course of action that belonged to your general concept of happiness, a course of action that sought nothing more than to take form: since a house was a basic necessity if you were to start a family, you wanted to become homeowners.

"Invest in stone, that's the only way!"

Said your father-in-law, when he learned of your decision.

There were plenty of houses for sale in Chambéry, but they were in noisy suburbs, so you extended your search area. The colour television had cost three thousand francs. You were earning twelve thousand at Bédani. In a good year François had eighteen thousand a month at his disposal, so together you were able to put aside five thousand a month. But even with the help of your parents and your Livret A savings account, no matter how you did the maths you were not rich enough.

"As a young couple, you need help along the path to home-ownership."

Said the banker.

"We can still make a decent down payment."

Pointed out your husband.

Your diary was full of notes such as "4 p.m., by Mammouth roundabout". Once you were at the appointment, you shook hands with the estate agent and followed his car to the house for sale. The visit lasted roughly twenty minutes, even if you knew from the moment you walked in that it wouldn't work. You made a checklist: insulation, heating, size of kitchen, light, terrain, neighbours, access, shops. There were some houses it was worth going back to see with François, and in the evening, out on the balcony, you would compare the advantages and disadvantages of each one, and sometimes go back for a third time; none of the visits were ever pointless, they all helped you to fine-tune your search for a house.

You remember; your in-laws would invite you to lunch on Sunday, and your father-in-law would say:

"Dear girl, there are only three things that matter when you're buying: location, location, location!"

It made him laugh.

For weeks your living room-kitchen was cluttered with estate agents' brochures, which you read until midnight, circling the listings with a pen, encouraging each other in your search.

"The important thing is to fall in love with the place."

"And it has to fit the budget!"

You went to the bank, as a couple, to take out a loan. The interest rate was high, but the other banks weren't offering anything better.

"At least he's our banker, he knows us."

"If there's a problem, that will help."

Then one morning there was a nice surprise, you "fell in love". François asked his parents to come along to endorse his enthusiasm, because there mustn't be any *hidden defects*. Then you had to draw up the sales agreement, free the accounts, ask for a certified cheque, go to the land registry to double-check the land-use plan, fill out a pile of administrative forms. Last of all, there would be the scene at the solicitor's, in an office with a photocopier, a secretary, all taking place over the space of a morning in an old house in Chambéry. The former owner was one Madame Remoulin; she was a widow and she had lived in that house all through her retirement. "But at my age," she said,

"I want to be closer to my grandchildren." She was a very thin and wrinkled old lady with a pleading gaze. You tugged on your skirt, you thought it was too short, while the solicitor read out the deed of purchase; you heard him say *referred to hereafter as the buyer, discharge of any pre-emptive right,* and *other conditions relative to the execution of this document.* Finally François handed over the cheque from the bank, and two sets of keys were placed on the desk. Everyone relaxed.

The old woman let out a happy sigh:

"I'm so glad you are the ones who will be moving in. I have quite taken to you."

"I wish you good luck with the move."

Concluded the solicitor.

Somewhat dazed, you and François went for coffee on the place Saint-Léger. You talked a lot, as if to ward off your anxiety (the loan was quite substantial), and your husband said yet again that you had made the *optimal* choice. You called your parents from the bar.

"That's it, we've got the keys!"

On the other end of the line, your mother:

"Well done, then, children. We must celebrate!"

The following evening you had dinner in Terneyre, very excited, very talkative as you tucked into the *blanquette*.

All through the process of buying the house, you had run the gamut of emotions: your joy at discovering that you and François had one and the same desire: to leave the flat in Chambéry and move into a detached house where you could raise "free-range" children; the excitement, each time you visited; your disappointment when, during the second visit, the house you sensed would become your home turned out to have a problem with the roofing, for example, and you had to rein in all your joyful brimming anticipation; the fear (stronger in the husband) of committing such a huge sum of money to a dodgy acquisition; a certain disquiet at the thought of this imminent and significant material migration, and everything it implied in the way of things to worry about – the second car you would have to buy, the entire accumulation of administrative procedures, which on some evenings left you feeling quite fed up, saying things like: "It's so much simpler to be a tenant."

Once you had the keys in your hands, you and François shared your relief and your pride, hopping up and down in the bistro. Before long your bank statement would reflect the amount withdrawn every month, four thousand five hundred francs, something that used to be called an "instalment"; this loan would oblige you, when it came time to do the Christmas shopping, to check your balance carefully, but you quickly got used to it.

"At least the money's not going to waste."

"At least that," you echoed, kissing François full on the mouth, "at least we'll be in our own house."

Your postal address, from then on, would be clos des Narcisses 12, chemin des Pins, 38110 Empan-sur-Nive.

Empan was a small town of five thousand inhabitants; a secondary road ran through it, leading to Valvoisin. The municipality took its name from a pre-Alpine stream whose bed had been channelled following serious flooding. There was a Romanesque church from the twelfth century, and all the necessary facilities: schools, bakeries, post office and *tabac*, a bank branch, sporting clubs. The centre consisted of a tangle of old streets where a seamstress and a butcher still had their shops. Two cafés with outdoor terraces lined the central square, known as place Victor-Hugo, and in the summer they were filled with workers and petty employees who came to eat the *plat du jour*; the rest of the year the square acted as a car park for a particular type of town centre shopping, such as changing a seal on the coffee pot, or buying a ribbon at the haberdasher's, or a stamp from the post office. The estate agent had pointed out the recent opening of a supermarket, which meant you could avoid the hypermarket in Chambéry. You could see its rectangular warehouse buildings as you came by car from the motorway; then you drove around the local car repairer's, and past some small buildings, houses painted with a dark distemper that were a sign you were nearing the town. You would turn in front of the window of the Le Bec Fin restaurant to head towards the LA FRUITIÈRE AGRICULTURAL ZONE, LAND WITH A BRIGHT FUTURE. In the middle of this rapidly expanding neighbourhood the mayor had built a sports stadium. You went up the hill. Left foot on the left pedal, right foot on the right pedal, lift your right foot, press down on the left, with your right hand take hold of the gearstick and press downwards; change gears.

Overlooking the municipality of Empan-sur-Nive, then as now, was a hill a hundred metres high. A very old footpath meandered across it, leading to a viewpoint that was popular on Sundays with a few older residents. On the far side, on the final slope, was the village's cemetery extension, created in an era when the sole inhabitants were farmers, unmarried cattle breeders. But the town grew quickly. Its proximity to Grenoble and Chambéry was a plus, because both those cities were known as *métropoles*, and as the water treatment plant lay on one side of the Nive, and the main road lay on the other, hampering the development of the town, the local council had bought up a considerable portion of the surrounding farmland. Once they had zoned it as *building land*, there was room to house all the people who had come from the city and who did not want to "find themselves in a cramped street when they were actually in the country". Now you drove along the old by-road. Recently paved, with a few sharp turns, it went up to the top of the hill. The Chemin des Vignes began by the cemetery, and light-coloured detached houses lined either side of the road; sitting in their plots in the middle of lush green lawns they looked like so many puffs of egg white on custard. Then came the Chemin des Pins, at its far end were the clos des Lilas, the clos des Bouvreuils and the clos des Narcisses; you slowed down. This adjacent suburb was called La Garotte, from the name of the pre-empted hill. The community of small towns ran a bus through these streets, the number 3; it came up from the village then went down again empty once all the secondary-school pupils had got off. The residents claimed they were very pleased, because there was more sunshine on the hill than down below. The one disadvantage was that the only road leading to the centre of the village tended to get congested in the morning.

Your house was located almost at the very end of the clos. A right of way through two properties led to a little forest track, and then you could be out in the fields. You loved going for walks there with your round belly, your husband, and later, with the children. The town stopped there. It was all so quiet, even quieter than you could have imagined when you bought the structure and the plot of land. When the weather was fine you could admire the summits of the Massif de la Chartreuse, and on days after rain you would find a strong smell of the country waiting for you, full of animal and earthy scents, as if the old farms, on disappearing, had left their imprint upon the air.

"At least we're in our own home," you said, and they were magical words from your lips. You'd think you were the first person to make such a discovery; what it meant to be in your own home; the first person to move in, prepare the ground, plant, decorate; you had forgotten that your parents had expended the same energy in Terneyre, in that house with the two bedrooms and living room upstairs, and the kitchen, garage, and storeroom on the ground floor. It was not long after your father had begun to work for himself, and your mother was taken on at the town hall, in the early 1950s, that there, in your childhood bedroom covered with yellow wallpaper, and in that house, all your memories began, and this entire story.

Their house was in the north of the Isère département, a region that used to be called the Bas-Dauphiné, not yet part of Savoie nor of the greater Lyon region, and where the fields of wheat and the pasture land, moulding to the gentle curves of the landscape, posed no difficulty when it came to accommodating future trunk roads. In every house, on every level, there was a corridor; an exterior wrought-iron stairway led to a small balcony. On days when there was no school you would play with your skipping rope out in the little courtyard, and your parents could see your head pop up then vanish again behind the privet.

The roof above the front door was in the shape of a circumflex accent, and continued horizontally to the adjoining house where a veterinary surgeon lived. All the houses were painted grey; they had been built in the 1930s.

You often stood in the kitchen watching your mother. You remember the way she prepared breaded veal: she would wipe the plastic tablecloth and take three soup plates from the cupboard. In the first she put a handful of flour, broke an egg into the second then beat it, and in the third she poured some breadcrumbs. She unwrapped the little package from the butcher's. She took a first cutlet of meat between the thumb and forefinger of both hands, and dipped it in the first plate, carefully turning the cutlet on both sides, which left the pink meat covered in white streaks. Then she soaked it in egg. That was your favourite bit. The cutlets re-emerged from the plate all sticky, and your sweet little face on the far side of the table was a picture of delighted disgust. The meat ended up in the third plate, where your mother tapped it so that the crumbs would stick properly. She repeated the operation as many times as there were cutlets, and in the end the tablecloth was splattered all over.

That house was an emblem of their social advancement; to be born in a valley full of cows, and end up, after the war, among those whose workplace is separate from their place of residence; your grandparents had been proud of their children. Your family had a good reputation. Your father did not drink. There were geraniums overlooking the street. The rooms were kept clean, particularly the living room, which was often locked. Your parents rarely invited friends over, and most of the time it was just the three of you.

You remember a little ashtray that was full of burned matches.

You remember when you got your first television. It was an enormous set, and it crackled. You had to turn a knob on the right-hand side, and figures would appear, first long, then flat, until they attained what your father thought was the right size. He would go and sit back down in the armchair, looking at the presenters, and General de Gaulle, and their faces were regularly bisected by a thin orangey horizontal line. They sent you up to bed.

Your entire childhood was spent there among those little semi-detached houses all in a row, among your girlfriends from primary school, and in the village of Terneyre and its shops; your maman, your papa, both coming home in the evening, and every house concealing a long garden round the back where families had lunch on Sundays.

And now that you were moving into another house, built at the beginning of the 1980s (you liked what was *modern*), the strange thought occurred to you that your childhood could have been spent in any number of places; in a building in Lyon for example, or on a farm in the Vercors; it struck you as strange that your parents had also signed a deed of purchase in a solicitor's office; you would think you were the first one who had ever done such a thing; that everything was new – the credit, the walls, the plants sprouting; that everything was a product of your will, when you had to decide where to put things – saucepans, coffee pot, clothes, but also books, records, which oven, which fridge, where should you put the shelves. Upstairs there were four rooms and two bathrooms; downstairs the kitchen, the living room, the hall, the toilets, a storeroom and a door leading to the garage, and the living space was much bigger, the kitchen much brighter, and, unlike the house in Terneyre, you could walk all the way round it, and you would soon be accompanied by your children who in turn would find it . . . strange – the thought that it could be any different.

It was the garden that gave you the most joy, just opening the shutters and gazing out at it made it all worth the effort. Like the other gardens in the area it was divided down the middle by a stone path where the two poles of a clothesline had been planted. But the clothesline had become slack and the lawn was in such poor condition that the mud stuck to the grass in clumps after heavy rainfall. Once you had finished moving in and male energy had been restored, you asked your husband and father to redo the lawn. You would have liked to help them.

"Darling, may I remind you that you are pregnant."

"Oh, this will only make it sturdier!"

You remember that afternoon when they sowed the seeds for the lawn, arms in flight, broad swooping movements, as if from days of old, and the long summer evenings that followed when, with a glass of Muscat wine in your hand, together you watched the grass growing on your land. Together, too, you restored the hazel tree, the arbutus and the walnut tree that Madame Remoulin had planted in the front garden. Naturally this all required work, and the next day you'd be aching, but at last you could organise things the way you wanted.

"It is lovely to be able to hammer in a nail without having to ask permission."

You hung petunias above the front door to make it more welcoming right from the start. You wanted a climbing plant to wind itself round the ironwork, but you were still hesitating between Virginia creeper and wisteria. When your friends came to visit during your maternity leave, as you gave them the tour of your domain you said,

"I think I'll plant a tree there, I don't know what yet."

They recommended a cherry tree, a mimosa, or a Judas tree.

"In the spring it's really wonderful."

"You have to watch out for frost."

"You could have a bay tree, for sauces."

First, as the weeks went by, you saw your house reborn as it became more beautiful, more welcoming. François had replaced the broken tiles in the outside wall, the flagstones had been cleaned, and the trees were pruned; you could not help but feel delighted as you walked through the door.

You went through that door every morning, each of you taking your car to go to work. François would get up earlier, and head off to deal with paperwork before it was time to open the agency in Chambéry; he was rising through the ranks at Réserva, and felt completely at ease now, almost powerful, in his insurance broker's suit. You had found work at Bédani (a furniture manufacturer), shortly before your maternity leave. When you were together again in the evening, you sensed that a similar desire came over both of you, the desire to be happy, the desire to succeed, the desire to transform your house into a home, and to do that, you were both prepared to spend another busy weekend, for neither one of you ever tired of the pleasures, still new, of home ownership.

For example: you wanted to have fitted carpets in the children's bedrooms. It would be better for the baby that was on its way, for warmth, for noise as well. Madame Remoulin had left the wooden floor in poor condition.

"It's true, with a carpet, if he falls out of bed, it's less risky."

"Don't laugh, we have to think of everything."

The salesman wearing a jacket in the store colours of the D.I.Y. store listened to your plan and directed you to the "Flooring and Surfacing" department. You ran your hand over the samples: loops of wool and polyamide; you finally opted for a burgundy carpet that would be suitable for a boy or a girl. Not to mention the fact that red would not show the dirt.

The plan was to fit the carpet on Saturday.

"We wouldn't do as good a job during the week."

"With a baby underfoot our minds will be on other things."

You equipped yourselves with the necessary tools: a linoleum cutter (an instrument which, years later, stripped of its blades, would serve as a space vessel for Xavier, now that he had seen science fiction films), a solid cutter, spatulas, and a tack hammer with which you banged on the newly laid carpet – something that would earn you, for several weeks, the saucy nickname "my little tack hammer". The room had been emptied of furniture, you were both wearing lightweight clothes that Saturday in a house still exempt of routine or heaviness, you and François were still young, capable of change, capable of working in harmony to complete the task at hand. You cleared the parquet. François spread the white glue on the floor. When it began to dry, you stood at either end of the roll of carpet, unrolled the first width, and laid it in the direction of the pattern. How nice it was to do this together, as a couple, with a man in charge of the job. You admired the effect from the corridor.

"It looks good, don't you think?"

You swapped positions. Your head by the wall, you adjusted the carpet beneath the skirting board, grunting faintly when it was hard. François coated the parquet with glue, going back and forth to the pot at regular intervals. In this way you laid out the three rolls, paying careful attention to the joints between them. You got into the rhythm. François was bare-chested, the room smelled of sweat. Before long, a handful of words sufficed for you to work in tandem:

"Come a little further this way."

"Like this?"

"Yes, that's fine."

"More?"

"More, yes."

"Stop."

"Now."

"Perfect!"

Then – in due course – you got pregnant. You had gone into labour hours earlier, and you had been breathing methodically, squeezing François's hand as he tried to make himself as small as possible in that room in the clinic. The young man happy to see his life – vaguely purposeless until now – changing direction, as he became irrevocably indispensable to someone. François would be proud to say "my son", "my children", with the certainty that he would never again be useless on earth; whereas you were absorbed by the effort to reduce your suffering with each contraction, you were feeling; something was about to cry, to live.

Subsequently, having lost along with your placenta some of your more frivolous attitudes, you would see yourself as if projected into a different humanity, a humanity whose essence was superior to that of the previous one. In the street you walked with your head held higher, your feet firmly on the ground: you were a mother – which did not prevent you, paradoxically, from being perpetually agitated, because, as you were constantly handling your baby, because you had him constantly in your arms or at your breast, constantly putting his dummy into his mouth or taking out whatever he had just put into it, you always had something to do with that little body next to yours; and unlike your husband who, when it came to his turn to go and fetch the children (on Tuesdays), had no trouble putting it off until the daycare was about to close, you were only willing to do with-out them if other chores, repetitive chores that must be dealt with immediately – calling in at the butcher's, buying a box of laundry powder – were there to make up for the children's absence. Because in that other humanity, you quickly had to learn to distinguish the errands you could run with the children from those it was better to do without them; learn to think constantly about the bread, the bath, the nappies, the shopping, the rides here and there; you had to learn to think ahead.

"It's the nights that are the hardest."

In the kitchen, in Empan, your gazes no longer drifted dreamily into loving mutual contemplation, but were ceaselessly, sharply, focused on Xavier and Nathalie. Either you had them eat first – wriggling offspring in their high chairs – and you sat down to eat afterwards, or you all ate together. But whatever you decided, there was always one of them underfoot, playful or grumpy and not yet in bed. Your meals now depended on how quickly they fell asleep; both of you were on the lookout for a reaction, always ready to spring to your feet and hurry up the stairs to see if something was wrong; a cry, a call; their father would go up to calm them one last time. And when he came back down, your conversation about the progress at the agency or his father's health had been interrupted once again; it was this babbling or that broken toy that had come along to be added to what your husband was saying; you listened while chopping the banana into little pieces for Xavier, or picking up a spoon that had fallen on the floor; you were constantly doing several things at once, and your visual and aural space were always filled with those little creatures, and this gave you the impression, on the rare occasions when the two of you were invited on your own to a friend's house, that there was a strange imbalance that would only disappear once the babysitter went home, once you peered into their bedrooms; the moment when you heard them breathing in the dark, your little sleeping brood.

A few seasons passed and you were pregnant with Nathalie. Again you gave birth, and felt how it wriggled, so moving, that damp, soiled, famished, laughing little body; you were so inhabited by your concern for your children that you could not possibly imagine how you had ever lived without them. The years spent studying in Lyon seemed so free that they became almost scandalous, and even your two-bedroom flat in Chambéry, devoid of either pram or baby bottle, relegated to the distant past; it was all completely foreign to this new M.A., you who were constantly overwhelmed by these two addenda to your life, both ongoing distraction and ongoing devourer of your time – even if you regretted none of it, of course.

"What an extraordinary thing it is to give life."

And yet you had suffered during the contractions and the birth, suffered from breastfeeding and the fluctuations in your hormones. When her little mouth came to suck on your nipple, it felt as if you were being milked by a greedy angel, that all day you were being harassed by a crying baby. And you sometimes felt an inadmissible desire to put the screaming baby into the rubbish bin, so that you could sleep and be free of its tyrannical dependence.

Since this was what it meant, starting a family; becoming a queen and a slave at the same time; constantly being concerned about others, adults and children alike, anticipating their needs, their schedules; you had to conscript your body in the service of the smooth operation of the family machine, an all-consuming octopus that had devoured M.A.'s entire personality, her entire person caught in the tentacles of this creature that required, in succession, a bottle, a piece of advice, where did the puzzle go and what do you want for for dinner this evening, my darling; until eventually it took a painful cavity to oblige you to go urgently to the dentist's, exceptionally delegating the dinner preparations to the father – who was always so kind when it came to helping you.

But that all passed, was forgotten, you slept at night, you had both been changed into parents by then, François was squeezing your hand ever tighter, the midwife at the clinic was urging you on, and at last: the cry, the birth.

It starts with becoming a homeowner, then settling in, then reproducing.

Once you were back from the clinic, once the children had been fed and put to bed, once the mimosa had been planted and the day was over, you returned to that tender evening relaxation on the sofa by the television; just the two of you. That moment of respite when François put his head in your lap. The film was over, you could no longer hear the children.

"They're asleep, our little kiddiewinks."

You pressed the OFF button on the remote control, and going from room to room you turned off the electric lights, the one in the living room then in the hall, François locked up, you went up the stairs. You peeked into your little girl's room, and in the boy's, you used the bathroom. You finished your round and switched off the light in the corridor. Your house had faded into the nocturnal shadows of your neighbourhood, pierced here and there by the yellow halo of a street lamp. You slipped under the duvet, deep into a mellow feeling of safety, your impression of comfort even stronger when, outside, the rain was falling against the shutters.

II

After the move came a period of happiness without words, without change or anxiety, a period that can only be told through simple scenes, for it was only the daily repetition, rather than the insignificant nature of it, that could etch itself so deeply upon your memory.

For example, that moment, every evening, when your husband came home. It was seven-thirty; it began with the crunch of tyres on gravel, together with the judder of the engine as it was switched off, then a silence, a slamming door; you heard those sounds from the kitchen or the bedroom. The front door would open, the click of the door handle followed by a louder noise, that of the door closing again, the bolt sliding onto the plate, a whoosh, a slamming followed by a cheerful jangle, for there were several sets of keys hanging behind the door, and their tinkling resounded through the hall, those keys tinkling together as all of them – car keys, to your mother's place, the extra garage keys – were shaken by the door closing again; they banged against the wood, giving out a clear jingle, then they would swing from right to left depending upon how hard your husband had slammed the door. When you heard these sounds you knew that the act of homecoming had been completed.

Your husband would be wearing a suit, he had a jacket, he had a tie. He was tall, taller than you, he was tired. He immediately put his briefcase down, took off his coat, removed his scarf or sweater, he always abandoned some element of himself; and in this gesture of shedding something, which you found moving, you were also moved to see how he had been permeated with the effects of work, his weariness, the tired creases in his suit, the traces on his face of whatever it was that had kept you apart all day long. You had come down from the bedroom, or in from the garden, or perhaps you had not moved from the kitchen, because you had to keep an eye on the saucepan on the cooker. So he would take a few steps forward and call out:

"Darling?"

Then all you had to do was open the glass door that separated you from him, and peer out; you saw him; you smiled at each other. As if in that moment the planted trees, the salted cucumbers, the rubber tyres of the car, the hot water running from the tap onto the sponge that you were squeezing with one hand and which you placed still wet on the edge of the sink before opening the glass door, before peering out; all of this had no other purpose than that smile you exchanged with your husband; as if he had not gone out that morning in order to have his wages at the end of the month, but solely so that he could come back to you; come back to you in the evening to smile at you; seven, sometimes eight o'clock on your watch; as if the children conceived, the children yet to come, the children enclosed in your belly and later on in their rooms only existed in order to justify that moment when the husband came home and you, his wife, asked him:

"How was your day, my love?"

And after a sigh of pleasure, as he removed his shoes to put on another pair, dried off the rain or got something to drink out of the refrigerator (since he had already come to be with you in the kitchen), your husband would describe his day in detail, dwelling on one particular thorny issue, and you had already tamed the jargon by then, words such as "contracts", "accidents", "premiums", and you could even give some advice about that thorny issue if he asked you to. Your husband, drinking his beer and talking; through the words you exchanged, through the gradual emptying of the glass, the workday retreated. Your husband worried he ought to help you with the meal; you refused his offer because you didn't want him setting the table; what you wanted, what your entire body wanted at that moment, was precisely what he was doing, just then, when he put his arm around your waist; simply that gesture of going round behind you, and circling your hips with his hands, then moving them up to your chest while you were stirring something in a saucepan, even though he knew he was disturbing you, that gesture of planting a kiss on your neck, a kiss you let him have; nothing could give you greater pleasure than that particular kiss, even when you were behind with the meal, or something was bothering you, there was no greater pleasure than that kiss that calmed you down, that ordered your world.

Thus, everything was as it should be. When he hadn't changed out of his clothes yet, when he was still handsome in his dark suit, you saw him as a responsible man, he had taken off his jacket, he had placed his hands on your body. You felt you were exactly where you belonged. Thus the world closed in on your kitchen, your relationship, your man coming home after a day's work, his words in your ears, his kiss, your family. The children had grown, they waited with you for their father's return; tyres, car door, jangle of keys rattling, banging against the wood:

"Papa!"

That shout was a sign that everything was as it should be, right down to the father's protest that he hadn't even had time to take off his coat, the feigned irritation of the man who is over-whelmed by children; his mock irritation showed that things were as they should be, as did those enthusiastic children's arms reaching out to him. The son and daughter were waiting, they'd had their after-school snack, they'd done their homework, and they were very hungry; they were waiting for the door to open, for the jangle of keys to cue the scene, then they would rush into his arms, asking for, begging for, giving, a kiss, a hug, "A cuddle, Papa", "Today the teacher . . ." and you would say, "Calm down! Papa's tired." Back on the ground and off they went, lively little bundles grabbing a piece of bread that lay forgotten on the table. That was when you could hear the man, the man's foot-steps, on the stairs: it was all as it should be.

He was home, he was yours again.

Now he was in the master bedroom, you could sense him moving from one room to the next, you knew he was in the shower, you could hear the water running through the pipes, you could see his body washed, rinsed, cleansed of work. Now the table was set, he came down those same stairs, relaxed, his clothes changed; you turned down the volume on the television, he asked you what was in the news and you answered, "Oh, nothing, just nonsense," or "Still that accident on the motorway, that's all they can talk about." And the world did not make its way any further into your home. Night had fallen. The signs of fatigue on his face had faded, he sat down at his place, unfolded his napkin, plates were held out towards the dish you had prepared – every detail of the scene, night after night, leaving deeper and deeper deposits in your memory.

And years later, things were still as they should be; when you felt a knot in your stomach at his homecoming, when you no longer smiled at him, and you thought of leaving him, when he no longer touched you, because it all made sense, obeyed a certain logic. Things would actually no longer be as they should if one thing happened, if he no longer felt the need to leave in the morning, or if he didn't come home in the evening, since that was what determined everything – your marriage, your family, your house – that closing door, that jangling of keys by the front door, the clinking that became a swinging motion, then the different keyrings knocking together, you could see them, from left to right against the back of the door, then more and more slowly, stopping at last, silent.

Thus every evening, together again. And every morning as you checked your schedules, you would exchange words such as:

"Anything special today, darling?"

"No . . . Oh, yes. I have to go and see a client at the end of the day. Drat, I had completely forgotten."

"Will you be long?"

"I don't know. The man is a pain. Don't wait for me."

"I can wait, I'll go ahead and feed the kids. Anyway, I thought we'd have pizza tonight, it doesn't take long."

"Well, if there's pizza!"

"I knew it . . . Where is your last client?"

"Not far from here, why?"

"Oh, nothing. If it had been Chambéry, I would have asked you to stop in and buy bags for the vacuum cleaner, you know, the place next to the antique shop."

"I can make a detour."

"No, no, it's out of the way. And besides, I'd rather take care of it, it's not at all urgent."

"Sure?"

"Yes, yes, I'll do it myself."

"See you this evening then, my darling."

"See you tonight."

That was how the days began; in general a kiss came next, then the sound of his car heading off, followed by yours. Always the same gestures, incorporated in your youth, the technique hardly changed: open the car with the key (later it would be, press a black button, and hear a beep), grasp the handle, open the door, the same gestures repeated every day by millions of drivers: take your seat at the wheel, close the door, turn the key in the ignition, put your right hand on the gearstick, press down on the clutch, engage the gear, relax your left foot, press on the right pedal: pull away.

Once you had dropped the children off at the crèche, you hurried to Bédani. You did the tasks the company assigned you, moving around your department, had letters typed up or checked invoices, added your own personal value-added contribution to a global system of production, in this case for the manufacture of furniture. Even if your mission in this system seemed less crucial than before (that is, *before the children*), you had to concede that working was a distraction, because, like those mosquitoes that are invisible during the day then come out in clouds when the sun goes down, your domestic worries inevitably came back to besiege you. At five p.m. exactly, in the company car park, your mind, only just relieved of its professional preoccupations, was invaded by the million and one things there were to do before you went home. You had to get organised. Your first obligation was always to pick up the children, but then there were always other errands, of greater or lesser urgency, and you had to draw up the optimal route to get them all done. Once you'd decided which way to go, your car, like millions of other cars, would stop off at the supermarket or the post office, as is the custom in industrialised countries, making a temporary use of the *car park reserved for customers*. Park, put the car into neutral, switch off the engine, set the handbrake, open the door, get out, lock the car. Come back, put your carrier bag in the boot, start off again.

Back at home, the worry of what had to be done at once: peel the carrots, watch over the children's homework. While you opened a tin, you would think of something else to add to your mental list of the next day's errands, the next day's route by car, and sometimes you would jot it down on a Post-it note, so as not to forget. It was time to boil some water, then came the evening news. You switched the television on to the local news, gave the children their dinner, they waved their spoons around, awkwardly; all these gestures executed far too quickly for you to stop and ask yourself any questions; you had to eat while it was hot, quick, time for bed, school tomorrow.

And every morning the conversation went the same way, with a few variations:

"Don't forget the Polskis are coming for dinner, don't be late."

Or:

"I'll be at Maman's at seven for Nathalie's birthday."

"Fine, I'll see you there."

These morning conversations enabled you to visualise and work out your itinerary in advance. You were in charge of so many things, no sooner had you made the list of errands somewhat shorter than it got longer again. But in spite of these masses of uninteresting petty obligations, you were happy, as a mother, as mistress of your space and your little world, happy to be demonstrating what an organised woman you were. Moreover, when François tried to pitch in on Saturdays, you made fun of him, when he said,

"Darling, I think Nathalie doesn't smell too good."

"Show me . . . Oh God, what a stink!"

"She needs changing, doesn't she?"

"Of course she needs changing, don't be such a ninny. Couldn't you have told me sooner?"

"Well, she was just off playing by herself . . ."

"Off playing by herself? Playing in her poo, more like!"

And you charged upstairs with your child under your arm, to finish a maximum amount of work in record time.

"It's a good job I'm here!"

It was a good job that, as you listened to a monotonous voice on the television droning on amidst endless close-ups about the inauguration of the City Hall in Empan, where the new façade would *blend transparency and modernity*, you were capable of keeping an eye on the water heating in the pan; capable at the same time of responding to the chirping of your bare-bottomed baby; of guessing that, downstairs, François had just sat back down in front of the television with a glass of wine and not a care in the world; capable of calling out to your husband as you pressed the poppers on the rompers:

"Could you please call my mother and ask her what time they are coming on Sunday."

François obediently got up from the sofa, dialled the number and said,

"Hello. It's us. How are you doing?"

Even their conversation on the telephone; capable of following it from the bathroom where you tossed the dirty nappy, the baby chirping joyfully on your shoulder, capable of guessing the sentences you couldn't hear, of interrupting their conversation:

"Tell them to bring a bottle of wine, eh, we're counting on them."

And as you went down the stairs, you added, more quietly,

"It always makes my father happy."

In those days it didn't bother you, or not for very long, that you never had a break. Inventing a marinade, discussing your daughter's progress, teasing your husband about his incompetence at household chores: you got the impression that at last you were enjoying a certain return on your investment, after so many years of movement, migration, studies, pregnancies. On Sundays you might be out on the patio together, François gazing contentedly at the irises. You had been idle for a moment already when he would say,

"Darling . . ."

"Yes?"

"There's a button that has come off the shirt you gave me, you know the one."

"The plum-coloured shirt?"

"Yes. I suppose it fell off."

"Can't you look after your things?"

"It's not my fault, it got caught—"

"Sure, sure . . . where is that shirt?"

"In the living room . . . next to your sewing box."

"I'll do it right now, while I have the time."

"Thank you, my darling. That way I can wear it on Monday, I've got an important appointment."

Followed by a kiss of gratitude. François went back to his newspaper, you went to find the thread, a needle, the guilty shirt. As you sat back down you put on an air of a monarch granting a favour:

"You can be a right pain, you know . . . As if the children didn't give me enough to do already!"

We don't generally remember times like this. By showing so much devotion, M.A. had lost some of her presence for us. And yet it would be unfair to say that during all those years you no longer existed, but your daily life consisted in being over-whelmed by the bodies of others – the bodies of the vegetables you bought and weighed and peeled and soaked and washed and scrubbed and pampered; the bodies of children and of the man, satisfied, nourished, cared for. Because all it took was for a member of your family to be contaminated by a germ, brought home from school, for you to take on the role of nurse, unflinchingly; to prepare a grog and watch over the patient, happy to have him or them entirely at your mercy, the husband or the child whose temperature you had just taken with similar authority.

And yet in the annual cycle, the summer holidays did constitute a break, a different cycle, which might explain why your memories of that period (unless it was the abundance of photographs which came to the rescue) were more precise. Once it was summer, mealtimes were more flexible, the children went on playing in the garden with Papy and Mamie watching over them; when François closed the agency, you would take two weeks away from Empan.

You rented a bungalow or a flat, your requirements were a quiet place, a well equipped kitchen, and easy access to *traditional restaurants*. You liked the sea, the mountains were François's thing, that healthy living side, eating *fromage affiné* and coming home with bottles of local wine in the boot. You had decided you would take turns, but in actual fact, as you were the one who arranged the reservations, you went to the seaside more often than to the mountains. You would leave on the Saturday morning at seven a.m. at the latest, the car weighed down with suitcases.

"Wait. Let me just check if the gate is properly closed. All we need is to get burgled ..."

You always went by car. Since the beginning of the twentieth century, cars, also referred to as *automobiles*, have been used for the transportation of human beings. These machines weigh roughly a tonne and are made up of four low, thick rubber wheels supporting a metallic body fitted into a chassis. Their proportions are roughly one metre fifty high by two metres wide by three to five metres in length. The car's body contains a seating area which we enter through a door on either side, with two seats at the front and a long seat at the back. The most important seat is the one in which the person manoeuvring the vehicle, known as the *driver*, sits. An automobile can contain three to five additional people, who are known as *passengers*, while human beings outside the car are known as *pedestrians*.

An automobile moves about with the help of an internal combustion engine connected to a control system in the form of a steering wheel and a dashboard mounted in front of the driver. In order to function, the engine requires a liquid fuel made from a petroleum derivative which is distributed at *service stations*: these are found all over the country. One's ability to manoeuvre a car is sanctioned by the possession of *driving licence*, which is obtained after a training period generally undergone in early adulthood.

Cars are built in the shape of rectangular parallelepipeds that are elongated at the front with a sort of nose (it is difficult to describe such an object without resorting to animal or anthropological metaphors). This long nose, known as the *bonnet*, hides the engine's mechanisms, which consist of black entrails: a mixture of battery, hoses, spark plugs, belts and tanks. On either side of the bonnet, two lamps help light up the road at night. Between the roof and the bonnet there is a large glass pane called the *windscreen*, through which the driver looks at the road. Other windows are fitted to the upper part of the doors, and they can be raised and lowered by means of an electric or manual handle.

Driving a car implies a great number of risks, given the speed at which such a heavy vehicle moves, and despite the vigilance of drivers and an ensemble of rules laid down by society (the most typical example being that of *priority to the right*), the daily simultaneous traffic of thousands of automobiles leads every year to collisions, also known as *traffic accidents*, that result in the deaths of thousands of people belonging indiscriminately to the category of drivers, passengers, or pedestrians. This quantum of deaths has nevertheless been accepted by society as a regrettable but unavoidable consequence of an automobile system that, globally, has proved satisfactory.

If we look at the back of the car, we will see what is known as the *boot*, in other words the part of the interior reserved for belongings, as a car is a very practical vessel for moving heavy objects about without any physical effort on our part; and it was precisely to the boot that M.A. consigned the family's suitcases before leaving on holiday.

The price of an automobile varies depending on the make, the type of engine, and the model. But the purchase of a new automobile always requires a significant amount of money – several months or even years of wages – which means that the possibility of getting a car damaged or stolen is always a much-dreaded misadventure. As a result the automobile, once it was in general use by the middle of the twentieth century, became a recurrent topic of conversation in homes in industrialised countries. There would be a great deal of discussion about the various initiatives, personal or collective, to assure its security (part of François's job consisted in getting clients to take out automotive insurance policies). In these conversations one could hear terms such as *traffic jam, ticket, filled the tank, exhaust pipe, hub cap, garage, change the oil, registration document, car park, indicator, gearbox*. With each new law governing road safety, new terms were adopted; in recent decades some of these have been: *seat belt, helmet, penalty points,* and of course *radar*.

One does not keep the same car all one's life. Students – those who have the means – begin with a car that doesn't cost much; when their children are born they buy an automobile with a big seat in the back; once the children are gone, they sell again, to buy a model that is smaller but nevertheless superior to the one they had in their youth. Drivers quickly come to identify with their car. We say "I'm parked over there" when we mean "my car is parked over there". We leave items that have emotional value inside the car in order to make it more personal. We give it a nickname and eventually grow attached to it, as if it were a member of our family.

Small children like Xavier and Nathalie become familiar with cars from birth. For years, they have an intermediary status between passenger and freight, and when they come of age, they too will be drivers in their own right. Some of them (usually the male of the species) invest a great deal of money in these vehicles, they clean them, change them, resell them, decorate them, and talk about them a great deal, but most human beings sit behind the wheel every day without thinking about anything in particular: the practice of driving is so common that we have reached the stage where we measure distance in the time it takes to drive rather than in kilometres.

And when the time came for one of these big trips, it was always François who drove. You were separated by the gearstick.

It would be a long drive, but it could be quite pleasant, thanks to the music from the car radio – providing, of course, the children didn't throw up when you went around a bend, which could turn the trip into a *veritable nightmare*.

There, you were on your way. The clos des Narcisses receded behind you, and so did Empan, and the motorway tollbooth, and the worries at the agency; you were lulled by the sound of the engine, you chatted with your husband who, whenever he could truly accelerate, enjoyed the sensation of power that stems from the ability to move such a vehicle at such great speed with only the slightest adjustment of arm or ankle; a sensation of freedom.

Thanks to François's foresight, you would reach the holiday flat before the major bottlenecks began. You got out of the car, everyone stretched, the children were restless, you took possession of the premises.

"This will be great, don't you think?"

"The rooms are rather small, but at least everything is clean."

Before long you expressed your desire for some peace and quiet. For dinner you could just go to the buffet, or to the restaurant, or just have a few tomatoes, everyone could help themselves from the fridge. Manage on your own, no cooking to do. Don't make any noise, children, please.

"I'm having a nap. You're disturbing me."

Once the suitcases were unpacked, it was time to let you catch your breath. Your husband looked after the kids, and as he helped Nathalie put on her little Velcro-fastened shoes he realised how deprived he had been of these everyday little joys. Whereas you forgot about them; you almost neglected them. You put on your swimming costume and hurried to the sea. After your first swim, which was the best, you had a shower, then a nap, then another swim, and so on, several times a day. Your mental lists disintegrated, at most you might look at one of the women's magazines you had bought the day before. What a treat those moments were, to be anonymous amidst the peaceful hubbub of swimmers, to listen to the ebb and flow of the waves you would slip into again the moment the sun had warmed your skin through. The children were playing with their father. You let out a long sigh. On this beach your body became whole again; as if your entire person – scattered in tiny pieces during the year, hard little pieces like tools, which quickly and efficiently took care of all the tasks that fell to you day after day – now it was as if your body were growing softer in the salt water, liquefying, becoming timid pools in search of each other, then joyfully commingled, restoring your integrity at last, the pleasure of being a whole person, a woman lying on the sand.

"I'll tell you what my plan for the day is: to do nothing."

They caught you singing as you came out of the shower. Naked, you looked for the biggest mirror you could find. Once you had found it, you gazed at yourself. You had always been drawn to mirrors. At your parents' place there was a big one, set into the door of the wardrobe; in Empan there was a full-length one. You went closer and smiled at yourself. The August light changed the colour of your eyes, there were tiny intriguing spots in your irises. The heaviness of the heatwave secreted a dense, almost palpable silence, and you were filled with a desire to kiss every patch of that skin, that shoulder, those few dark beauty spots; you looked at yourself in the mirror and were pleased you had stayed slim after two pregnancies; as the days went by your suntan give you a new aspect, something you had never seen in Empan; and while your worries about Bédani or the shopping at the hypermarket faded, you lay in bed and patted your calf, a little golden ham you would have liked to bite into; you were not often caressed in that spot, you noted, although a pretty calf is very erotic. After another swim, you went on touching yourself, one leg and then the other, your round knee, your thighs, your belly, your two breasts rising from your brown torso, your upper chest flushing redder as you slipped your hand into the hollow of your navel, turning your fingers, stirring amidst the seaweed, around that soft invisible duvet, a delicate slit surrounded by shining hair that was fading to blonde, almost invisible.

"Mmm, the water feels good today!"

These holidays were the only time of the year you had *to yourself*. Your playfulness was reborn, and you were suddenly overcome by a desire to do things that were slightly out of the ordinary. You called loud and clear for breakfast in bed, you went with Xavier to the dodgems, you ate Italian ice cream or suddenly started a pillow fight. Then it was time for your herbal tea; don't anyone go near my chaise longue; all the mosquitoes went after you. François smiled:

"There's no-one else like you."

He gazed lovingly at you, and indulged your slightest whims. Thus one evening you felt so beautiful that you convinced him to go with you to the Rive Bleue casino. You'd been intrigued by the place, with its flashing lights, ever since the start of your stay, and you didn't want to leave without having seen it. In you went, and together you changed a hundred-franc note into a huge pile of coloured plastic chips, while François said,

"My darling, I can't believe the things you get me to do . . ."

You went down to the lower level, with its dazzle of multi-coloured neon lights and blare of brash music, and found yourselves next to an oval table where a sort of hopscotch was printed on its green baize. Players were putting chips on numbered squares: they were playing *petite roulette*. There was a couple next to you, as well as a young man, a woman in her fifties, and an elderly man with a blasé expression. You assumed they were regulars, and you immediately tried to imagine their lives. Had they made a fortune in oil? If they lost vast amounts one night, did they try to commit suicide along the quay? Did the elderly gentleman argue with his mistress before he came? Did they take drugs, putting on a disabused air, on board a yacht anchored in the Mediterranean? You observed them from under your brows until one of them caught you looking. So then you concentrated on the little roulette ball, *impair, manque*, all those numbers. First you bet on the six, then on the two, and you lost both bets with a distraught little look, your pulse racing; you tried again and then suddenly you were winning, once, twice, three times. Your pile of chips grew, François opened his eyes wide. And these were small amounts, you knew that you would lose in the end. You had come "just for fun, to have a look", you said to François to convince him, but before leaving the place, somewhat stunned, feeling distinctly that you were going against your own morals, for a few minutes you would experience that moment that all gamblers know: when the initial quantity of chips has grown slightly and the sum of additional money excites one's greed and liberates one's imagination. You wondered what would have happened if you had put not just a few dozen but hundreds, thousands of francs on the table, if one hot night you had stayed there until morning, if you had won thirty-six times your initial bet, and put it all back on the baize and gone on winning, if you had become rich, rich beyond measure: then your life would have changed dramatically.

For a start, you could have satisfied your basest needs. To buy a camcorder, a triple heat toaster and a food processor; you could have changed your wardrobe, and furnished your bedroom with the maxi bed from the Habitat catalogue, and curtains trimmed with braid, you could have redone the stairway in marble to decorate your living room, which you would have enhanced with a big picture window with remote control opening. Then you saw yourself in a long gown going down to your kitchen at dinnertime. Just within reach you would have a thousand exotic fruits, a thousand extravagant desserts, a chocolate pyramid, juicy strawberries, a gleaming vanilla sauce, creams, mousses, fruit cakes and jam and bread, the most delicious little tarts, vol-au-vents with quail, walnut bread, legs of lamb, crayfish, you could eat as much as you wanted and it would all be served to you on a silver platter, you had only to hold out your hand for a glass of champagne, and one word would suffice to resolve any problems; the word *problem* would no longer even exist, because in your fantasy you would have chefs in your home, and manicurists, a butler, beauticians and hairdressers, and they would all treat you with great admiration and respect; you would no longer have to take care of anything, there would be no more papers, no more bills, no more annoyances, and in your great benevolence you would give to the poor, after making a moving speech in the presence of other philanthropists at a grand high-society gala where you would be queen, you would take a jet to a Moroccan *riad*; there waiting for you would be your new friends, all good-looking and in good health, and your conversations would always elevate you; one morning you would fly to a faraway island where the blue of the sea was like a floating sapphire, while sitars played the same serenade over and over. You would stay at table with your guests for a long time. You would drink liqueurs, there would be a scent of anise, lemon, honey, and cumin, as you sat on soft cushions, the flickering glow from the candles reflected in the inlaid mirrors, you would listen to Mozart in Dolby stereo. Once night had fallen, you would go alone onto the patio to contemplate the shimmering lights in the valley, and the weather would be balmy, of course. In the distance a bird with indigo plumage would sing in the moonlight. Then a man would come to join you, a man embellished by money, made more powerful and free; you pictured yourself reclining on elegant divans; making love in your chambers under filmy canopies, on immaculate sheets or, to your surprise, on private planes, reality would be nothing more than a long aftertaste, something both sugary and sweet and salty that you would savour with half-closed eyes, you'd be wearing Chanel, drinking red wine at sunset. One morning, your lover would be waiting for you at the airport on the tarmac, you would get into his car and the two of you would go off to know eternal love, there would be no more past, no more taxes, no more baby bottles to heat up, your hands would always be soft and your legs freshly shaven, you would never lose your keys again, you would not put on weight, now that would be happiness.

"Darling?"

François was looking at you. Everyone else in the living room was staring at the wall. Your husband was hanging the painting, "Provençal Mas with Lavender".

"A bit further to the right."

"Like this, how's that?"

"Perfect."

"Well, what do you think? No regrets?"

No, no regrets, apart from coming home, and after the return journey on the motorway, feeling your body *get back in the rhythm*, emptying the suitcases and putting them away, you were immobilised by assorted domestic obligations – water the garden, start a load of laundry, not to mention the fridge, which was empty. When you saw the chemin des Pins again after the summer break, you always felt a little bit down. Because once you'd exchanged whatever tiny bit of news there was for the month of August with your neighbour Monsieur Pommier – Oh, there were some youngsters on the vacant lot, getting drunk, and the police came – once you'd opened the mail and been all round the house to make sure everything was fine, you knew nothing new would be waiting for you. It would take you only a few hours to tell your parents what you'd done on holiday. François was already getting out his papers, with his preoccupied Sunday evening look, you had to find some clothes for these children obstinately set on growing, Xavier would be starting infant school this year, are we having Sunday dinner at your mother's?

The homecoming was not without recriminations:

"Honestly, can you not take better care of your suits, I'm not the maid around here!"

"So now I've got to go to the Halle aux Chaussures again, what a nuisance!"

"It was so lovely by the seaside."

François took you in his arms. As he was not in charge of "stocking up the house" at the Intermarché, he could not understand why you were so moody.

"We'll go again next year."

"I work until seven, how do you expect me to do anything?"

Your conversations resumed their morning routine. Obviously, you were the one who would stop at the dry cleaner's, next summer you would find another *gîte* to see if the sea wasn't more beautiful elsewhere, and anyway next summer, from the vantage point of early September, always seemed impossibly far away; your blues always lasted that little bit longer with each passing year. You would try to persuade François to go away again, one more time, even just for two days. You could send the kids to their grandparents'.

"The weather is still so beautiful."

"I'll try, my darling, I'll get organised."

While waiting for this last break, you made some changes on the ground floor. You put the yellow trivet you had bought at La Grande-Motte on the tablecloth, you decided to go to the swimming pool twice a week from then on (with Chloé, who now lived fifteen minutes away; her move had been a source of true joy). But all too soon the trivet lost its charm, one week followed another and, as the weekend in Les Baux-de-Provence had *been just what you needed*, once again you let yourself be

113

overwhelmed by your family, and your resolution to do some sport was engulfed by your role as housewife, as your body went back to its familiar gestures, you felt yourself being constantly devoured by everything there was to do.

Starting a load of washing, for example: fill the drum with dirty clothes, choose programme number six, "whites and colours", turn the knob, press the start button, close the door to the laundry room. You didn't actually need to listen, but your ears heard the succession of inarticulate sounds the washing machine made; they began with a clear gurgle of water filling the drum, the hum of a motor starting up, then a spell of silence, then the drum beginning to turn; there was the familiar sound of the motor combined with the flip-flop of clothes knocking inside the drum in ten-second phases, followed by a pause, then a new rotation, and from time to time a click, when a button struck the metal wall of the machine. You recognised every new cycle of washing, the motor turning in short bursts before stopping again; starting; stopping, and in your ears was a constant hum, the sound of a washing machine running.

But there was some happiness to being back in your own place, with the garden in flower, your kitchen, your friends, the happiness of drinking muscat wine on the patio on a picture-perfect evening. The children talked fondly about their new teacher, they climbed trees, and their shouts, like the cadences of the washing machine, were something you recognised; you could tell if one of them had fallen, or if the boy was getting annoyed with his sister, like the influx of additional water, followed by the hollow sound of a hose draining until the knob clicked on to the next cycle, emitting another sound. You could hear François telling how you had bought "a proper artist's painting" in Provence, and you could hear the rotations starting up again, the clothes were soaked, rotation; pause; rotation; pause.

There was something vaguely dreary about that repetitive rumbling, but what could you have done to reinvigorate your life with each homecoming? It was impossible, unless you were to lapse into *implausibility* or *psychological instability*. So, yes, a painting you had bought during that romantic escapade, an escapade which silenced your reproaches for a brief while, did indeed add a certain novelty to the living room.

"But, hey, you must have paid a small fortune for it, it's art!"

"It's more *noble* than a photograph."

"It's not the same thing."

"You forget the price, the quality remains."

Said your friends.

"Provençal Mas with Lavender", which François hung in the living room, was a painting in acrylics, with a wooden frame, representing a farm in nature. The lower two-thirds of the painting were filled with a broad expanse of green, offset at the top by blue and at the bottom by a layer of ochre to indicate the earth. Then the viewer saw violet, or to be more precise, six sorts of mauve tubes representing a field of lavender, and to the left were spots shaped like little trees, in all likelihood olive trees. Right at the centre was the Provençal *mas*, a pastel brown and beige block. One's gaze was drawn to the thick black outlines around the rows of lavender, the walls of the *mas* and the olive trees; no doubt these lines were an expression of the artist's individuality, an attempt at distinction from classic landscape painting. The sky, with its impasto of white clouds, veering towards red, and the light coming from the right: the viewer was meant to imagine a sunset.

And otherwise, once you were back from holiday you might sign the children up for early-learning activities: judo classes, pottery courses or gym lessons, depending on what was on offer in the magazine *Living in Empan*; you could go and fetch the roll of twenty-four photographs you had taken during the holiday, and sitting behind the wheel of your car you would open the envelope, in the end you were glad François had got you to pose on the beach – but no matter how hard you tried, there would be nothing going on back here other than programme number 6, "whites and colours". Now the motor would speed up, the plop-plop of the clothing would come to a halt, to be replaced by a sudden shrill noise of acceleration, the motor would pick up speed, the rhythm of the spin cycle would be faster, increasing the level of sound in the house, until there came a still louder bang. The knob had moved forward a notch. Then once again the calm of the drum turning: rotation, pause, rotation.

The laundry had started half an hour earlier. You closed the envelope with the photographer's striped logo, you put the keys in the ignition, thinking, This evening we'll have noodles; there was some leftover stew from Sunday, that would do fine. The washing machine continued its cycle until another influx of water, then the engine went from a rumble to an increasingly strident whirr, louder and louder, faster still, and faster still again, until the entire machine began vibrating in place on the tiles.

"What's that, Maman?"

"Don't you see, sweetheart, it's a painting."

"Yes but why are you and Papa staring at it like that?"

"Because it's pretty."

In the gallery where you had found the painting, there was a small sign describing the artist: "With a melodious, tonic palette, symphonies of green, purple and yellow, Laure Cordine paints subjects and landscapes from the south of France. Her canvases are true to life, because they lovingly reproduce a harmonious lifestyle, set in a landscape of generous nature. Born on 19 September 1948 in Nice, Laure Cordine had always been drawn to painting, but it was only when her second son was born that she enrolled at the Beaux-Arts and revealed her innate talent as a colourist. Since 1975 Laure Cordine has been pursuing her career with steady enthusiasm and constant innovation. Her paintings are sold all over the world."

You showed the photographs to your friends, and later on you put the album away on the shelf next to the others, all neatly ordered. Because all it took was a whooshing sound that lasted too long or was too high-pitched, or the absence of a spinning sound after a certain while, for you to head, frowning, towards the laundry room, to probe the white plastic in search of some possible malfunction; but no; everything was as it should be, and the machine went on.

You recall how much you had liked the painting, you and François, that time you went to spend two nights in Les Baux-de-Provence. You walked along the paved village streets. There were so many art galleries that, although it was not something you and François were in the habit of doing, this time you felt compelled, by an open-mindedness peculiar to tourist activities, in conjunction with the purchasing power of a couple who, while they may no longer enjoy the *enchantment of the early days*, still know how to get away for a romantic weekend; so you ventured into one of the galleries. You walked around among the paintings, then went back out without saying a word. It was only at the restaurant that you spoke of it again – of the silent contemplation, of those canvases, and you had both noticed – initially surprised, and then touched – that you had been affected, "How should I put it, aesthetically", by those paintings. Because your husband was receiving significant bonuses at the time, because there was something lacking in your decoration of the living room, and because, finally, you liked the idea of making your shared taste visible, a shared taste which, so people believe, reinforces a marriage, you went back the next day. After much careful deliberation you chose the painting that you, M.A., liked best, from among sunsets in olive groves, fishing ports, and other typical settings, including a "Village with Poppies", you chose the "Provençal Mas with Lavender". Although it was a very costly purchase, you nevertheless felt, with delight, that you were doing a good deed, making a frank and honourable commitment as a couple towards art.

And with the four of you gathered by the wall in the living room, this too is a tableau; since with each autumn homecoming everything started again, a clear gurgle of water, lasting, lasting, the monotonous sound of the cycles starting up again, the motor picking up speed, the sonorous whoosh becoming increasingly shrill, depending on the phase of the spin cycle, everything churning in your ears until the knob moves forward another notch. Click. A short pause. And the motor again. You no longer know when it started, perhaps forty minutes ago; it is time to go and fetch Xavier from school, it is time for dinner, and now the button on a pair of trousers is banging against the metal drum; you set off in the car while the cycles continue; a few seconds of motor, a few seconds of silence; you prepare the meal until a little clicking sound; the programme was finished. A changed silence returns to the house.

When you went into the living room, it felt as if the entire room had been transformed. As you looked at "Provençal Mas with Lavender" you were once again right there in that village with its labyrinthine pedestrian streets, and what you remembered was that it was followed by a sexual interlude in the hotel room. You had to wait for the red light to go off before opening the washing machine. As the years went by, the painting remained associated with a vague contentment, then gradually became nothing more than a pretty landscape, which you will eventually no longer notice but still respect, if for no other reason than you recall how much you had paid for it.

Now you are kneeling in front of the washing machine, with the basket between your knees, reaching your arm through the open door. The washer surrenders a tangled mass of clothes, like a bevy of children on their way out of school, you unfold them, with one hand you wave to Xavier among his schoolmates, he gets into the car and you continue along the circuit for that day, then you hang those clothes on the line in the garden. The weather is mild for September. The laundry line is completely filled, your fingertips are all damp, in the kitchen your little boy is having his snack, he watches as you come back to him with the empty basket on your hip, the dampness on your fingertips mingled with the satisfaction that has taken hold of you at the sight of his little face smudged with hot chocolate – that feeling of having accomplished things: you have done a load of laundry and put it out to dry.

III

On the big calendar hanging above the telephone, that big calendar with pictures of marmots in April and snow in December, you wrote in black felt tip on the square for Friday, November 9 one simple word: "Dinner". That evening friends came to dine at your home. You had sent out the invitation after an earlier meal with the same group, since you had tacitly agreed to take turns inviting each other round, and you all expected one of the wives to suggest a date that would then be confirmed by telephone and written in black felt-tip pen on other calendars. For you this little word was the promise of an evening that would be a change: it would entail a lot of work, to be sure, but it would be a pleasing diversion from the flow of your week; an event. Or at least you hoped it would.

As Friday drew nearer, a slight anxiety came over you. Because the fact that four, six, or sometimes even eight people would be coming into your living room, even people you knew and liked, made you nervous; because they did not only come to eat and drink, they too came for a change from their everyday life, and to spend what is known as *a good evening*; and for all to go well, for them to go away content with their evening, it meant you had to make an entire series of minute decisions and execute them in perfect tempo; in order for everything to unfold according to the expected ritual, it meant that you had to be (that simple word in felt-tip pen) perfectly organised. Because the responsibility for the evening rested with you alone, even if it was your husband who would close the door behind them when they went off into the night. That was why that little nervousness was part of the programme.

You had to agree on the menu. You consulted François, who said, Make what you want, it's always good, and he would take care of the wine. You then went through your cookbooks and, depending on the season and your mood, you made your choice and drew up a shopping list on the basis of the recipes you had chosen. The day before the dinner, you went to the supermarket, walking methodically up and down the aisles in order not to forget anything on your list. Back at the house, you put the bags full of shopping on the kitchen table. The children were lured by the rustling crackle of plastic, there were multi-coloured bags, boxes, and biscuits for the aperitif, things they were not used to seeing in the house. You told them not to touch, that it wasn't for them; it was for tomorrow, Maman and Papa were having friends round.

There was nothing mandatory about these dinners, no-one in the group had imposed them, not even your husband, who merely made suggestions ("It's been a long time," he would say, "since we've seen Laurent and Brigitte."). But at regular intervals, as if by magic, different guests, friends or family, would sit round the table in the living room. You were careful not to schedule these dinners too often. "Because it's a lot to think about" (you told François), but you organised them with good grace. In spite of the additional work it gave you, you took pleasure in your role as housewife: it made you the orchestra conductor of these evenings.

Everything happened in either the living room or the kitchen. The kitchen for you, the living room for the guests. When you got back from work on that Friday the 9th, you would remove any papers left lying around on the table in the living room, and choose a tablecloth. Everything was still quiet. At around six o'clock you went into the kitchen, you chopped some onions, melted butter, scraped the carrots, you minced and stuffed and salted and peppered and added shallots, you brought to the boil, you peeled, you removed pips, you added the *bouquet garni*. All these gestures repeated at the same moment in other kitchens, all these gestures that so many women have made for so many other guests, all these gestures, now you were making them; and just as you used to watch your mother making them as she listened to the radio, now at the end of the table Nathalie was drawing and watching you. She saw her mother; a cookbook open on the plastic tablecloth; leaning towards the page smudged with flour to read the recipe, a dish cloth in her hand to wipe her fingers, her mother leaning over, an apron around her waist: all was well.

The hall smelled of plums and melted chocolate, it was time for François to come home from the agency. He had managed to get away not too late, he kissed you and asked you what he could do. You assigned him a few small tasks: bring in the chairs, put the extra leaf in the table, take care of the wine; he did as you asked. You told him what was on the menu. Suddenly you remembered that there were two of you, and that that evening you would not be having your ordinary dinnertime conversation, you would be exchanging the precise gazes of the initiated. Your husband had his role to play in your organisation, he must steer the conversation away from prickly topics, fill glasses, pass the salt, slice bread; you knew that he would play his role; just as you knew you would avoid overcooking a dish or buying substandard cheese; he would avert any tension, and thanks to the little tasks he completed, your husband would contribute to the harmonious equilibrium of *the couple who are having guests round*, so that when you luxuriated in the after-party contentment, when you were in bed and he kissed you, saying that the dinner had been a success, perhaps adding his thanks, he would be proud of himself and pleased with you.

So you told the children to behave themselves during the meal, because it was not just your image as chef and spouse that was important, but also your image as a mother, that too was important. It was half past seven, time to lay the table. It was a quarter to eight, the vegetables were cooling in the Teflon frying pan, you hurried upstairs, pulled on a skirt, changed your blouse, and rushed to put on your make-up in the bathroom.

That was when, in the silence of the tiled walls, you were overcome with fatigue. Now that everything had been done in the kitchen, you had only one desire: to sleep, to sleep without having to smile or dish out the food. You felt yourself grow weaker as you stood by the mirror. You went even closer, you thought you looked pretty, you made up one eye and then the other, hoping that all would go well, of course it would, everything would be fine. The little mascara brush was still stroking your eyelashes when you heard steps on the gravel, and the doorbell announced that the first guests had arrived.

The door opened wide.

The guests: the sound of shoes scraping on tiles, echoing greetings, others responding, faces entering the room and cheeks touching, bodies chilled by the outside temperature, the odour of perfume, bouquets and wine bottles, deposited in your arms. François shook hands. Everyone sat round the coffee table, waiting for the aperitif. The evening had begun. You were already back in the kitchen, the bowl for the olive stones was missing; a circular inspection of your domain, your friends were waiting for you in the living room, you had to go back. But now that same weariness came over you. Now you really would rather wait here for all those "strangers" (as your mother would have said) to sit round the table. It would be so much simpler, you need only serve them, like a simple maid, you could stay in the shadows, hear the rhythm of the discussions from the kitchen, you could spend your time checking on the roast, getting the desserts out ahead of time; these details passed fleetingly through your head all evening long, it would be so much more restful to deal with them here, alone and hidden, rather than to have to, at the same time ... But it was nothing, scarcely a thought, now you were hurrying, picking up the tray, and in the living room the men cheered the arrival of the port.

Sentences were uttered, then others, regarding basic information, work, children. After a glass of kir, your nervousness slipped down a notch; although throughout the meal you would remain anxious, your mind split between the living room and the kitchen, your body making regular trips from one to the other. These trips provided a rhythm for the dinner, neither too slow nor too quick, so that the successive arrival of dishes followed at a steady pace. At precise moments you got up and headed into the kitchen. You had to know how to measure out these successive entrances, so that your friends did not grow bored or feel pressured; for example, now that you had begun the aperitif, and merriment was well under way, you could come and stay longer in your domain. But other footsteps followed in the wake of your discreet ones, more audible, those of the other women. Do you need any help? No, no, I'll be fine. You laughed, you complimented each other on the dresses you had bought during the sales, and which your husbands had not even noticed. You went back into the living room together, but you were the one who declared:

"If you'd like to sit round the table now, dinner's ready."

And it was like the first movement after an overture. Each of the guests found a place to sit, and after a short silence the conversation would be woven again around several more general topics, to do with the holidays, politics, or meteorological phenomena, and from this topic a theme would emerge and dominate most of the conversation for the rest of the evening. As for you, you forced yourself to remain in your chair (you had been so active over the last few hours, so it wasn't easy), and you watched as the salad bowl was handed round the table. When everyone had been served, it all became simpler: it was time to eat.

But it was only after the roast had been sliced and handed out on plates, and you had emptied three bottles of wine between you, that the last vestiges of your nervousness vanished; when, in the warmth of full stomachs, you noticed that all had gone well; and, besides, that the table was a mess, invaded by crusts of bread, noises, and greasy cutlery placed right on the tablecloth; it all proved that your invitation had ended up what it was meant to be, a success. The children had gone off to bed after politely saying good night, and you were in the middle of the cheese. Smiling, you talked with the friend sitting next to you. François thought you were beautiful.

In the kitchen, the fat in the roasting pan had congealed. You sent your husband to fetch a missing dessert spoon. He got to his feet for the first time, and on his way back he kissed you, in front of everyone; they complimented you, and joked politely; it was a symphony coming to an end; all that was left to do was to fill the coffee pot while chair legs scraped as they were being pushed back, and the smell of cigarette smoke wafted through the room, then there were a few yawns in quick succession. As a first departure precipitated all the others, coats were put back on, and cheeks were kissed in the hall, crowded once again. Cars started up, and the front door closed against the cold. Suddenly it was quiet, and this quiet was surprising.

The two of you set about cleaning up. François with slow gestures, while yours were quick and efficient. You wanted to go to bed, to get out of the kitchen, it now seemed to you that the day had been unusually long. You went up the stairs, you felt rather heavy, rather sad as you closed your eyes, kissing the man at your side who was already asleep. It was only a meal, after all, even if it had been good.

And so, the morning after, there was always an aftertaste of disappointment. You would hide it, invoking with François the best moments of the evening, commenting on the anecdote that Whosit or Whatsit had told, and you felt no compunction if you were judgemental about your friends, but before long there was nothing left to preserve, the moment had passed. Perhaps you would have more fun at the next dinner party, hosted by another woman, but that was still a long way off, and besides, that meal would be followed by the same disappointment.

You were waiting for something. You persuaded François to go away for the weekend, you went to the cinema, or you frenetically scrubbed the bathroom. You would have liked different words to be written on the calendar every week – the date of a show, the hairdresser's, the purchase of a new piece of furniture, an event of any description, you put a great deal of care into planning everything, and if despite your efforts you happened to have an empty week on the calendar, already on Sunday a gnawing despondency came over you. At the sight of a week with no handwritten entries you were on the verge of tears.

Already as a child you had been acquainted with expectancy. The summer holidays, a radiant horizon of sunshine and play, surrounded by loving adults. Then the days got shorter, soon it would be time to go back to school, you were a little bit frightened, but there would be so many new things! You told your maman about your girlfriends in the class, and when you came home from secondary school, you would show her your timetable. By November, as the autumn holidays for All Saints' had been dreary, Christmas seemed like a star in the dull sky of your everyday school routine. Your anticipation was powerful, and so was the let-down. February was anything but jolly, but soon it would be spring. Little things made you happy, it was enough just to go for a walk in a grassy place with your parents, and then it was summer again. You went off to see Papy, you fed the rabbits in their hatches. Once you were at university, it was your exams that marked the passage of the weeks. You had no responsibilities other than to hand in your papers on schedule, your parents sent you a cheque, time went by, lightly, every year was different, you travelled, you discovered love, life was like one long toboggan ride. Then there was your internship, Chambéry, the move, you were taken on at Bédani, you had to learn, obey, integrate. You got your wages, the alarm clock rang every morning, only the weekends were left to have fun. But then your love for François brought a new quickening to your heartbeat. You went dancing together on Fridays, you went out to eat, you saw a lot of people (now you wonder what has become of them all), you got married. For nine months you put on weight, then emptied out.

The birth was a veritable event. From between your thighs came a baby who filled you with strange sensations you had never experienced before. For your second pregnancy you let nature get on with it (François added with pride that nature had been very insistent) and you had a daughter. So everything was perfect. Your shared dream of starting a family had become a reality. But above all, other new things were about to happen. Thanks to your round belly you had appointments in your diary: paediatrician or midwife; the entire year headed in a precise direction, towards what was known as "term". Because unlike other years, which are drifting, confused, or uneventful, a year of pregnancy carries its justification in its very entrails, and has a finality about it that will be engendered after an attentively negotiated series of stages; a year of pregnancy carries within it, in a way, that *dramatic tension* which the publishers on the boulevard Saint-Germain obstinately hope to find in every manuscript, yet once they have at last determined its absence or its potential they then go on to ask the author to accentuate its arc; like those food lovers who are obsessed with one particular flavour and want to find it everywhere, and once they have tasted it at last in the dish before them, insist it must be the dominant note, because it alone, and not the subtle mixture of the chef's spices, can possibly explain the rapture of their taste buds; like those publishers, M.A. had failed to understand that what fills a life is a way of being, the present tense of the sentence in which one is breathing, not an event situated in the future which, after being consumed, will leave us standing disappointed in front of the refrigerator.

And so; once the birth was behind you, there was this relapse, this hollowness, soon busy with everything there was to do, buying the new pram, filling the drawer with nappies. In those days your fatigue was so intense that all you aspired to was quiet, the days did not yet have those empty squares on the calendar, white squares to be coloured in. Your daughter against your breast, comfort all around you, friends, parents who said *Stay in bed, sweetheart.* Then the visits related to the baby became less frequent. There was one last hope as long as you were breast-feeding, something to look forward to, but no matter how you kept putting it off, sooner or later Nathalie would have to be weaned. The space you had felt opening between your hips closed again more tightly than before. The weeks went by, each one identical to the next, with the agency, your work at Bédani, and preparing the evening meal. Of course, one day your little girl was walking, and saying "Papa", one morning Xavier started primary school, but the children's laughter was only a pleasant background noise, nothing spectacular. You eventually grew weary of it.

And yet with the birth of your son, how you had loved shaking the bottle of baby lotion and squirting his little bottom, making all the new, tender, material gestures that motherhood sets in motion.

A child had arrived in the house.

You had to get organised, with special food, with his waking in the night, and your worrying about whether his bottom was clean or dirty. And when there was nothing left to do for that new little body, babbling in his cradle, he was there at your disposition; you had given him a name, you would bring him up. After the "Xavier" page in the album, in golden-yellow ink, there came the "Nathalie" page. The second child was greeted with greater simplicity. You were a mother now, you were more *in control*, her insistent wailing would eventually stop, at worst she would wear herself out. Thus you had become a family. You talked about car seats, holidays at the grandparents' place, birthdays, family allowances, and every July 14 you went to see the fireworks. There were lovely moments. The two children looking up at the dazzling sky, and your husband with his arm around your waist, the bursts of light, your little family cell lost in the crowd and the wonderment of those colours, when the entire sky sparkled with light descending in showers of invisible carbon meteorites.

Until that Saturday morning when the first class photograph arrived.

You remember: you looked at that group portrait, little children all in a row, and naturally you compared it with your own memories. Not that long ago, you were the child being taken to school in the morning, you were the one smothered in kisses, you were the one someone was waiting for when school was over. It was the month of May. It was hot. You were sitting between Xavier eating his cereal, and Nathalie sucking on her bottle. Your gaze paused on the refrigerator door, and automatically your mind began to draw up a list, you knew what was missing from the shelves, liquid yoghurt, butter spread, and then your mind veered to the trip you'd make to the supermarket on Saturday with your two children on the back seat. Because from there on out it would always be the same thing, always these mornings and these meals, always as a family, this constant concern for other people . . . So this was what you – their mother, for now and always – were sentenced to. And you understood that the deep plates on which your existence was founded, the ones that had begun to shift when you turned seventeen, those plates had stopped in a certain location to leave you here, in this house in Empan-sur-Nive, with a husband and two children; and in the future it would be much more difficult to bring about any change to that order. Never again, without resorting to an entire complicated organisation, would there be those selfish, quiet mornings when you could just drink your coffee and dream about your Saturday evening, about what you were going to buy with your most recent paycheque, never again, because of these children who had left your womb in order to sip their milk at thistable, would you be able to think about yourself alone.

Thus, those endless spells of waiting from your childhood took hold of you once again.

You booked the flat in Cassis or La Ciotat already in January, and you wondered if you ought to sign up for a course in gardening, or paint the corridor a darker colour. You were looking for a purpose, even a small one, even a stupid one, something that would be like a beacon to light up your calendar, a word in black felt-tip pen, to indicate a before and an after. Your hunger even fed off minor accidents. They called you from the crèche, Nathalie had fallen and hurt herself; the trip to the doctor's; your heart beating faster; the ultimate diagnosis, "Nothing serious, madame." You went home, her pale little face, you put her to bed, at dinner you described the event to François. He listened, his eyes bright. That week would stand out, it would be the week when Nathalie fell at the crèche. Even unpleasant things were useful for warding off the emptiness.

In December you could let yourself be carried away by the Christmas festivities. To the children's delight, which you shared, you brought out the garlands, and the scent of fir reigned in the house, the air was lighter, something cheery and mysterious filled the days leading up to the 25th with excitement. But every year ended for you with a feeling of frustration; all that work for this, for a migraine, without even getting the presents you might have wanted (it was enough to make you think that no-one had the slightest inkling of your secret desires). Because workplaces were closed, the days that followed were long, the children tried out their toys and squabbled. Then it was time to wish everyone a happy New Year, and after that, eventful days were even fewer and further between, you changed the clocks to summer time, bought a new lamp, had an argument.

On Sundays you loaded everyone in the car and went hiking in the Chartreuse. The sun on your skin imposed its serenity, you walked, the kids babbled, François carried the backpack; maybe then; for a brief instant, between two trails marked red and white; without a thought, for an instant, satisfied. But as the sun set, once you had knocked your shoes against a stone to avoid dirtying the inside of the car, off you drove, and you turned your head towards the window, while a cold sadness welled up inside you. The weekend was over. Beyond your window you saw the houses encroaching on the last vestiges of countryside, and then came the roundabouts, the traffic signs, and all the well-being acquired from your walk dissipated as you drove past the huge Darty warehouses, and the question of dinner was before you once again. You bought two "everything on it" specials from the pizza van, and your son grabbed the boxes for the pleasure of the aroma that emerged and of feeling their warmth on his knees; in this way he was stockpiling good memories, unaware that his mother was, without any pleasure, watching the road climb towards La Garotte, the rows of villas, the chemin des Pins, your house, your car entering the garage. François opened the door. You hurried over to the calendar. The week was empty. How could you illuminate the long passage until the following Sunday?

You could not voice your feelings of dissatisfaction, because – and images from all over the world came to remind you – everything had been programmed for you to be happy. In your country there were no floods, no war, no epidemics, people died at the age they were supposed to die, no bankruptcy in sight, just a tough career ladder for your husband, and your concern about the children's future orientation. Later on, your mother would die in a room with dirty curtains, you would be sacked from your job, there would be a burglary, but you would never experience anything extraordinary, you would never win the lottery or be taken hostage, which might have made you famous. The ordeals you would face would be only secondary annoyances, the difficulties one confronts among adults and which can be resolved, provided one remains reasonable; to be sure, they would leave their mark on your skin; the skin of your hand now reaching for a glass in this kitchen; but those are ordinary wrinkles, not the scars of those who have been seriously wounded.

But for the time being; once Xavier was settled in his school, you signed him up for judo; you were overwhelmed every minute of the day by the demands of the household, living in your middle-class white affluence, calling your parents twice a week, going to visit them on Sundays, finding a day nanny for Nathalie, making love once a week, doing it doggie-style once a fortnight, a weekly fellatio, a biannual cunnilingus; so, for the time being; everything was as it should be. You had reached the place you wanted to be in when you used to talk about it, as you sat smoking on the pouffes; to be married, have children, "working at the same time because you have to be independent", so why didn't you feel genuinely satisfied?

"You always want more."

"You're never happy."

Your husband was irritable. Even on holiday, something uneasy was creeping in, even in the sun, even in the *farniente*, when you had absolutely nothing to worry about, now the slightest little thing could cause that sense of utter fulfilment you used to feel by the seaside to fracture. A seagull was pecking the ground with its beak and you instantly thought about the parquet floor that needed changing in the guest room. And yet how you would have loved to be like the women you saw on the posters! With a radiant smile, a skip in your walk, making love languorously, preparing the dinner in a flash while keeping up an amusing conversation. No such thing. Already in the morning, there would be something to exasperate you, a hollow feeling; and then that expectancy, always. There was something missing. You became irritable, you shouted at the children, you promised you would take them for a walk and in the end you collapsed in front of the television.

"Is something wrong?"

"I feel a bit down, that's all."

François tried to understand your moods, but he didn't know what to do, you daunted him. He would come home tired, all energy spent on a growing number of clients. You watched him come in, diminished, like a soldier on leave, drained, with no originality, in only a few years his features had swollen, he snored at night, and chewed his meat inelegantly. He had become incapable of making the gesture that would have sufficed; rather than a thousand words, if for just one minute he could have been sure of himself and granted you enough importance to lose his temper. You would have preferred his anger to this constant, pitiful withdrawal, this pretence of appeasement; as if with tender gestures he could calm the spiteful anger that you wanted to suppress but did not know how.

IV

So, when one day Philippe at the office looked at you more intently, and began to smile more systematically, when one day he complimented you on your suit, and as you were leaving his office you could feel his gaze on your back, precisely focused, when one day you understood, basically, that he fancied you, you felt more alive.

You remember; it was easier to get up in the morning. The car started right up and once the children had been dropped off at their respective institutions of literacy and child-minding, you rushed off to work. You had to take the *route nationale* in the direction of Valvoisin, go through the tunnel under the motorway where you saw the sign BÉDANI FURNITURE next to the sign for La Révole, drive up as far as the administrative building, a sort of glass cube next to the production warehouses, then go up two flights of stairs. The room where you had written, telephoned, drawn up summaries, done the maths, obeyed orders, and dozed, was a quiet place, and it was in this room that for the first time you would have what is commonly referred to as an affair.

At the time, the company was a prosperous S.M.E., the product of a rather clever idea on the part of its founder. At the end of the 1960s Marc Bédani repaired an old dresser with some bits of wood his father had brought back from Vietnam and left in a corner of the family cabinetwork and furniture restoration workshop. He made a piece that was an original mixture of the two types of wood and, according to his elderly parents, this made it look "rather over the top". The dresser was left at the entrance to the warehouse as a sort of curiosity. Several clients stopped to look at it, and that very week it was sold to a young couple who were teachers. Young Bédani, sensing that this could be a market worth expanding, went abroad again, brought back a few varieties of rare wood, and promptly began to manufacture furniture for the home, later known as the *Bédani-Exotic* range. The idea was to play with the different hues of tropical wood and local varieties. This meant it was somewhat tricky to make, but there was definitely a demand. As Bédani had suspected, young households were soon besotted with his furniture and its unusual, slightly modern aesthetic, which they preferred to antique family dressers. A few years later the company left the family workshop and opened a factory on the *route nationale*, near the village known as La Révole, a name which for many of the employees became synonymous with the company itself. But the half-exotic, half-French furniture was still subject to the dangerous fluctuations of international transport, "not to mention the political instability of the supplier countries", he told his wife after Sunday mass. So that was when Bédani had another innovative idea: to make new furniture *that looked old*. His workers would make dressers, sand them to give them a sort of patina, then bash them fiercely with bicycle chains. This treatment gave a worm-eaten allure to a product which with its holes and dents now looked old, while offering all the solidity of a new piece of furniture. In its presence customers felt the lingering impression of paternal wisdom and good-natured indifference that an old dresser lends to a room, similar to chests of drawers or any furniture that has witnessed the passage of many lives before our own and which will long outlive us. In fact, Marc Bédani anticipated something that would soon become the fashion, the *return to authenticity*; he even called this range *Bédani-Authentic*. A drop in the price of wood contributed to the rapid rise in the company C.E.O.'s fortune – unless it was due to the growth the country enjoyed at the time.

When you started working there in 1979, the company was still expanding. Exotic wood arrived at the warehouse: rosewood, wenge, sandalwood, as well as planks of French oak and walnut. Your work consisted in helping your head of department find the best prices on the market, monitor the status of deliveries and make sure suppliers honoured their contracts. To this end, every morning you found yourself in the presence of a rather heavy stapler, and a telephone with its little buttons, one of which was stuck, to your annoyance. Against the back wall was a steel filing cabinet where you kept the manilla files with their sets of initials such as LCR 1980, RT8-6, AP45. This was your office, your place; on the door was your name in white letters, preceded by the inscription: HEAD OF IMPORT MANAGEMENT.

Philippe had been hired in 1985. He worked on the third floor, where management was located. The corridor leading to those offices was the only one in the company that had plush fitted carpeting that absorbed the sound of footsteps (the decorator had no doubt wanted to create, already from the moment one entered the vestibule, a quieter atmosphere than that which reigned on the lower floors, since power is instantly recognisable in the dimmed lights and luxury appointments cloaking its brutal domination with a safe and comfortable softness). On his door was a shiny brass plaque: DIRECTOR OF HUMAN RESOURCES – PHILIPPE QUINIO. He was in his thirties, sporty, charming. He had been hired less than a year before the company started gaining new prominence in the regional economic landscape. You did not know much about him.

Anyway, in the beginning it was only a game. You were glad that chance had made him single you out from among all the women in the company, and there was something both restful and liberating about this unexpected familiarity.

"The atmosphere at work has been more relaxed lately."

You even said to François one evening.

Philippe Quinio was married, he had a ring on his third finger and twin daughters, and your badinage would surely be of no consequence.

You remember; it all began the day you took him some report or other. His secretary had just put a cup of black coffee on his desk. He was about to take a sip but, suddenly clumsy, he spilled it on your skirt. You cried out in fear and surprise. He hurried over.

"I didn't hurt you?"

You wiped your skirt with a tissue, not realising you were revealing a patch of thigh.

"It's nothing serious, really, it's nothing."

140

But he again apologised, standing next to you and adding, with humour:

"But I could have hurt you! Ah! I will never forgive myself!"

And from that moment on, Philippe Quinio would find it very entertaining to act as if he were under an obligation to you:

"Oh, madame, you may have forgiven me, but I shall never forgive myself!"

Every time he ran into you in the entrance, he would hold the door for you. You brushed past him, close to his torso, you could smell his perfume (*Absolu* by Bourjois, you later found out), and out of the corner of your eye you could see how nicely put together he was. Then there were jokes while waiting for the lift, or kind remarks about your hair or your smile, and every time, you found you had something in common, even if it was only watching the same programme on television the night before.

For a long time you'd had no friends at work. The previous years had required a great deal of pugnacity on your part to defend your position, for its remit was constantly re-evaluated every time you came back from maternity leave. You had managed at last to consolidate your place, and you now thought, without ever dwelling on the issue, that you would stay at Bédani until you retired. This mind-set allowed you to speak more freely to the workers or executives you might meet behind the scenes. Basically, you became more *sociable* – as your grandfather would have put it – than the other employees; because it is quite obvious that what in modern society is considered *freedom of speech* is virtually absent from human relations at work; at Bédani, simply to comment on the fact that the administrative buildings were small, or that the latest business investments were *excessive!* might be viewed as a failure of loyalty; only those salaried employees whose long-term employment seemed established could allow themselves to make such remarks; those who hoped to transform their internship into a permanent position or, at the other end of the ladder, those who wanted to obtain a promotion, were hardly capable of creating ties with the others, as before long any true friendship would have required them to say – in a tone of complicity which in the long run might make something like a collective agreement or even unionisation possible – that the C.E.O. ought, for example, to have "soundproofed the cubicles", "moved the site", or "done a better job of redistributing the profits". But you found it easy to discuss things, you did not shield yourself, and only after the fact did you become aware that, unlike you, Philippe was one of those who, out of an instinct of self-preservation, always hung back, regardless.

But for the time being; sipping a milky drink with a sugary smell called "Cappuccino" on the drinks dispenser, Philippe asked you why you had decided to live in Empan-sur-Nive, and what activities your children had on their Wednesday afternoons, and this gave you the impression he was interested in you. Philippe had got into the habit of stopping by your office on a regular basis. You knew it was him from his black sunglasses, they cheered you, those elegant glasses he kept on his head at all times, it was heartening to know he was there. His simple presence in the building added an erotic bonus to a job that had become easy and repetitive.

Another episode fired your imagination. One Tuesday Philippe sat down across from you in the cafeteria. You were very surprised, because there was an unwritten rule that at the cafeteria senior executives sat well apart from the administrative staff, just as the administrative staff kept their distance from the carpenters. You had lunch together. In spite of his jokes, you sensed he was less jolly than usual, you were thinking there was something strange about his attitude, when Philippe; suddenly; in a sad voice:

"I always enjoy talking with you. You make me feel good."

Your cheeks flushed:

"Is there something wrong, Monsieur Quinio?"

At first he looked down, contrite, then all around to make sure no-one was listening, and finally he turned to you with a tender gaze. Philippe had had an argument the night before with his wife. She had again reproached him for working too hard, selling that "damned furniture".

"But everyday life is not enough for me, I always have to put in as much as I can, otherwise I get bored."

You listened to him, feverishly; time went by. Now Philippe was talking without stopping. All you needed was to encourage him with one or two words in a low voice for him to continue confiding in you. You were alone in the cafeteria, perhaps just the shadow of a kitchen worker pushing tall carts stacked with meal trays.

"It does me good to tell you all this. I'm sure that you at least understand me."

Quinio eventually stopped speaking. He was looking at you, silently, his gaze lost in yours, while a lock of hair fell loosely over your forehead. There was something more fragile than usual about his face, his voice seemed sincere. Finally he got to his feet and said:

"Do me a favour, would you mind if we say *tu* to each other?"

The afternoon went by in a flurry of projections: what did all his confiding in you mean? That he was in love with you? No, it couldn't be, you had just been there for him, a timely listener. But other images assailed you, exciting, forbidden; you forgot to buy bread on your way home.

You remember; every morning you would buckle the children in on the back seat, five minutes later you dropped them off at the childcare centre in Empan, then alone at last, you would luxuriate in your thoughts of him. You thought about his eyes, his hands, his voice, what time it would be when he stopped by your office, the shape of his tie the day he had kissed you on the cheek four times, his luxury watch, the report he had asked you to fill in even though visibly it didn't need to be filled in. Every day your thoughts ventured further; at the roundabout in La Révole it was time to banish these images, in the car park you really had to stop this schoolgirl behaviour, in the lift it was not reasonable to want to run into him, in your office you snapped out of it: time for work!

And so, by means of polite visits to your office, and a slow occupation of your thoughts, Philippe aroused your desire. Before long, all you wanted from these forecast reports, supplier accounts or preliminary statements was a pretext to stop in and see him. One Monday when you were surprised to find him absent, a colleague informed you that the management team had gone on a business trip. This was a blow to your morale: he hadn't mentioned it at all! To make things worse, it rained all week. François seemed old to you, the children oppressed you. For the first time in years, you went to the cinema with Chloé, and even bought yourself a choc ice to lick during the film. It reminded you of your life in Lyon.

"How free we were back then!"

Back from his *business trip*, Philippe did not stop in to say hello. You were biting your nails, and could not understand his change of attitude: after all, you hadn't invented that tender gaze in the cafeteria . . . After a week had gone by, annoyed to find yourself thinking only of him, you found the temerity to wait for him in the car park. Naturally it was somewhat ridiculous to hide behind the steering wheel, in expectation of his car, but fortunately it didn't take long. As he was parking his Audi, you got out, slamming the door noisily, while pretending you hadn't noticed him. He was the one who came over to you. When you saw him come closer, with his elegant shirt, his dark glasses, his smile, you felt a warm bubble explode in your belly. This man's importance in your life had become disproportionate, was what you had time to think. Philippe kissed you on the cheek:

"Oh, am I glad to see you!"

The conversation you had that morning made you happy for the entire day. Philippe apologised, it had been crazy ever since he had got back. For a moment you talked about his trip and then, as if it was involuntary, the man put his hand on your shoulder and said it again:

"Yes, really glad to see you."

You couldn't breathe. You were looking at his eyes, trying to speak, while out of the corner of your left eye you saw his hand, still there on your shoulder, still there, then quickly withdrawing, brushing your chest. You flushed, you wanted to say something, but that male hand was once again safely at his side.

"Have a good day."

Your desire became constant; as you drove you imagined the wildest scenes; at the end of a meeting, once the technical managers had gone out, Philippe would lock you in your office to declare his love; you would run into each other in town, you imagined his kiss, he came into your office, the traffic was getting heavy; you grabbed him, he thrust himself upon you; ah.

Your fantasies stayed with you as you prepared the dinner; they were in your mind once you'd put the children to bed, they pursued you into your own bed. Something unknown and exciting was happening to you, taking shape in the distance, like a rainstorm you might dream of running through, stark naked. In your opinion, what you felt was inadmissible and immoral, but you could see yourself crossing each progressive threshold. Now you could go into his office whenever you liked, you said *tu* to him in front of everyone, the slope you were on was perfectly clear, but you were drawn to that slope; because it is never desire alone that compels two people towards each other, nor is it the pride of knowing one is attractive to a person one considers one's superior; it is, rather, a sort of tug of novelty, and in M.A.'s case, it was a veritable hunger, an individual remainder of the once collective ambition to *change life.*

Oh, but what a terrible word it was, adultery! When it crept into your thoughts, you shuddered with horror. No, you said to Chloé on the telephone, you could never do such a thing; it was just a flirt, you knew your limits very well; well, maybe you were having more fun than you ought, but François was not much fun, Chloé had to agree with her on that. And in any case, adultery was for loose women; duplicity was not at all your style, you were an honest, well-bred woman; and in any case, despite his marital strife, Philippe was a father, and the family was sacred. Basically, your friendship was something *lovely and original*, under no circumstances must it become a *betrayal* or a *crime* in the children's eyes, that would be foolish, it would mean the failure of the productive and happy marriage you and François had together, in everyone's opinion, not to mention the loan on the house.

Because the day you went to the *mairie*, and then the church, to take your oath of fidelity, you thought it would be easy to keep this commitment, you thought that your excitement, constantly renewed, would suffice to ensure constant cavorting while your bodies shivered with moans of joy in a shower of sunbeams. Right. The time had come to accept the fading of passion. But after your first pregnancy you had made love again with relish. Those nights, after an initial wrinkling of the sheets, François would open the drawer in the night table where he kept his condoms. You nibbled his ear, and went on arousing him while he, increasingly agitated, pushed his hand deeper into the drawer – which was still half open the next morning. Sitting on the bed before you got up, you would close it with a smile. Those were good times.

But over the years the sex had become insipid. Both of you would go up to bed more tired than ever because of the children. In a bed whose purpose was rest above all, you wished each other good night with a quick kiss. If François prolonged his caresses, you slid your hands under the blanket and touched his cock. It grew hard; this aroused you. He was only too happy to be able to unburden the stress accumulated at work and, already heading in the direction of your vagina, he kissed you in a way he thought was languorous; in and out; it was over with very quickly, got to get up early tomorrow.

Of course you liked the sensation of being filled with him, of course you had your almost automatic changes of position and speed, of course. But when he climaxed, it brought your own pleasure to a halt. Then you would nestle against him, very feline, but all he said, albeit content, was "I'm worn out". If you tried to get him going again, he would repeat that this evening he was exhausted, that next time . . . You were no fool. His desire had lost all curiosity. When was the last time François had really caressed your breasts, really kneaded your buttocks? He no longer touched you as if you were a precious gemstone he could polish for hours, saying your body was a territory where he would gladly spend his entire life. Now, when he mounted you, it led to a sort of combat that lasted twenty minutes, with each of you trying, through the other, to satisfy a physical need. His victory alone was a certainty: it was mechanical.

Yet you had proved your willingness to *keep the desire alive* after Nathalie's birth. As the summer evenings readily made you feel warm inside, you used to caress him. But on two occasions his sex stayed soft in your mouth; it was not the right moment, or so it seemed. After that you gave up trying to take any initiative. François made love when he'd been drinking, when there wasn't much time, when it was impossible to make any noise. It wasn't unpleasant, far from it, it wasn't tiring, or drawn out, and besides, you loved the man, was what you told yourself in order to silence the unappeased, pulsating tension that was there still between your thighs after his ejaculation. Because before long – after you had prepared the meal, cleared the table, tidied the kitchen and put the children to bed – and given the fact you found no release in it, nor were you thanked for it; before long this coupling made you feel as if you were serving a second sitting.

One evening when he had yet again unburdened himself, leaving you with that unpleasant frustration gnawing at your pubes, you ended up begrudging him his pleasure. Even if this meant he did not consider you an equal, but was using you as a receptacle, he could at least have gone about it like a real master, you would have liked to have been a bit shaken up – why not? – and seen the effect it might have on you to be mistreated now and again. You dreamt of some roughness on his part. No doubt you would have respected something in him, had he been capable of that sort of domination, it would have helped you find something interesting in the whole thing. But François did not take responsibility, he was spineless in his penetration, he was the man who is easily swayed by the unreliable rigidity of his cock. Because in the end, it was his cock that decided everything: he merely followed its erections, however hard they were or long they lasted, he responded as if by remote control, taking no account of what you might desire. The next morning you closed the half-open drawer in a very bad mood.

Another year went by and François now only put off his sleep once a month. Was he bored as well? You did not know. To find out, you would have had to take responsibility for your own dissatisfaction, but you did not know which gestures, which words to use, how to convey it to him; take him by the arm; put his head there? You would have had to talk about it, but no-one had taught you how to talk *about that*. You felt trapped, the tension was rising, and spite, too. Every week you postponed doing anything. Pleasure is quickly forgotten.

So when this flirtation at the office took a more dangerous turn, your very malaise with François gave rise to an irrepressible desire to make love with Philippe. With him it was bound to be better, because it would be different.

It all happened in one day. That Thursday you were busy with your morning tasks, you were even running a bit late. Philippe had got back into the habit of stopping by your office every day to say hello, and now he came in and closed the door behind him. You were beginning to talk when you slipped behind him to put a file away. You could sense him breathing, a presence. His arms circled your waist. You turned around, your reflex was to back away, but Philippe; he pressed you for several long, delicious seconds against the cabinet; kissed you right on the mouth. Then, as if shocked himself, he rushed out.

Your vaginal temperature had soared.

An hour later, the blaze inside you still raging, the telephone rang:

"It's Philippe."

You didn't know what to say.

"Listen, I've surely done something foolish, but perhaps it would be better if we talked about it."

Still you said nothing.

"Would you like to come by? So we can talk about it?"

Your mind went blank, you could not speak. Then he said, his tone more natural:

"Are you alright? Is everything O.K.?"

You swallowed your saliva.

"The problem is . . . I can't get much work done!"

You laughed. On the other end of the line Philippe was laughing too, and the knot in your stomach dissolved. Everything was simple again.

"Alright, yes. I'll come at six o'clock."

A sort of tranquil joy, in the guise of a number of dilated blood vessels, stayed with you until five o'clock. But when the three other departments on your floor began to close, you panicked. The kiss that morning seemed almost unreal; did it really happen? In any case, you must not go to his office for any reason, other than to put an end to this accident, you must *go no further*. The sound of your colleagues' footsteps on the linoleum startled you.

"Are you coming down with us?"

"Uh . . . No, go ahead, I have some things to finish."

How could you go home with the fire still raging between your legs? It was beyond your strength. You called your husband to tell him you would be late. No problem, he would go and collect the children. On hanging up, you let out a sigh; some peace at last, available at last.

You stood up. Through the only window in the room you could see your colleagues' cars leaving the car park to head for the motorway, some of them would drive more than fifty kilometres to get home. The workforce at La Révole had increased dramatically. Three years earlier the management had received the "Prize for the Most Innovative Company in the Rhône-Alpes Region". A cohort of politicians had come to congratulate the top managers on their company's *economic vibrancy* and *exemplary social responsibility*. Marc Bédani felt as if he had sprouted wings. He wanted the Exotic and Authentic ranges to be distributed in specially earmarked stores, where a bevy of students had been hired straight out of their sales force courses at the polytechnic. He had taken out a loan. He had hired Philippe. He had paid an advertising agency to create the slogan "Bédani, Your Lifelong Furnishings", and display it at the entrance to every major town in France. All this expense had impacted the balance sheet. A new injection of funds was urgently needed. Antoine Scalli, the founder's son-in-law, was the man of the moment. He came from a family of industrialists; when his fiancée took him home to meet her family, his fortune was of considerable interest to his future father-in-law. (A gracious, spoiled child, Caroline had succumbed to the charm of that little cretin she had met at a society party. Marc Bédani, still very much the peasant where his tastes were concerned, did not take to his son-in-law, but he had made a great effort to integrate into the boy's milieu, and as he said at the time to his wife, "You can't go fishing without catching a few gudgeons.") After the wedding, Antoine Scalli, who had an M.B.A. in management, acquired an interest in the company of up to 42 per cent of the capital. He signed a huge cheque. Bédani senior was pleased: "The main thing is for the company to stay in the family," he said to his son-in-law. Scalli was appointed business manager, and his office was next to Philippe's, whose door you were now staring at before you dared to knock, three times, quietly.

It was five minutes past six. Philippe began with a joke, the blinds were lowered, his desk was cleared of papers. You sensed he was nervous. This morning after the kiss he had fled, was he sorry? The thought frightened you. And yet he had kissed you, you had felt his tongue, but what if now he said that you must stop seeing each other? The thought crossed through your mind as you uttered banal phrases, sitting in the armchair across from him. You talked about the most recent financial results, which reflected certain weaknesses due to recent risky investments: "They mustn't jeopardise the company's future." Philippe played along for a moment, then finally he stood up and went over to you. There was a silence. You could hear his intake of breath.

"Look, I don't know if what we did this morning was very clever—"

"We shouldn't have!"

You said it very quickly, to protect yourself, because you were panicking, again you could feel a fierce heat coursing through your body all the way to your face. How you desired him! Philippe seemed unsettled by your response. You had a fleeting image of little Xavier waiting for his Danette while you opened the fridge; waiting for permission. You lowered your eyes, you could not help but smile. Philippe came closer still and put his hand on the armrest next to you. To your great happiness, he said, insistently:

"We shouldn't have, I agree . . . but I'm not sorry we did."

Something intense and happy exploded in your belly. You could smell his perfume, mingled with the odour of washing powder and tobacco. You looked up and your eyes that had been level with his belt now saw his face in detail. He was strong, young, *you fancy him*, you said to yourself, *you definitely have the hots for him*. His hand touched your knee.

"Tell me you're not sorry?"

His mouth had come to a halt a few inches away, the mouth that had kissed you only that morning. And this time you went after the next kiss.

He really did have *a perfect body*, you remember thinking, the moment his hands were upon you, your blouse on the floor, his hands going up under your skirt, and you could bite his shoulder, touch his sex, help him get undressed with an aplomb you did not know you had. You remember that terrible desire, in your hands, the desire that at last you could follow to its conclusion, follow until he took you, turning you, with his hard, sure cock, into a little wet thing who can be fucked for a long time, forcefully, as you lay contorted on the desk, hearing a name in your ears which never before had seemed so pornographic.

The building where you were making love housed the expanding administrative staff: import and export departments, sales, customer service, advertising. These were the "risky investments" you had mentioned and which were a source of major concern to senior management. The cash contribution from the Scalli family had been quickly absorbed, but Quinio did not seem worried. He was pleased with the way the company was developing, he urged them to spend, even to implement an entire restructuring process. He watched the delivery trucks go by his window and the regular to-and-fro made him dream of even greater expansion. Philippe thrust deep; it was good to have him fuck you, as good as you had imagined. You lay naked on the desk, exultant, unbound.

You made love again, then Philippe eventually got dressed. Outside, the sky was shot with fine red streaks that made the view over the motorway almost surreal. The company, normally teeming with people during the day, now seemed empty; only the warehouses were still active. You recall you went down to the car park together, Philippe kissed you one last time, but he refused to let you hold him: "Someone might see us."

It was eight o'clock. Sitting in your car, you looked in the rear-view mirror. "I've cheated on my husband," you realised. How could that be? You, the faithful wife, how could you do such a thing, in such a place? "Once, not twice." You said these words to yourself, several times over, while your sated body cooled off.

You could have avoided the entire affair. Because there had been signs, after all. Philippe, once he had climaxed, did not seem disconcerted. He had taken the trouble to remove from his jacket a hair of yours that had settled there as if to kiss him, with a care for detail of which you were incapable, while you lay half naked, in a state of bliss, on the edge of the desk. You could have made love for hours with that cock, but Philippe put an end to the session in a tone that brooked no reply:

"We'll see each other tomorrow, love. Time to go."

And as you drove you swore to yourself that it would stop there. You'd had your pleasure, but you both had your own lives, it could not lead anywhere, you must not go on. The drive home was quiet. "Once, not twice," you swore again. You went into your house full of virtuous resolve. And in the space of three sentences your husband had annoyed you, the children were howling, the dinner was not ready. Dazed, you put four plates on the table. Such banality seemed impossible, a bad dream: were you not a changed woman? The children were easy to fool, but François, there was no way round it, he was bound to notice. Well, he didn't. Like the day before, he told you about his day at the office. Unbelievable! You had just made love to another man, and here was everyone tucking into the same apple flan!

V

So: you were having an affair.

The thought that you might be doing something bad had vanished. Radiant, you explained to your friend that you were incredibly attracted to him, *it feels so good to be with him*. And Chloé told you:

> to listen to your heart,
> to be careful,
> not to endanger your children,
> to trust your feelings,
> to go with the passion,
> that love was beautiful,
> that lying wasn't cool,
> that he was a charmer,
> and do you still love François?

Any remorse evaporated in the presence of the desire that flowed to your skin every time you touched him, the joy that illuminated you; because having a lover never makes one sad, on the contrary, adultery stems from the desire of one of the partners in a couple to be happy, still; but on their own; and since deep down no-one knows whether supreme happiness is attainable in one's lifetime, physical pleasure remains one of its earthly traces, a trace we cling to, as long as we have the strength.

The next day Philippe told you he had been blown away by this unexpected encounter, he'd never experienced such a thing, he'd fancied you from day one, he'd tried to resist, because my two girls are just magnificent, if only you knew, I'd like to spend all my time with you, but he had to be home for supper by eight.

"You've got me, love, I give in!"

"The problem is that I want you, all the time."

You protested, you could still *stop everything right there*, but no sooner did one of you suggest it than your lips met, and off you went.

The tectonic plates shifted slightly. You found another vocabulary inside you. Just saying, "I want you all the time, too," to him filled you with a strange power. The geography of the area you lived in changed. Now there were the two franchised hotels, his sports club serving as an alibi, and the meeting room on the third floor; between these points all sorts of combinations could be worked out that had only one purpose: to bring the two of you together. Philippe took you several times in a row and when you heard him say, "I'm knackered," you felt proud. Time was measured differently. Already on Sunday you would put a neatly ironed skirt on the armchair in your room, for the next day. The tedium of work had vanished, going to the office offered nothing of interest other than these virile interludes, on those days when you found yourselves naked in each other's arms; like that time the first week, when you did it again by the photocopier; Philippe slipping one leg between yours, a hand in your knickers, you said *You're crazy, Watch out*, he took you against the wall, you were impaled with bliss. This was what it meant, to feel more alive, *like in a film, Chloé*. Two or three times a week now you stole away to the hotel. He waited for you at the first roundabout, your two cars continued in convoy, he pulled into the car park. In the beginning, these anonymous establishments left a bad impression on you. Philippe would go into the lobby, ask for a room for two hours, pay cash. You admired his self-assurance.

"You only need to act self-assured."

He said, as if to excuse himself.

The rooms were charmless; the bed linen was decent, and there was a basic bathroom, and once you became familiar with the neutrality of the place, it had a liberating effect on you. In that room you were no longer mother or spouse or employee, you were no-one and no-one knew you were there; so you would take off your stockings, watching Philippe as he watched you, he removed his tie, your lips moved down along his torso. You made love. In the next scene the pair of you, in a state of bliss, mingling your sighs, his hand on your belly; and you sometimes got the impression, in the dark behind your closed eyelids, that you were once again that young woman bathing in the sea in Spain, or lying with her head on the sand, one of you saying I feel good, or gazing at the mountains when you were a little girl, running through the fields, your thighs scratched by the long grass, falling breathless, afterwards, to the ground; since you could hear those same bursts of laughter, and in your ear you felt the same tickling of the grass; you opened your eyes; it was Philippe saying, I feel so good with you. He was so in love then!

On Saturday you went to the Hôtel Ibis in Grenoble, it was *incredibly erotic*. Sundays were dreary, the objects around you were back where they belonged, unchanged, and you couldn't call each other. You folded your clothes on the armchair in the bedroom and waited for Monday. At the company you would wait until you saw him. Your chest expanded when at last he appeared, you would hide away somewhere to kiss, then the D.H.R. went back to his floor. But Philippe had got into the delightful habit of sending you faxes with naughty drawings, and when the old teleprinter behind you began to wheeze, it was a horse you were hearing, galloping towards you with a message sealed in wax.

That was how it was in the early days. You had the energy of ten people, you joked, hummed, everyone around you thought you were in fine form. Lying was not difficult, because on that famous evening of the apple flan you could have confessed everything, but François had not said a thing, too bad for him – and anyway, dammit! in the end, *it was just too good*.

Something inside you was opening up, something was being reborn. Like those raindrops that fall to the ground and bring out heavy odours of humus the earth had kept secret, Philippe's sperm irrigating your life brought about an awakening of longing and desire that had long been buried in your sleep. You took up sports again. You changed your wardrobe. Above all you wondered at what point you had stopped wanting to *have a career*. When you had decided – if you had ever even decided – not to be that businesswoman you had dreamt of becoming when you began your studies, that ambitious woman who would step off a plane wearing a trouser suit to go off in conquest of the

Asian market. You questioned Chloé and she said, "Hey, come on, don't you remember what you said when Nathalie was born, how happy you were with your job at Bédani, because you wouldn't get this chance to look after your children at the same time anywhere else, this possibility of 'having it all'." Yes, that is what you said. But now you were bored at work, you couldn't just do that and nothing else. You began looking at job offers, and possibilities for further education. Philippe encouraged you wholeheartedly.

"You must never start dozing off in your career, otherwise you're dead."

"Go ahead, go for it, it's a question of wanting it."

The subject often came up in your conversations. You shared your aspirations with him, and asked him for advice about what you might do, perhaps at another company – and why not in another town? To give you an example, Philippe compared you with himself, he told you how he had enhanced his C.V., and you ended up talking exclusively about him, his magnificent career in human resources. You listened and never get bored ... because here was a man with ambition!

But the finest memory of your romance was undoubtedly your weekend in Brussels. For the first time you dared to leave the house for a night: you claimed you were going to a conference. You met Philippe on the station platform, you kissed, the train pulled out – *just like in a film, Chloé*. The huge city swallowed you up, you went to dinner in a restaurant, your fingertips touched between two wine glasses, Philippe took you to a bar where he'd been going since he was a young man; bulbs of garlic hung above the counter, the waiters had shaved heads, the music was deafening. Your lover bought you whisky, he drank like a man, he was handsome, *he looked good enough to eat*. When you left the bar, you pressed yourself up against him, you said "Come on, let's go", you kissed him in a doorway, you were both drunk, you went back to the hotel.

You pushed him down on the bed, your hands unbuttoning his shirt, you were intoxicated by his sex, tonight you were in charge, you said. You recall those things you have never experienced again since that time. That rage beneath your skin becoming sensitive, the electric current flowing through your hands, something liquid, warm, something that drew your fingers, and then. A swollen tongue, you took Philippe's hand and guided it, following that quivering that came in waves, feeling alive, and then. A growing, tingling sensation, an unreal need for caresses, on every spot on your body, between your breasts, and then. Sparks, to the back of your legs like a pressing itch, almost painful. You straddled Philippe, hardly opening your eyes, your hips guiding you, your entire body gathered into a single burn, you rubbed yourself against him; and again; and then. Your breasts, your skin, now your belly, you touched, pressed, accelerated, until there came an intensity, rising inside you; you moaned, you squeezed your fingers and at last. A groundswell, breaking; the fierce tumult of a passing roar; dilatation; the world and the joy inside you; brought together. A shout. From your entire body, from the tension in your belly, you shouted. Then that same body becoming fluid, red light behind your closed eyes, ecstatic, more light, now your legs were closed, you fell to one side, borne on a heavy, benevolent wave, a deep sigh before another wave, come from far away; reconciliation; descent. You were tired, you let the seaweed carry you away, you were hardly moving, floating in a state close to tears, and while you re-surfaced from the night of flesh, there came a scent of perfume, a rush of tenderness for this man, and for life.

The hotel was in one of those majestic Haussmann-era buildings with small wrought-iron balconies overlooking the avenue. The breakfast buffet was copious: croissants, *pains aux chocolat, pains aux raisins,* fried bacon, cereal, hard-boiled eggs, fresh orange juice, mortadella, fromage blanc in small bowls, fruit salad, coffee, black tea, green tea, Earl Grey, Darjeeling, cold milk, slices of comté cheese, jam, fresh yoghurt, all you could eat. Philippe laughed and said he'd never seen you so greedy. A poster in the corridor showed pictures of the movie stars who had stayed at the hotel. It really was the works.

Or perhaps the best moments of your affair were when you waited for him in those soulless rooms. You would meet on Tuesdays and Thursdays at one o'clock. Now you were the one who asked for the room, the innkeeper often gave you the same one, you took a shower, Philippe arrived a quarter of an hour later. And because the man was coming, you got yourself ready. With a fine pencil you drew a black line at the edge of your lashes, extending it outward from the corner of your eyes, in order to *lengthen your gaze,* you touched up your mascara, and put some colour on your lips. A glance at your watch, it was time to put on the sexy skirt you had hidden in your handbag; earrings; you brushed your hair again, pulled on your stockings, moist-ened your lips, sat down, got up, waiting for him, for his eyes, his verdict, that first gaze your lover would bestow upon you:

"You look absolutely gorgeous."

You had your reward. When he arrived, when he took you by the hips and gazed at you:

"You look absolutely gorgeous."

A long kiss, interrupted by a few words, two or three topics of conversation which had now become habitual, then your kisses deeper and deeper, he shoved you onto the bed and then everything was all undone: stockings, skirt, make-up, hair, and you laughed and laughed. After a few months you realised that this thing that only yesterday had seemed unthinkable – having a lover – was not only possible, but quite manageable, a condition that had its own conventions and misunderstandings, just like a conjugal relationship. That was when you began to love.

You loved the smell of washing powder that rose from his shirt, the taste of coffee in his mouth, the way he lit his cigarettes. You loved it when he said:

"My little Walkman that I wish I could take with me wherever I go."

"With you, I feel like a man."

"I adore your little bum."

You loved the way your heart pounded when you asked for the room.

You loved to watch him putting his belt back on, afterwards. It had fallen to the ground, unbuckled, the leather trapping the light in its curves. Philippe picked it up and slipped it through the first loop on his trousers, his right arm across his torso, then he made a sweeping movement in the opposite direction with his shoulders, reaching behind his back to guide the belt through the remaining loops, then tucking his shirt in, pulling up the zip, taking hold of the belt again and in his hand the buckle clinked, shining, he threaded the leather beneath the metal and pulled; you watched him in silence; and now he tugged on his shirt, and it puffed out slightly, and the round tip of the strap was tucked through one last little loop. Then Philippe noticed you were looking at him, and he smiled, embarrassed, almost modest.

You loved him, that was certain. Should you tell him? Chloé listened to you for hours, alarmed by the power that radiated from you, because in the end:

"Where is it all going to lead?"

Ah! Don't think! To close your eyes and see him materialise, to think of all the things you had in common, while you were walking towards his office, and knocking on his door with your little code, to feel the tiny, sensitive ties that bound you to him, the rootlets that love was sending ever deeper inside you, and to whisper in his ear:

"I'm yours."

"You get me so excited."

"My man."

Sometimes you thought back to the first time you saw "the new D.H.R." in the corridor, how you hardly noticed him; at the time Philippe was just another executive. Now love gave your gaze an ardent enchantment which made you adore the slightest detail about his person; like a visitor to a museum who indifferently walks past a painting then comes back to admire it if he finds out that it was the work of a master, now because he was your lover Philippe Quinio's entire person had become wildly original. He was younger, funnier, richer, more energetic, more sensual, he was a good lover, he was touching, he wanted your relationship to last, he was *a truly exceptional man*; you began watching the television programmes he watched, you listened to his music, you replicated his opinions and even his linguistic tics, "Pigs might fly"; "No big deal." Philippe was left-handed, forced to use his right hand, he took his coffee with three sugars, he had lived in Finland, when driving he kept one hand on the gearstick, he was allergic to pollen; he; he; he; he.

Until one day at the hotel, when every pore in your skin finally said:

"I love you."

He looked at you, surprised:

"You mustn't, love, you mustn't."

Philippe was touched, however. By virtue of giving him everything, of always saying yes, you had triggered a feeling of happiness in his heart, the sum of all the narcissistic and sexual delights he had found in your presence, a feeling that resembles love and that is surely one form of love among so many others. So on the following Thursday, when he was having you doggie style, as he collapsed on your back it was his turn to say, *I love you* . . . Unbelievable!

VI

There was a hole, a hole in the accounts. To make up for their deficit, the company should have positioned themselves more aggressively in the domestic furniture market, which had recently felt the onslaught of competition from Scandinavia. Bédani senior wanted to launch new products to attract the clientele eager for flatpack furniture, but there wasn't enough money. The company had had delusions of grandeur, and now it was in a bad way. Antoine Scalli and Philippe Quinio came up with strategic and capitalistic plans, summed up on a few coloured transparencies and submitted to the C.E.O. during manly presentations with the overhead projector. There were two solutions:

1) Build a new factory in the industrial zone at L'Isle-d'Abeau. Property was cheap there, and there were more than enough main roads. But Bédani refused to leave the historic site of La Révole which – so he said, contrary to all common sense – could produce more. In any case, they did not have the necessary cash.

2) Open up their capital to their long-time competitor, Cornellus France furniture, who had a foothold in public markets. The Bédani family would become minority shareholders in

the new holding company, something that was difficult to swallow for the company's founder.

After lengthy debate, the C.E.O. decided to go with this second option, on the condition they keep the site at La Révole with the number of staff virtually unchanged. As soon as the merger was signed, they would build a joint factory at Cergy-Pontoise, as close as could be to the demand from Paris; production lines for the Authentic, Exotic, and Cornellus Comfort ranges would be set up there. The architecture of the new factory would be more functional than in La Révole. As soon as this option was approved, Philippe Quinio embarked on a struggle with the other executives for the position of director, because from the point of view of those who rule us, every new factory, every new institution, before it can even fulfil its social purpose, is first and foremost a new *lode of power*.

But for the time being, the holding company had not yet been created, no-one had said anything about it. Well, almost no-one: the day Marc Bédani reluctantly gave his approval to start negotiations with Cornellus, Philippe knew that the worst was over. Thrilled, he shared the news with you. Initially flattered that you were being let in on what went on backstage in management, you listened to the capitalistic projections pouring from your lover's mouth, then went pale when it became clear to you that Philippe's dream was to leave La Révole. And he said it all so lightly! That was when you realised: you were only a passing fancy.

It was a *cold shower*. What an idiot you had been! On your way home, you tried similarly to view Philippe as a simple object of pleasure with an imminent sell-by date. Now you remember what he had said: if he managed to become the director of the factory, he would have an increase in salary, he would have opportunities, it would be better for his daughters' studies, not to mention the recognition the position would signify; even if Bédani were to close, unthinkable at the present time, *business is business*, sweetheart, with such a prominent position, my career is secure . . . Philippe was clearly a selfish, pretentious man, driven by childish impulses; he didn't deserve you.

"You know I don't want to hurt you."

Was what he had said, at the start of your relationship.

It was a cowardly thing to say, *because how can you not want to dramatically change the life of the woman you love?* Other memories resurfaced, more bitter, of days when he had ignored you. At home, François found you "looking a bit peaky". When you told him there were rumours of a merger he became very worried:

"These things often mean that people are laid off."

"Not to mention the crisis . . ."

"What if you end up unemployed?"

You hadn't thought about that. You could trust old Bédani, he wouldn't let you down, you said to François. Besides, what did you care? Your unhappiness was not of a basely economic or collective nature, no; your unhappiness was of a higher order, more immaterial and more personal, more sentimental and more cruel: it was Philippe's expression, full of delight as he told you about the future holding company, without a thought for you, *without a thought for us, Chloé.* Oh, you'd been roundly punished . . .

(It wasn't that Philippe didn't care for you, it was just that, for him, his career and your affair were not of the same order; they were on two levels as different as, say, those of a strawberry tart and a government action, he could find no shared logic between them; to be sure, one day his feelings would come into conflict with his professional opportunities, but only later, inevitably, or through an interplay of consequences that did not trouble him for the time being – unlike you.)

You felt a resurgence of tenderness for your husband, always kind, always considerate. During this conversation, you took his hand. Almost without noticing, you made love again. After a series of platitudes François said:

"Don't hesitate to ask me again, I don't pay you enough attention."

His words left you utterly despondent, and when Philippe came back from his umpteenth business trip, and held you in his arms and slipped his hand under your skirt, all your anger vanished; your lover desired you, he was handsome, powerful; the thought that he might abandon you filled you with anguish, but if he hadn't had that ambition that was tearing him away from you, you would surely not have admired him as much.

On September 30, 1987 the merger was announced to the press accompanied by a lavish spread of petits-fours. For months they had struggled to establish the most favourable holding company for each party, and now, all smiles, "Kevin Cornac (president of Cornellus-France) and Marc Bédani (from the company of the same name)" were shaking hands in the photograph published in *Meubles-Pro*, the professional journal of furniture manufacturers. In Cergy, construction on the factory had begun;

they were still waiting to hear who would be appointed director, but Philippe had turned pessimistic.

"A lot of the senior management at Cornellus are better positioned than I am."

But all the same he spoke of applying elsewhere, as his present position did not offer any *room for advancement*, he would leave in any case, Île-de-France was the place to be, you had to aim for La Défense in Paris. He sodomised you on his desk, turned you over, and shafted you from above. Your orgasm was unbelievably powerful. How could you give up a man who gave you such unbelievably powerful orgasms? That was when you first envisaged the unthinkable: to leave François.

To leave your husband... It was both impossible to do alone, an act that required the intervention of an outside force, armed soldiers like the blue helmets, or a natural catastrophe with an uncontrollable whirlwind and dark logistics that would assume responsibility for your separation; something that would be disconcertingly easy at the same time; because a few words would suffice – you shivered at the mere thought of it – all you had to do was go into the living room and shout, "I have a lover!", and after a break-up scene that would leave François prostrate in a leather armchair, you would leave with Philippe for Cergy or Seattle, wherever you could love and manufacture furniture together.

You went back to see your lover with this idea in mind, to convince him to make the move. You gradually informed him that your marriage was fraying around the edges, that you felt like travelling, that the Paris region was wonderful. Philippe didn't understand. You didn't want to seem hysterical, but after all; now that you thought it was possible to get away from the path you had been following ever since you moved to Empan-sur-Nive, and from which you had not strayed, like your electric gate closing faithfully along the aluminium rail riveted to the threshold to your property; now he had to understand.

It was a sort of madness. You thought you had been chosen. You had a mission, that of revealing to Philippe that his happiness lay with you. His wife represented the past and mediocrity, but you were Freedom, the Future, Salvation, and of course Love. And besides, Philippe loved you more than he knew. The higher he climbed in his career, the more he would need a companion who was equal to him, you would be his ally, his muse, he would rely on you in order to become a great international business-man, but his watch said eight o'clock and it was time for him to go home.

"My wife mustn't suspect."

His wife! His wife! His caution was exhausting. Did he never feel like *throwing it all in*? You suggested spending a weekend in Brussels, but he couldn't, because of work. A flood of tears followed.

"You don't love me!"

Philippe had to reassure you, at length, and apologise for not being free those very days.

"I have too much on my plate, with the merger."

You asked him for his schedule for the weeks ahead. As he felt you were becoming more demanding, he was evasive. As for the hotel on Thursday, he had to tell you three times that he would come, and if he didn't come, you reproached him. And so Philippe began to grow away from you. He had liked your proud side, your legs, your pretty little face, but when you began to play the saint polishing her idol he grew weary.

"You're getting tyrannical, my little love."

Philippe eventually began to fear you, was alarmed by your excessively passionate soul, which he felt was about to devour him. He postponed a meeting, then a second one, his wife was sick, he had family visiting. The fax machine no longer coughed out messages, no more little hearts distorted by the refracting effects of the telecopier.

And you waited. You waited for the day when at last you would be together, a phone call, a message, a note, a kiss; Thursday was in four days; he'd be back from his trip, in the evening you would stop by his office, you waited for the moment when at last you could hold him in your arms ... But when at last the waiting was over, it seemed at the same time to regenerate that waiting, like one of those mythological monsters that sprouted two heads when one was chopped off, the beloved moment of being with him signalled the departure for still more exacerbated waiting; you watched Philippe come into the room; already your heart sank, in sixty minutes he would be gone again!

The union informed you of the new staffing structure at La Révole: thirty cabinetmakers and six administrators had been let go. Oddly enough, your position was kept on.

"That was a close call, my love."

François was visibly relieved. You didn't understand a thing. What did it matter to you if you lost your job? Losing Philippe was far worse. You could not accept the prospect of going on working at Bédani without him, with just your husband and the kids, it would be impossible, *it would be death, Chloé.*

So one Thursday you spoke up at last:

"Philippe, I can't go on with this hypocrisy, I'm a woman of integrity."

"If we love each other, we have to be brave."

"Leave your wife."

"It will be hard in the beginning, but afterwards we won't regret it."

And other sentences you had taken a long time to prepare, so eager were you to convince him. You spoke a great deal, moving around that hotel room half-naked, feeling as if you were acting in a grandiose scene. Not only was your lover listening to you, but every man on the planet, from Apollo to Priapus, by way of Robert Redford, they were all around you, they were going to understand what sort of woman you were, one of those women who restore love to its original power. You opened up, the way you had never opened up. Philippe didn't say anything, astonished by so much grandiloquence. Then he sat next to you on the mattress.

"I don't know what to say."

"It's difficult."

"I really wish I could."

His gaze was lost in yours, tempted by something new. Then he kissed you and fucked you so hard it hurt. You let him, convinced that this impromptu penetration was a proof of love. But no promise was forthcoming that day, or on the days that followed.

Your madness grew. You began to lie to yourself. If Philippe called you, it was because his wife bored him, if he did not call you, it was because you were endangering his marriage, if he cancelled today's meeting, it was because he was going to tell you something important the next day. Because you would get there, *you were going to be together*, it was just a matter of days, as soon as he finally admitted to himself how much he loved you, you would speak to François, *you would tell him everything*.

Two weeks later, Philippe abruptly came into your office. He had that proud expression in his eyes, just like Nathalie when she came home from school with good marks. He was being officially transferred to Cergy for the position of "assistant director of human resources". It wasn't the position he'd wanted, but it was clearly a promotion: his salary and his department had doubled in size.

"At last! I've been waiting for this moment for so long!"

Caught up in his own happiness, he took you in his arms, while your heart slowly lost its grip, dropping into the abyss, which turns out to be immense, in such cases, between one's lungs and one's stomach. At last you stammered:

"And what about us?"

He took your hands:

"Will you come and see me?"

"In Cergy?"

"Why not? It's not that far."

"But what about my work, my husband . . ."

"I thought you wanted to leave them behind."

You cried:

"You want me to leave them?"

"Of course not, that's not what I said!"

"Didn't you understand what I told you the other day? I want to live with you."

"For God's sake!"

175

Philippe threw his hands in the air.

"For God's sake, love, I'm moving away! I'm moving away with my entire family!"

Yes, but he had a tender expression in his eyes when he said that. I'm sure I can still make him change his mind, you told Chloé, when his departure was imminent. It was time to leave François, *that will put Philippe up against the wall.* But every evening as you drove back to the chemin des Pins, you were overcome with anxiety; every evening the keys jingled against the door; you couldn't go through with it. Chloé was afraid you might do something stupid. Your husband thought you looked worried.

"All those redundancies . . . The atmosphere can't be very jolly at work."

"No, it's not much fun, that's true."

They were terrible weeks, looking at the price of property in Cergy in case you did decide to move, not sleeping, finding it unbearable to live with a man *who no longer makes your heart beat,* with that knot in your stomach, waiting, reduced to nothing but waiting. Another day you said:

"Philippe, don't leave. Please, oh, please, stay with me."

You would not have believed you could say such a simple thing. Unlike in the previous scene, these words brought no relief. You had just made love, his favourite positions. Your lover was there, on the bed, putting his watch on his wrist, a gesture you found so virile, because he was handsome, because you loved him, because he was going to slip from your grasp. Then he said something that you immediately forgot, words which you cannot reconstitute today; basically, he accused you of being selfish. How could you ask him to turn down that promotion?

"I have to go, I had no part in it, after all."

You began sobbing, quietly. Philippe put his hand on your shoulder and said these words that later would hurt so much:

"I didn't know you'd grown so attached . . ."

You were still crying when he went down to the hotel car park.

To go home, Philippe Quinio had to take the motorway as far as the number 6 exit in the direction of Villefontaine. That town had been one of the first to suffer the assaults of the bulldozers when in 1969 the government decided to build the new town of L'Isle-d'Abeau. The plans fomented by young engineers repatriated from Algeria ravaged the bocages where the old peasant families lived. Once the first buildings had been erected, the region launched a public relations campaign vaunting "the city in the country": in every railway station there were posters where L'Isle-d'Abeau, by means of a graphic illusion, was located at the heart of France, or even the world. The politicians expected a great deal from this new city, it was supposed to host a future baby boom and *revitalise the Bas Dauphiné*. But before long the promoters from the public buildings and works sector had simplified the engineers' idealistic plans. No *new man* arose from the levelled hills. The town had no life, people often said, and to this day only the Carrefour hypermarket and its shopping mall have offered a semblance of a space for socialising. But because they lived some distance from Lyon and Grenoble, the inhabitants of L'Isle-d'Abeau had the same notion of a densely populated city, a noisy dump of a place where children did not have playgrounds worthy of the name, where the "local youth" (who shall remain nameless) were in danger of burning your car, and where there was no private parking at a reasonable rate. The majority of inhabitants were what the Institute of Economic and Statistical Information called *commuters*, workers who spent more than an hour every day behind the wheel. They did not have a problem with this: in your car, you're still at home.

Philippe Quinio was now driving past the sports arena and the new concrete church. Despite the different urban layers, there was an urban sprawl to the place which made it look, it is true, somehow in-between, neither town nor country. Philippe had been right to move here when he was hired at Bédani, *everything is so convenient*, his wife had said, and if the company had had greater financial autonomy, building a factory in the industrial zone at Tharabie scarcely three kilometres away would have been a much better solution, much less risky than this merger with Cornellus. His tyres crunched on the gravel in the garden. Cardboard moving boxes were piled every which way by the front door, Philippe opened the door and called out a resounding "Evening!" And indeed, they were just sitting down to dinner. The father smiled at his daughters. He kissed his wife then picked up the lid on the pot to see what fate had cooked up for him that evening . . . His wife tapped him on the hand with a smile and a wooden spoon.

After the meal, she said:

"Darling, you won't forget to take the bin out to the grey skip?"

The husband went to throw the bin into the grey skip. He stopped for a moment outside his house. A roundish moon was shining in a vaguely black sky. Philippe took out his lighter, a cigarette, then lost in rare thought, took a few steps down the street, which at this late hour was dark and quiet like an empty motorway. Basically, he had been happy here, he now realised that it grieved him to leave; the Paris region would never offer such *quality of life*. Philippe walked a bit further, gave a sigh as he thought of M.A., her cheerfulness, her little arse – ah, the way she moved her hips when she was on top of him, she was so good at it – but a barking dog roused him from his melancholy. Philippe went back the way he had come and closed the gate behind him.

VII

After three days in hospital you felt as if you had always been there. You liked the fact that you could:

eat your L.U. *soft centre raspberry* biscuits in bed;

ask the nurse to lift my pillow a bit, please;

watch soaps on television with that air of regression on your face that made the nursing auxiliaries say: "She's resting, that's good";

weep at night – and think about him.

Although you were already weeping less, your terrible sorrow seemed to have hardened in this clinical space, transmuted by the power of the hospital into a scientific name, a delightful, anonymous syndrome: post-dural-puncture headache.

Because your collapse had been total. Love had not conquered all! Love had lost! The sound of the coffee pot echoed the scandal: he left you, he left you, whispered the boiling water as it slid over the filter. His absence was so sudden, *you had got on so well together*, the separation was unbearable, *you had given so much*; you foundered in a sort of prostration. You despised men, the entire planet, tears filled your eyes without warning.

There were brief moments of relief. No more adultery, no

more secretive behaviour, you could get back to a normal life. Philippe was gone, much good may it do him, François seemed to you to be a much better person, an honourable, moral man, it was a good thing you hadn't left him. But in the evening by the television, precise memories of pleasure came back to you; the touch of a hand on your breast; a breath; an acceleration. In that soft sofa François was very bland.

The prospect of the weekend filled you with terror. To get them to leave you alone, you pretended you had a severe migraine.

"It's crushing, absolutely crushing!"

François did not insist, and you managed to get out of going to dinner at your in-laws. Once the family car was around the corner, your face began to distort. You recall that moment now; standing in this kitchen, looking at your wrinkled hands; the saliva in your throat increasingly acid. You would go upstairs and throw yourself on the bed. There were tears, there were cries, you shook, hiccupped, yelped like an animal, *Why? Why?* This was what rose to your lips, and an immense pain emerged in fits and starts from your trembling body, you called out to the loved one – *Philippe!* – and you struggled, refused, refused reality. *Philippe!* In the damp sheets your body believed it was touching his body, and again you smelled his odour, and out of you came wrenching *I love yous*; there you were again confronted with his absence, absence like a sadistic knife eviscerating you, the separation you had so dreaded, it had come, *I'm in a black hole, Chloé.* You sobbed pathetically, your twisted lips plastered to the sheet. The world beyond your duvet seemed like a hostile mass of towering peaks, and you were lost, stammering, you would never have the strength to confront it, you wanted to stay where you were all your life, yes, all your life, *I can't take it anymore, I can't take it . . .* Oh, you felt so sorry for yourself, oh, how unhappy you were, why wasn't your maman there, why weren't you still a little girl pampered by Maman or someone strong who would take you in their arms, someone? The thought of Philippe living far away from you, in Cergy, went through you. The sobs started up again. Was there nothing you could do? And what if you went there, what if you showed up at his house? Now your moans came even louder. No, all of that was beyond your strength, and besides, what was the use, your lover was a coward, he was selfish, he had lied to you when he said he loved you, *what a bastard, I hate him, I hate him*, you said over and over, but the thought didn't help you at all. You turned over to try to find a more comfortable position on the mattress, you put your cheek on a cool patch of pillow, like after lovemaking, like when the two of you, naked . . . Off went your crying fit again, and as you looked for something to embrace you bit the bolster and wept for a long time.

A few hours later, all that was left of you was a sad frazzled little thing. Outside, the rays of the setting sun enhanced the thin cottony trail left by a plane in the sky. You managed to unfold an arm and blow your nose. You went downstairs to eat a yoghurt in front of the television. That was where François found you two hours later, in a bit of a stupor but presentable. You answered his questions mechanically, like a robot.

"I've got the most horrible migraine, there is nothing to be done."

You ate frozen dinners in silence. You went to bed immediately afterwards.

"My head . . . I've got a headache."

"Please don't switch on the light."

Seeing your husband sitting on the blanket, feeling his warm hand on your forehead, you felt a sudden urge to confess everything; you were in desperate need of consolation. He was as kind as a brother, he would surely understand. You groaned, he thought you wanted to get up.

"My little love, you don't look at all well."

When you heard his words, you lost all any remaining strength and fell back against the pillow, pale with guilt. François rang the emergency services. Two hours later, although your headache was beginning to recede and you were about to call to your husband to reassure him, you saw the doctor's car pull into the drive. You were frightened: you had to look ill now. The doctor examined you. Had you been tired for long? Did you have these migraines in childhood? Did you feel like throwing up? You said yes to everything. The man took François to one side. You had been suffering for several days from severe persistent headache, there was a chance it would go away by itself, but he could not rule out the possibility of meningitis; he was sorry, but it was his duty to warn him. From your bed you gazed scornfully at these two cuckolds.

After the doctor had left, François collected a few things and took you straightaway to *Les Urgences* in Chambéry. The hospital was barely twenty minutes away by car. Once you had arrived, the signs indicating "internal medicine", "pulmonology", "tropical and infectious diseases" – seemed like so many destinations for a long-haul flight.

In your bed in room 504, your exhausted body let go. You let them look after you, you were glad to see the world subjected to the ravages of your heart. At least you had managed to stop time.

You stayed in hospital for two weeks.

The wallpaper in the room had a pattern of pale and dark pink peonies, each of which had at its heart a pistil surrounded by five petals; you stared at them obsessively, the way you obsessed about this one thought: *Philippe will leave her, Philippe will call me.* Because you were convinced that once he heard, through colleagues, that you were in hospital, Philippe would call you, then come to see you. You could already imagine the words you would say during your emotional reconciliation, opening the next chapter to your love; because it simply could not be, there was *such a strong bond* between you; it simply could not be truly over, you said to Chloé, who replied that for the moment Philippe had *really gone away* and it would be better to *move on to other things.* You despised her, what did she know. Moreover, now you really were suffering from migraines. Following a neurology test, an intern had given you a lumbar puncture, and the operation had triggered an intense migraine reaction (the famous post-dural-puncture headache). Consequently you were given morphine. It had the effect of making the peonies bigger, and the days went by, irrevocably, you were astonished to find you still believed, astonished to see the petals come closer then withdraw, looking for stamens to cling to; you asked for an additional dose and the intern put you on a drip, and after that you stared at the pistil dancing before your eyes, you fell into a state of insipid stupor, you looked on as that first evening on the desk faded into the flat wall, Philippe's flower in your hand, as you squeezed the pipette to inject your blood with something that might cause your wretched hope to vanish; but how long does love take to disappear?

"Oh dear, it looks like they've given you too strong a dose of morphine."

Said the nurse, seeing your face.

The pain was not as strong when you were lying down, you could think about Philippe, you could add faces to the peonies, your lover's image invaded you in meandering, intermittent thoughts, you thought about him when you watched those American soaps on television where husbands left their wives, saying *they could not stand their life anymore, that it was all pretence*; on the second channel, adolescents embraced, and your enfeebled heart still hoped; you imagined running into him again, and he would tell you how much he loved you, you were the love of his life, he had understood it at last; then came the weather report, a mother saying goodbye to her son who was on his way to war, the conflict in the Middle East was escalating, to François Mitterrand's regret, everything you had experienced together was so beautiful; he loved you, he would return, Philippe the soldier, Philippe the millionaire, Philippe the president, but why didn't he call you?

The doctors came to tell you: *they had made an appointment for a scan in Lyon*. Because migraines and vomiting could also mean the brain was hiding a tumour, *even a benign one, madame*. To be thus informed of your imminent death was a delight: it would, in a way, be like dying because of him.

Two days later, four paramedics wheeled you out to an

ambulance flashing with lights. For a moment you believed you were on your way to paradise; at last; Philippe had committed suicide and you were going to meet him there; from the firmament of legendary loves you saw your poor widower going alone to grieve upon the two adjacent tombs that had brought the ill-fated lovers together, sheltered in autumn by the long branches of a willow tree.

At the university medical centre they made you wait. Then you went docilely into that sort of big white *doughnut*, as the technician jokingly referred to it. The return trip was difficult, there was traffic on the motorway, you slept for the rest of the day. The next day, Professor Loberre came into your room looking pleased with himself (but he always looked pleased with himself). He was holding a big white envelope which he brandished before you.

"No sign of any tumour!"

François hurried to look at the scans. Dark pictures showing nothing, neither lesions, nor lies, nor passion, nor hotel rooms on Thursday at noon; just a grey spot with two little curves at its centre, like a black butterfly. No tumour, no cancer.

You really did fail at everything.

How long does love last, how long? When the loved one disappears from our life, how long do we go on loving on our own?

"He's going to call me, I'm sure that at least he'll call me."

François came by every evening, Chloé between noon and two o'clock, then your mother took over. These were sweet moments, like in the old days when you used to have a fever and she would come up to your room with hot chocolate. At six o'clock you watched *her game* together on television, then she left you with the regional newspaper. You read everything. From the opening times of the local library to the summary of an educational visit to the Jardin des Plantes, the slightest details of life in the outside world, filtered through a simplistic, merely factual wording, filled you with fraternal feelings for humankind; as if in a world where the most passionate love had proved pointless, it was of some comfort to know that the Les Petits Loups outdoor centre had taken on a new instructor whose smile now spread inanely across the printed black and white sheet.

You looked out at the flower garden, where ducks watched as the convalescent patients walked by.

Then it was time for dinner. White uniforms and carts resumed their busy rounds. Philippe had not called, you stared at the wall which, on the other hand, really did exist, as did every object in that room. You picked at your food, disappointed, betrayed, you gobbled down your dessert, *I don't want to believe it's all over,* and yet another tear slipped from your eyes.

How long would love last, how long?

One night when you had insomnia you switched on the radio (it was the only way to stop thinking about him). And you heard a classical concerto, a slow movement of violins in ascending octaves, and in the empty room you suddenly felt this immense thing, that you had carried for a long time, you felt this thing fracture and fall away behind you. There were more tears, but they were different, less plaintive, more final. The next morning, Dr Loberre asked you a series of questions:

"Do you work a lot?"

"How many times in a week do you eat meat?"

"Do you feel weak when you have your period?"

Given all the tests that they had done, they found that your blood was lacking in iron, and that you might be anaemic. As the post-dural puncture headache had abated, you left hospital with a prescription for Forci-Ferron, and some paternalistic recommendations:

"You must take better care of yourself, madame."

The return was calm. You were glad to see the garden and the children. *Time to turn the page. I can't let myself go anymore.* François kissed you, ardently, his body in your bed, he was there again for you, warm as a hot-water bottle.

"I was so worried, darling."

You made love again, tenderly, and in spite of everything, it did you good. François attributed the episode to the stress caused by the merger between Bédani and Cornellus. That was only partly untrue, and you adopted this version for the others around you. The hardest thing was to go back to work at Bédani. Every cupboard, every lift had its memory of him, and you were constantly banishing his ghost; in spite of your efforts you sometimes stopped in the middle of what you were doing, and if a secretary or a courier happened to walk by, they would have found you staring blankly at a silent fax machine, as if suspended in time. To Chloé you decreed: "It was just sexual." You had to cling to that thought in order to reject the idea of a telephone call, or a business trip that might have brought Philippe back to La Révole, or a transfer . . . Fortunately, nothing happened. You would not see him again, this man you had loved so passionately. And before long you were restored to your lucidity, and you wondered how you could have believed *even for a moment* that he would leave his wife and children for you, when every morning every salaried employee parked his or her car in the same place in the company car park as prescribed not by any corporate rules but by the power of habit.

VIII

You took refuge in the children. You had never abandoned them. Even after your most powerful orgasmic release, when you sat naked astride Philippe, your sex devouring his to the rhythm of his insults as they aroused you, excited you, your skin swelling with blood, your flesh clamouring; your entire self resounding with that triumphant cry; even after that, you had gone on changing the batteries for the plastic tortoise.

Xavier was nine, Nathalie was seven, their height was in keeping with the growth curve on their health record. For dessert the boy liked peach and apricot yoghurt best, and his sister strawberry. They were your property, every mother says as much: They are my greatest joy; every day brings something new; you have to enjoy them before they grow up.

You remember; your superiors at work let you rearrange your schedule so you would have Wednesdays off. You used to go to the park. You would sit on a bench while the children played. Everything was quiet. You could hear the birds chirping high up in the trees, and in the distance there was a constant hum of traffic, and from time to time there came, briefly more noticeable, the sound of a fire engine's siren, or a road mender's chainsaw, or a scooter shifting into a lower gear. To forget

Philippe and his ingratitude you wanted a third child; François was surprised, but he went along with it.

And then; once you had recovered and François had transformed the computer room into a room for the infant (a girl), Wednesdays became even more important. Looking after your flock completely absorbed you.

"I've been trying to pay more attention to Xavier and Nathalie so that they won't get jealous of their little sister."

"It's great, Nathalie can play all by herself."

"Xavier has been asking for cuddles now and again, you understand, he sees his mother constantly glued to the baby . . ."

Was what you told their father in the evening.

In the magazine *Parents* you found ideas for all sorts of creative games; in the winter you baked cakes, made collages; in the spring you went back to the park. You got out the pushchair; you hung your handbag from the handle and you put the yellow bag with their snack underneath, you put the baby in the pushchair, you went behind the pushchair and you pushed. The rest of your progeny followed, taking irregular little steps. Your family could be seen walking for twenty minutes or so between the mini-zoo and the artificial lake before you stopped at a bench in the sun. The two older children went to unwind on a stretch of grass where they could fall down without getting damaged; the infant slept.

Yes, it was a quiet time. You took a book from the yellow bag, you read for a while; you closed your eyes; then you could hear, as if superimposed, shouts, footsteps, nearby, far away, birds, a train whistle; in the springtime you saw the crocuses stretching their little orange tongues skyward, your book of haiku told you to live for the present moment. Above all not dwell on the past. Say simple things:

"Mind you don't get your coat wet."

"There's no point asking for the merry-go-round today."

"Would you like a pear?"

And they would say:

"Maman, I saw a frog!"

"I'm too hot."

"Can I climb the tree?"

In the park, the cries of dozens of children created a sort of permanent background noise which numbed you. You pulled the blanket over the baby, closed her mouth with a dummy, opened your book again. But before long they wanted your attention:

"Look, Maman, look!"

And so you looked up again with that smile mothers must have when they gaze at their children.

Since your parents had retired, your mother sometimes came and joined you. You would slip away for a moment to buy some candyfloss while she looked after them. On your way back, with the treat in your hand, you could see the scene from a distance, the three children round their grandmother, every appearance of happiness. No sooner had you gone through the little gate to the playground than Xavier and Nathalie rushed over to you, tearing long translucent strands of candyfloss which they stuffed greedily into their mouths.

"Calm down, children!"

Without saying thank you, Xavier ran off to climb on the cabins, aeroplanes, bridges or any other construction meant for children aged seven to twelve, while Nathalie sat astride a rocking horse and, with a blissful smile on her face, rocked back and forth for a long time.

You sat back down on the bench next to your mother. She was reading *Le Dauphiné*.

"Well, what news?"

And she said:

"Oh, nothing, the usual."

And you:

"Things alright, otherwise?"

And she said:

"Oh, you know, at our age, something always hurts somewhere . . ."

From time to time a shadow passing:

"Your poor father is very tired."

Then, later:

"Wait, wasn't there a slide here last year?"

"There was, I guess they took it away."

"Ah, didn't I tell you I thought it was dangerous."

These conversations were interrupted by calls to tie a shoe lace, you told them to finish their biscuits, to put on their bonnets. You were milked, first one breast then the other, by your younger daughter, whom you had named Juliette.

Your mother was happy to be with you. The children loved these Wednesdays. It seemed it was enough for them, simply to have you there, smiling, encouraging them. They were having fun, they would shout out, Yaaaay! They had another chocolate madeleine, they had no memories, no burdens; and if there were moments of sorrow or tears, a few minutes later off they went to play again, memory for them was clemency.

At half past five your family could be seen heading home. You had to hurry things up a bit. You tossed the plastic container from the madeleines into the rubbish, the bath was filling with water. Right, everyone in the bath! They laughed, they got undressed, they played in the water. And you, at the sight of their bodies, so naked, covered in foam when you soaped them: it reminded you of another nakedness; and you soaped them even harder.

Once Juliette was weaned you left her with her grandparents and you all went skiing for the day. Your favourite resort was only an hour's drive away, the sun was still low on the horizon when you arrived, François parked right next to the shop where you hired your skis. With your day passes hanging from your parkas, you headed together for the nearest piste. You glided over the snow, each member of the family in a different colour parka, you talked constantly to Xavier or Nathalie, taking care they didn't fall, congratulating them after a well-controlled descent, discussing with your husband *which piste to take*. After an hour, you felt the intoxication of the mountain air.

"Such wonderful peace and quiet."

The day ended round a hot chocolate. Everyone slowly removed their boots, the children squabbled over the last Bounty bar. You closed the boot, and François pointed out, amidst a very characteristic smell of snow melting on waterproof clothing, that people from Lyon must have come up that day, or that you had been wise to make an early start, the weather was deteriorating. Then came the trip home. The snow vanished, the roads grew wider, the children fell asleep to the hum of the ventilation, while the car went back down into the plain of life's worries. In

August, the copper thread from the ski pass you had bought that day, still hanging from the zipper of the parka where you had found it twisted and wrapped in torn bits of paper, came to remind you of the passage of the seasons.

"Time will help."

Chloé had said.

After the bath, you read them books where giraffes were lost in the savannah. They had put on their pyjamas, they were sucking their thumbs, they asked for a kiss. They needed you. And you applied plasters, you filled baby bottles, you watched them grow up and squabble. From the garden came constant cries:

"Maman, she won't let me play with the yellow lorry!"

"Nathalie, you have to share with your brother."

"You heard what Maman said: give it to me!"

"Here!"

It could go on for hours, Xavier pushed Nathalie, she cried, it all started over again the following day, slightly different perhaps, but not by much; one day the little one was walking, said Papa. But there too, it was all just starting over.

You would have liked nothing better than to be a perfect mother, one of those women who fry chips every Saturday and say, "The important thing is for you to be happy, my dear," when their son informs them that he is homosexual, you would have liked to be more generous, to laugh at the funny faces of those children who were the reason for your three episiotomies, to think they were absolutely wonderful, your little darlings. But they were only children, and there were some Wednesdays, after an entire day spent shut inside with them, when you felt a tension under your skin that suddenly made you shout:

"I said no! No biscuits!"

"What on earth is this! Do you think I'm stupid or what?"

And you would leave them there, in the middle of the Mousline mashed potatoes, only half risen.

"I'm going to bed. I am tired, tired, tired."

Your husband, his presence required more than ever at the agency, had left you fully in charge of the educational territory, but he did worry about your mood swings, for in the long run they might have a negative impact on the children's development.

"You have to take some time off. We could rent a *gîte*."

"It will be a change of air, it will do us good."

As if you could leave your anxiety behind, on the motorway; as if you could rent a *gîte* in the Ardèche; as if you could set out, the five of you, on a hike. At a certain point, you would climb over a fence and sit down outside a hut with your picnic.

"This must be an old shepherd's hut."

One of you would say.

After a few sandwiches, the two eldest would start putting together a bouquet of autumn leaves, as per their father's pedagogical suggestion. And you would raise your eyes to the sky, breathing the air rich with perfume, letting your gaze rise unimpeded to the calm, restful blueness.

"It's true, I needed a break."

François was relieved. He often felt guilty that he was not more present at home, since all he wanted was your happiness, he said. Because he still loved you, in his way, without anger or variation, but as a man devoting his entire self. He cherished you even more since the birth of the baby girl he called *my little princess*, and which had made of him the father of what was, administratively speaking, *a large family*.

As if you could stay several days in that *gîte*, getting used to the tinkle of the sheep's bells ringing as they went back to their pen; everything seemed so tranquil there, everything in its place, the scarecrow in the vegetable garden, the ladder against a fruit tree, everything smelled good, of pure and natural smells, the smell of lavender, of smoke. In moments like that, you thought some sort of happiness might yet be within reach. Oh, not an ecstatic happiness, no, but small fragments of happiness, more fragile, more modest. You let your husband hold your hand when you went for walks. If you had been born in the country, in a place like this, your life would have been so very different, that was what you thought at moments like this. No doubt, with no possibility of choosing, you would have found your role in life fulfilling, a woman who was tender with her husband and generous with her children, like the one in the advertisement showing a sturdy farmer's wife endlessly pouring milk into a copper cauldron.

After the walk you would drink a lemonade on the village square, the five of you outside, "all five of us", was how you put it now, you would survey your little troupe, every member of your family around you like a second skin. They were your insurance against solitude; François had always been there. You were almost grateful to him on days like that. He looked at you with a vibrant tenderness. You were about to say something kind to him, when your gaze was drawn to an old woman sitting on a balcony above you.

She was speaking to a neighbour who was hidden by the corner of the little house. You could hear words like "rabbit stew", "Renée", "in the old days", "crush it a little in a bowl", but all you could see of her flat was an earthenware plate on a peeling wall. You were frightened by the extreme hoarseness of her voice, and the intense whiteness of her hair, and that face entirely riddled with wrinkles. Were it not for the drab housedress she was wearing you wouldn't have known what sex she was. Then you saw her hand, an enormous hand covered in protruding blue veins, resting on the edge of the balcony where a black telephone cable ran, as thick as remorse. You traced the line passing from one house to the next around the square, continuing its circuit until it came to hang down the façade of the café where you sat with your family round a table, your eyes staring at the old woman's hand and the monstrous shape of it, almost arachnoid, her fingers folding slowly in towards her palm.

PART THREE

It would seem that it is in man's nature to possess the faculty of discontent.

JULES DE GAULTIER

I

Five years went by, the washing machine broke down, the guarantee was no longer valid. Otherwise, everything was working. The fridge, the freezer, the iron, the vacuum cleaner, the computer, the games console and, before, long a printer; the electric coffee maker, the mixer, the oven, two colour televisions, the convector heaters when winter came; objects were sturdy until they gave way and you had to replace them. You sat on folding chairs, you lit the rooms with halogen lamps, you thought the pepper mill with its solar battery was great fun. Outside you had the gate, the fragrant herbs, the fruit trees, the table football and of course the barbecue. Visitors were impressed by how lovely your garden was. The lawn grew in thick tufts and the neat rows of iris bulbs bloomed every springtime in a fireworks display that elicited the neighbours' admiration. Your son, your firstborn, had become a fine adolescent. When he went with you to the supermarket, you would watch him go off down the aisles in search of kitchen towels, for example, then come back to the shopping trolley and say: "Mission accomplished". When he came home from the lycée he would make a beeline for the fridge: "I'm starving!" Then he went upstairs to play on the computer, Nathalie shut herself in her room, while Juliette, the little one, was still under your feet. But the minute the weather turned fine, all three of them would play table football on the terrace. Then you would say to François:

"Why don't we have some friends round?"

Your husband took care of the fire, and you prepared the meat for the grill; before long Xavier obtained his baccalaureate, and you celebrated the event one Sunday in July, your old mother brought her apricot tart, still the same, you blew out the candles, you took pictures; and the house, after all it had been through, had consolidated its walls around your life.

Your fortieth birthday, however, had not been much fun. That was the day you learned you had been made redundant. As Philippe had predicted, the factory at La Révole was unable to coexist for very long with the one at Cergy, the order book was empty, word had it that the crisis was making ever deeper inroads into people's budgets. As he had a nose for defeat and a penchant for money, Marc Bédani cashed in his dividends and vanished into thin air. This was followed by redundancies referred to as *plans to safeguard employment*. One morning in 1994, you went to sign up at the job centre; despite the kindness of the agents, you came out feeling somewhat humiliated, somewhat guilty. But as everyone began to feel sorry for you, instead of feeling sorry for yourself, you found it more worthwhile to show some courage. Which you managed to do.

"What's the point in whining? It doesn't help to make things better. You have to look on the bright side, I was bored at that job."

"My wife is a saint."

Said François to his friends.

By the time La Révole closed, there were only seventy employees left. Some of them could not accept the state of things, there was some unrest, graffiti on the warehouses, the biggest one proclaiming THEY'RE CLOSING A FACTORY THAT WORKS, and the last four letters – ORKS – were visible for a long time from the motorway. The site was bought by a budget chain for household goods, La Foir'Fouille, "Everything for Two Francs", but it must not have been in a strategic location, because the store closed a few years later, and it is now occupied by a go-karting circuit.

The hardest thing for you was going out on strike.

"It just adds disorder to confusion."

Your daughter reproached you for not putting up a fight, but you preferred taking things *philosophically*.

"What's the point in whining? You have to look to the future."

At the hairdresser's, you consented to having your hair dyed.

Thus began a period of struggle, an opportunity to test the solidity of what had been built. Family and bank account would be the foundation you relied on in order to *bounce back*. You had founded a family, after all, you had *put some money aside*, after all; and unemployment proved less upsetting than you had thought it would; past the age of forty, one no longer reacts to events in the same way, one's heart must be tooled by other sorrows. And then there is the shopping trolley to fill, the fridge to empty. Juliette was a growing girl.

"The amount of food that girl puts away!"

"Xavier, if you go out at night I want you to call and let me know."

"Yes, Nathalie, you can go to the cinema. But don't be back late, I don't like knowing you're in town, I worry."

You felt better when you sensed they were nearby. When you gathered for dinner, you felt like a hen on her eggs. Some families would have been shaken, bank accounts drained, the situation was not easy and François grew very anxious when his own position was endangered. There were major mergers in the insurance sector. Réserva had been the victim of a takeover bid and subsequently sold several agencies, including François's, to the AssuréVie Group. He had to start all over again in another district.

"That's what globalisation is about."

Your husband suffered, more than you had, to see his social status in jeopardy. You could sense his anxiety from the way he slammed the door when he came home, and you spent entire evenings together talking about the budget, you imagined every possible scenario, even that of moving if it was no longer possible to pay back the loan. François took you in his arms.

"I wish I could do better by you."

"We'll manage, I'm sure we'll manage."

To relieve his stress he went cycling every weekend. He set off on his racing bike, wearing his tight cycling shorts, with Fabien in his wake, a former client who had become a friend.

They drank a beer together when they came back.

"Have you been to the Col de l'Échelle?"

"It builds your calf muscles, doesn't it!"

"Not as much as the Ventoux!"

Fortunately, these hard times only lasted a year. François managed to make his mark at AssuréVie. As for you, you were taken on as administrative assistant with Coead, "The Future Go-Ahead", a huge computer company whose premises were in the industrial zone in L'Isle-d'Abeau. The arrival of the multinational had created quite a stir in your job market, and the local politicians viewed this manufacturer of high-frequency co-axial connectors as the economic pillar that had been so sorely missing from the new town.

Your admin position was subordinate. Never again would you enjoy the sort of authority with which you had reigned over your half corridor at La Révole. But you got used to it, you even found a certain pleasure in your submission. By bringing an end to the *career aspirations* Philippe had aroused in you, your redundancy had given you not only the somewhat cowardly restfulness which rewards any renunciation of higher ambition or anticipated freedom, but also the secret satisfaction of breaking up once again, of your own free will, with your former lover. There were other rewards, such as that of belonging to a company quoted on the stock market; you had dinner coupons. Everyone was obliged to say *tu* to each other in the company, in order, so they said, to avoid the more onerous aspects of hierarchy. In short, it wasn't a bad job, "given the current situation".

"Which just goes to show, there is always work for those who are willing."

"In any case, my wife has been brilliant."

"Our kids are very mature, they've been a great help."

So said M.A., with the support of her family to whom she had given so much, if not love – but who can tell? – then time.

*

But one morning a day at work would be cancelled by a phone call. You hardly recognised your mother's voice.

"It's your poor father, your poor father . . ."

The former mechanic had suddenly felt unwell in his vegetable garden; he had gone upstairs to lie down, then called out. A few minutes later it was all over.

"There was nothing I could do, there was nothing I could do."

At the funeral, people said things like: *It was such a sudden death, too sudden. He was still young. Poor man, he won't have had time to enjoy his retirement.* You hung up, you turned to François and you wept on his shoulder. You found yourself up against the irreversible nature of death. Yesterday you could talk to him, this morning it was no longer possible. All these years you had had a father, and now just as your tenderness for him was manifest, suddenly you no longer had one.

There is no conclusion to life. Only that morning as she came down from the bedroom and sat in her chair, your mother, looking lost, spoke these words:

"You know, I really was so fond of your father."

And you too had been fond of your papa. Why had he not played a more important part in your life? He had been too discreet; dying was the most discourteous thing he had ever done. You wanted to wear black, and organise a fine ceremony, but already the next day you had to go with Juliette on her school study trip to the countryside, and with Nathalie to a sports competition. The house in Terneyre did not seem to have changed, they still had the same telephone number, and your mother's voice was still at the other end of the line. You needed some time to get out of the habit of asking, at the end of your conversations, "And how is Papa doing?" It was something you had done for so many years, whenever you rang your mother. You had never exchanged a word, you and your father, except through her, he had always been the man in the background, behind the receiver. And now he was dead. He became a person in his own right. How strange it was. *It's so sad to lose one's husband. He was a good man. What a terrible thing to happen!* You watched as the coffin was lowered. *What a terrible thing to happen!* These last words, uttered by the neighbour, revived a memory.

It was a quiet Sunday. You and your father were at his garage. You had gone there on the pretext of repairing a part on the coffee grinder. Your father whistled while he fiddled, he was using a metal saw. You hovered around him in your little skirt. Suddenly his tool slipped and in the image that immediately followed, your father's finger was pointing downwards, and his hand was squeezing his wrist covered in blood. He shouted something at you. In the next sequence, you were running to the house, your father told you to go and tell Maman, quickly; you ran and you saw red all over the floor in the garage, you ran as fast as you could. When you got to the rue des Sartes, you saw your mother hanging out the washing; you saw her gestures, the usual gestures of a sunny Sunday. You knew you were going to destroy something when you shouted. You called your mother so she would turn round, and in that instant her face was already tense with worry, as you cried without thinking:

"Something terrible has happened to Papa!"

It was an expression out of a book of fairy tales: it had been a tranquil day, everyone going about their business when suddenly there was a catastrophe, a man was assassinated, war was declared, the world was in turmoil because of an accident; thus, in a frenetic whirlwind, great events plunge people into a different reality where all tranquillity is destroyed, where hearts beat faster, where days are full of adventure, unrest and passion. Then comes a sequence of trials, so that the hero can restore that lost tranquillity. The group emerges reinforced, each member has understood the value of this new happiness that has changed for ever from their prior happiness.

And on that day it was left to you to break the news:

"Something terrible has happened to Papa!"

Your mother plied you with questions. Suddenly you said, as if you had recovered your wits:

"Papa cut his finger! Papa cut his finger!"

The neighbour, who was working in his garden, overheard and drove you to the garage; you sat in the back, leaning forwards between the two adults as they asked you for details, and you could sense the special atmosphere; the atmosphere of an important day; you wanted it to last, but when you reached the garage you barely had time to see your father lying on a seat in a lorry. The neighbour said:

"You stay put out here."

So, since you did not know what to do, you burst into tears. You cried harder than now, that day you were burying your father. You were crying because you were only ten years old, because you had been very frightened, but also because you could tell that was what you were supposed to do, according to the script of an important day.

Basically, you knew your father's injury wasn't that serious, that it would soon be healed, but you tried to make that feeling of something exceptional last by showing your tears to an imaginary audience. The next day at school you could tell your girlfriends all about it; but for now you were outside the garage, crying, sitting on a tyre, with the distinct sensation that you were living through a memory, the memory that you were recalling on this day, now that this something terrible had truly happened; the death of the father; reduced to his sad reality, now that the coffin had at last been buried in a tomb.

Later your parents left the garage and you went home. The doctor made a bandage.

"He won't be able to work for a few days, madame. I'll give you a certificate."

In all likelihood the evening meal was more affectionate than usual. But just as you were going up to bed, your mother called out brusquely:

"Listen here, you! Don't you know you're not supposed to say that?"

"Say what?"

"You know very well what I'm referring to."

She looked at you and said:

"Your father just cut his finger, that's all. You mustn't frighten people like that!"

You understood. When you had giddily said the words, "Something terrible has happened to Papa", you knew it was one of the ways you could announce a person's death. But you had let yourself be carried away by the expression; because you had had a happy childhood, an uneventful childhood; for once something had happened, what would you not have done?

On Sundays when you had a barbecue, Chloé, Fabien, Michelle and Clément drove over with a bottle of wine. Everyone kissed hello, it was very informal, the women tossed salads, Jacques helped François grill the sausages, no-one kept an eye on the children until their shouts interrupted your conversation. Then an adult would get up and go to resolve the disagreement, then sit back down, exchanging a few words in a low voice with his or her spouse. You talked about the children's schools.

"He is much more assertive than his brother."

And this was how you celebrated; a new job, a birthday, a baccalaureate, a baptism, your mother's seventieth birthday, it all ended up as a barbecue at the clos des Narcisses. Only a few more years and you would have finally paid off the loan, and your friends, driving home in the evening, would say what a steady couple you were in the middle of all these divorces, oh dear, oh dear. You had resumed a minimum of sexual activity, you expected nothing from it and therefore it was less frustrating. Whatever your husband did, day or night, there was nothing that could surprise you anymore. The thought that he might have some deep inner turmoil, something lurking furtively in the shadow of an inner estate was foreign to you, even a bit ridiculous, he coughed up too much phlegm in the sink. You had no idea that François, too, had had his doubts, about your love, about your marriage, that he suffered from your mood swings. He had even said to his mother one day:

"My wife is not always all that easy."

Several years after your wedding, François had realised that his life would always be bound to you; his life, which meant the quality of his mattress, the various destinations of his car, the food that ended up in his stomach, the body he would embrace and then neglect, all of that would be you, and this permanent association had yielded neither lasting tension nor stimulating difference. Even if you often annoyed him, François had got used to this regime. In any case, he was too old to kindle any desire for another woman. Your optimism during his period of professional hardship had secured him to you once and for all. As for you, you were so used to seeing him show up at a precise time, like a cuckoo emerging from his clock, that you worried if he was late. The thought of parting had become inconceivable. Your friends were right: rock solid.

Now the sun was setting, the lawn gave off a welcome chill. The children had gone back inside to play Nintendo. Outside, the adults were discussing driving licences and penalty points, or the influence of violent images on the brains of young television viewers. Later on, another friend would talk about his old mother's decline, and there were sighs all round. Cigarettes were smoked, the bottle was finished, and the white hue of the plastic garden table that looked dirty during the day now softened in the evening light.

"Isn't this the life, then?" said François.

That was how you all got together, as a family or among friends, round that table that had proved so satisfactory all these years, a garden table you had bought at a big D.I.Y. centre a few roundabouts from there. On other Sundays, François would set his tools down there before smearing the trees with Bordeaux mixture. Your mother insisted on making jam every year. In this other photograph, which was taken after your father's funeral, the entire harvest has been placed on this very table, several salad bowls filled with apricots, the three children, and Mamie and François, everyone smiling.

Night had fallen. You had stuck the labels onto the jars of jam, and you went back out to sit on the terrace, watching as the wind ruffled the sheets on the laundry line. François was trimming a reed with his penknife. You wondered if you might not plant some mimosa at the end of the garden next to the walnut tree, that would be pretty, François replied that it would indeed be pretty, a mimosa bush. And in your memory all these scenes mingled with older or more recent images; almost identical scenes where the light travelled from one side of the lawn to the other; as the washing was only getting the last rays, you took it down, glancing over at your dark violet irises that ringed the garden and the family circle.

II

Until that strange moment when, although everything was going well, suddenly M.A. was no longer present among us. Her body sat next to us at the table, her head tilted as she listened to someone, a lock of hair slipped in similar fashion over her smooth brow; but, a slow abdication.

François observed this distance at Christmas dinner.

"I find you've been acting strange lately, my darling."

When you left your office, you no longer hurried to come home. You could be seen driving past the proper exit to continue for a long time down the motorway, searching for some emotion that did not come, which might yet give you the impression of being here, of been alive. You watched the cars on the other side of the barrier and you wondered what sort of life they had, those people you glimpsed behind the wheel. When you finally drove up to La Garotte, you felt a rather mad impulse to park outside someone else's house and not your own; you could imagine the scene, walking in to find another husband, another bedroom, another situation.

Now you were in the kitchen slicing tomatoes, and you didn't hear what François was telling you.

"Your head is in the clouds again."

You were having a strange experience, where nothing concerned you. At other times, the sharpness of a certain vision was unbearable: in this kitchen you saw this tomato, and you wondered why it was round, or what would have become of this chopping board three thousand years from now, and why you spoke French rather than sign language, and other questions that, asked out loud, would have seemed incongruous. You were sleeping poorly.

Now you were in front of the television, watching a D.V.D. At your side Juliette was relating something that had happened at the lycée, but eventually she gave up.

"You don't really seem interested in what I'm telling you, Maman."

"I'm sorry."

"It's nothing, it will pass."

One evening you took the ring road to the airport at Satolas, and you could be seen wandering for a long time, aimlessly, around the international terminal. You had your bag with you, and your I.D. papers, you needed only to buy a ticket with your credit card and you could be gone within the hour; at that particular moment, whether you stayed or left was no longer of any importance. It was only a telephone call from François, enquiring whether you needed bread that evening, that put you back on the path to us.

You ended up at the doctor's. Your condition had got worse. At night you woke up soaked in sweat, you felt electric waves going through you that then became migraines. François urged you to see a doctor: whenever you had a headache he feared the worst. Not to mention the anxiety brought on by the television campaign for breast cancer prevention.

The doctor examined you, asked you your age and said:

"You've had three children, madame, it might be time to slow down a little."

You didn't expect this. For the medical profession this meant take a break, but it was tantamount to death. You listened to the doctor, came back several times for tests, he suggested this or that treatment, you opened your eyes wide. Did they really have to treat you like an old woman when you were barely forty-eight years old? And anyway, why wasn't this happening to François, this end of fertility? The doctor dished out advice for elderly people: do some sports, stay out of the sun, eat soy, watch your thyroid. You felt like insulting him: it was alright for him with his beautiful white hair, what did it cost him to get old, he just looked all the more powerful. Whereas you were suddenly leaving the herd of desirable women; they had warned you that you would get fat. Better to have fallen ill, undergone an operation, contracted leukaemia; anything rather than this ordinary decrepitude. Because once you started conversations about oestrogen and hormone therapy, the charm of a curable illness vanished, just as the spark in men's gazes went out, and the children left home to study in the city. It was completely exposed, this gaping hole that had hatched inside you.

Therefore, vexed at having mistaken the precursory signs of a hormonal phenomenon for a flight of melancholy, you began to complain acrimoniously. You fussed all the time. François soon came to miss your previous, rather unpredictable moods, which had merely baffled him. Now when he came home it was to a never-ending jeremiad.

"My boss was nasty to me again, it's terrible, I can't stand him anymore!"

"My legs feel so heavy . . ."

"The fireplace is smoking, can't you do something?"

"I cannot figure out these euros, I'm sure I got ripped off at the checkout."

You blamed your family: it was their fault if you had grown old so quickly, it was because they had not known how to discover the secret inside you. Your life would have been different if you had married another man, if your children had not required – as was still the case today – so much care. You should not have embarked so hastily on that third pregnancy, you would have done better to go after Philippe – that's what you thought from time to time. Had you been foolish enough to marry the first man who said, "You're pretty"; although surely on a windy day in a big city an elegant diplomat would have singled you out – you – and would have taken you with him; in the gilded palaces of the Republic you would have been seen wearing a sheath dress, a powerful ambassador's wife surrounded by servile journalists and Ferrero chocolates. No such thing; instead, you sat grumbling next to that poorly swept fireplace, subjected to the swelling in your saphenous veins – not to mention the treeroots that were displacing the flagstones in the garden.

"There is nothing left to look forward to in life."

"I just drag myself around, is all."

Chloé replied:

"You seem so negative, I'm surprised. Get a hold of yourself! We're not that old, after all!"

You could fight it, after all; you could buy anti-ageing creams, go to the hairdresser's more often, swim, travel, but this sad numbness always overcame you, as stubborn and nasty as an ineradicable smell in the fridge. You saw yourself going shopping after work, all alone at the hypermarket, going through certain sections without even stopping, putting your basket down before you got to the till, always performing the same gestures, arriving at the chemin des Pins, locking the car, hunting for your house keys, opening the door to the villa.

The house was often empty. François was at work, Juliette was at the lycée. The two older children had not been living at home since the start of the academic year. Your only distraction consisted in calling your mother, but she was getting deafer and deafer. You promised to go and see her the next day. You had actually done some shopping for her. When you hung up, you were overcome by a rush of anxiety. You had to get back out of there, quickly.

You put on your jacket; you went for a walk in the neighbourhood.

On leaving the house you walked along the neighbour's bright orange wall, easily visible from a distance; you followed it for fifteen metres, on your right you left the black iron gate of the pedestrian entrance, then a white garage door, then a wrought-iron gate, a thuja hedge, a low wall covered with a row of tiles where an electricity meter was located. At the end of the street was a crossing. One car was parking, another pulling away, a third drove by. You looked for something to distract your attention, something else on which to fasten your gaze besides the variation of fences and the movement of vehicles, something that would dissipate your anxiety. A four-wheel drive turned to the left, now the gate was yellow, the wall to which it was attached was two metres high, on the ground there were smudges of

tar left by recent council roadwork. This was the only walk that you knew, the one that led to the retirement home and back again. The fields that once surrounded your house had all been built upon; a few kilometres further along, in the new *free zone*, there was a sprawl of corrugated iron rectangles, housing small businesses – plumbing manufacturers, heating specialists, "industrial air-conditioning" and other "carpenters for professionals". In the residential neighbourhood there were the same garages with white doors, the same light-coloured roughcast, the same communal dustbins; and the empty car park, its surface dotted with spots of oil.

You hurried your step to dispel your anxiety, here was the stop sign, there was a little wall with a grille, an interphone, another wall. These walks were nothing else, going along a fence, walking down an empty street, moving to one side when a car was parked in the way, your anxiety had returned, you would have liked to run but you didn't, you merely walked more quickly in the hopes of expelling this urge to scream that had been with you all day. There was a car turning, there was a car going straight ahead. Now you were at the bus stop, for the number 3 bus, symbolised by yellow zigzags on the pavement, there was an advertisement, a smiling face illustrating toothpaste. You came to the crossing that led to the Foyer des Lilas, the zebra crossing was wider there. There were blue parking spots for the disabled, and ramps for people with reduced mobility, there were flower-beds; as you walked by the house, you pulled up your collar.

No horizon, no animals, hardly a bird singing.

A woman was taking small steps in your direction, no doubt a resident from the retirement home. She was wearing a brown skirt and a dirty bonnet on which yellow letters spelled the word FUN. Her ugly clothes were off-putting. The pavement was too narrow for you to pass each other, you stepped down into the street, and then you noticed that the old woman was talking to herself. This encounter made you want to go home, you would feel better in front of the fireplace, because it was quite chilly out. You tapped something on your mobile phone, François replied with a text message, in the end your walk had distracted you, in any event it had tired you out. In a mirror hanging from a pylon – one of those which are put up to help motorists manoeuvre – you saw your reflection, and you turned away.

"I think I look awful these days."

"I still find you just as beautiful, my darling."

"You, you – what you say doesn't count!"

After a white gate, a coniferous hedge, a sign indicating the presence of two elevated walkways, the sun suddenly spread onto the pavement. You looked up. In the distance, Empan's water tower stood motionless among the trees that had not been felled. You looked down on a car park where there were a number of vehicles: grey, metallic blue, dark grey, black, blue, black, metallic grey, white, and light grey. On the road there were several patches of asphalt, grey, dark grey, dark black, signalling the council's road works, for cables, sewers, electricity. Walking back the way you had come you noticed the power station:

DO NOT ENTER – DANGER OF DEATH. And what if you committed suicide? It would be as easy as taking a plane – but you were not desperate, you were just constantly humiliated, like a victim seeking retribution for some unnamed injustice. You saw a little beige gate, freshly painted, and bamboo outside a lovely big villa.

"Our house looks so bland. It's ageing badly."

"Don't exaggerate, it's perfectly fine. You said so yourself, last week."

Last week, next week, will everything always be like this? Always that parked car, always that garage door, the grassy border, those red geraniums, and that letterbox in its niche, always that grey dustbin, that streetlamp, that pavement, that little wall, that manhole cover, that gate, always that garage, this wall, and that wall, this sign saying CLOS DES NARCISSES and always this orange wall you walk alongside for fifteen metres before you get home.

One day when you were burdening Chloé with the weight of your complaints, she advised you for the umpteenth time to go and see her acupuncturist. She was such an extraordinary woman. She stuck you with needles and massaged you with her hands. Your lack of vitality was due to a deficiency in your spleen, all you had to do was tone that meridian for several sessions and everything would go better, don't worry, madame, physically you are in quite good shape.

For a few days your smile came back.

Another day, in the waiting room, you saw an advertisement for yoga classes. ARE YOU LOOKING FOR INNER PEACE? COME

TO THE AQUARIUS CLUB. The expression *inner peace* resounded strangely inside you. The contrary of peace was war, and for months you had felt as if you were waging a permanent battle: against age, against a loss of self-esteem, or simply against your reluctance to go to work. The therapist opened her door and interrupted your thoughts. She was already quite old, quite ugly, and her fees were

quite high. You asked for details about the yoga club.

"A lot of the patients are very pleased. They do serious work there."

The club was in a suburb of Chambéry where there were a lot of parking places. A little bell tinkled as you opened the door. Two men standing by the till fell silent for a moment and then, after a hasty greeting, continued their conversation. You studied the bookshelves, they were filled to overflowing with books about astrology, tarot, psychology, personal development. Near the till was a corkboard where the club's various activities were posted. The yoga classes were held upstairs every Wednesday evening, the first session was free, everyone was welcome. The man who seemed to be the owner of the place (Thomas, you would learn later) was on his own now. You asked him for some additional information. He confirmed that the first session was indeed free, and was actually about to begin in half an hour's time. But you didn't feel like going on your own. You asked Chloé to go with you. You had a cup of coffee at her place, and then after you had caught up with all the latest news (work, children, shopping, husband), you launched into your usual lamentations. Life was hard. Everything annoyed you. In spite of the needles the acupuncturist planted in your skin, you felt old, old, old. You couldn't go on like that. The yoga would surely do you good. Chloé approved of the idea but didn't want to join you, she didn't like gym, personally, and besides, she was about as supple as a breadboard. You insisted. You didn't want to go without her. She refused again:

"I don't believe it, you're acting as if you were afraid!"

Eventually you let out a tiny "yes", and as if out of nowhere you began to cry. You were shaking with great irrepressible sobs. You wanted to get hold of yourself, you even tried to laugh; it's nothing, nothing at all; but the tears flowed freely, wildly, down your cheeks.

It lasted for a long time. Chloé took your hand and waited. Finally, when you had calmed down:

"I'm sorry to tell you this, but I think you're depressed. It's not that serious, but you have to get treatment."

It was like an apparition. All the previous signs suddenly became legible: your restlessness, your suicidal impulses, the pain of living, it all contracted into one word: depressed! You had never thought of it. But you were already rejecting the idea. No, no, that was an illness reserved for people who were unhinged – you were just going through a bad patch in your life due to menopause, otherwise everything was fine. It was true that the slightest little thing could set you off these days, but you had a job, a salary, children who were doing well in their studies, you had no major problems; was what you told Chloé, forgetting that for months now you had been inundating her with your complaints. She insisted: spells of depression often came when the most difficult was behind us.

Intrigued, you mentioned it that evening to François. Contrary to your fears, your husband did not make fun of you. He just said, in his efficient manner,

"If you want to be clear in your own mind, make an appointment with the doctor, he'll give you his opinion."

A shiver of doubt went through you. You asked François if he thought you had changed lately. Yes, sometimes you were a bit aggressive and he was sorry to see it. So for the first time in years, you apologised to him.

"But it's nothing, my darling."

He scraped the crème caramel on his dessert plate.

"I just don't like to see you unhappy, is all."

The words kept going through your head: *unhappy, depressed* . . . It was something to think about. Two days later you asked the acupuncturist to "recommend a shrink".

"A psychoanalyst or a psychotherapist?"

You blushed.

"If you don't need to be completely reimbursed, I would suggest you begin with a psychotherapist."

She gave you the name of Luc Cassale. He had a gentle voice over the telephone. Just to say, "I haven't been feeling well lately, someone gave me your name," was enough for you to make an entry on the calendar for two weeks later. Cassale's office was on the rue du 4-Septembre in Valvoisin. Your first appointment went well, it was the beginning of a long series.

You arrived five minutes early. Cassale made you wait a quarter of an hour. The previous patient went out through another door at the end of the corridor, there were voices, footsteps drawing nearer. The doctor shook your hand, looking slightly above your hair, you followed him into his office, he had you sit in an armchair that was too far away from him for your liking, you studied the shelves in detail while he hunted for a file among the numerous papers on his desk, you took a tissue from the cardboard box, wiped the dampness from your palms, tugged slightly on your skirt, coughed. Cassale raised his head, then finally looked you in the eye. There was a silence and you spoke.

There were times when you decided to unravel something precise; to go back over the feeling of malaise that had stayed with you all week long, to analyse your anger; and there were other times when unexpected sentences came from your lips. These sentences acted as guides, depending on what you had learned by searching on Google (you typed, "What should I tell my shrink?" and unearthed a host of forums where you lingered for hours). On you went, one sentence led to another, you said heaps of things. It was exhilarating to find out how much there was to say about oneself. Later on you had less to say, you were somewhat alarmed by what you were discovering, you would stop for long stretches and wait to be prompted. But Cassale was one of those therapists who do not say much. The first month this attitude unsettled you, you wanted for him to understand everything, right away, and set you on the path of inner peace. That was not his role, he said. It was up to the patients to do their own work. There were other days when a simple remark on his part left an impression, insidiously, and you had to stop off for a short while at the local bar.

These sessions allowed you to rediscover Valvoisin. You had not been there in a long time. It has to be said that as far as shopping was concerned you were fine with the shops in Empan, Chambéry and above all the hypermarket on the *route nationale*. Now every Monday you parked, almost atavistically, in the same parking area where your father used to park on those rare occasions when you drove up into the town. The old centre had not changed much since then. Nevertheless you could sense the traces of a desire to urbanise that must have dated from the 1970s – the station, for example, no longer served as a landmark for people who were out for a stroll, and the old department stores had been demolished to allow the *nationale*, quite literally, to make inroads into the *urban fabric*, but otherwise you recognised the melancholy, idle atmosphere of dereliction you remembered from your youth. There were very few major businesses. Valvoisin lived primarily from its schools and administrations; there were also a considerable number of plaques indicating "State-Registered Nurse" in the streets of the traditional pedestrian neighbourhood with its purple paving stones and chain stores like Camaïeu, Body Shop, Boulangerie Paul and Monoprix. But it must not be altogether unpleasant to live there. The price of housing or baguettes was lower than in Lyon, and the local women dyed their hair a colour which, however erratic, still managed to be in fashion.

Some years earlier, a *pâtissier* in the centre of town had invented a cake consisting of a walnut cream filling between two layers of pastry. The artisan had called his patisserie "Le Bourmoix de Valvoisin", and he sold vast amounts of these cakes to holidaymakers. Once word got round, the city seized upon the propitious cake to transform it into a tourist attraction. A local history buff serendipitously uncovered in some archive the story of King Louis who, on his way to Italy to wage war, was held up by a violent storm and asked for a meal from the local residents of the time. And lo, there was Louis IX savouring the cake with a smile of contentment, as could still be seen on the sticker created by the local P.R. people to seal the packets of little grey cakes.

Near Cassale's building there was a bar where pensioners and people on disability benefits came to drink up their allowance. After certain sessions you stopped in and mingled with the clientele. There were familiar affectionate insults, there were comments on recent television programmes, political or otherwise, beer was consumed, *Le Dauphiné* was read. Among the various special offers – a dozen hamburgers for the price of six – the local paper reported on the events of life in Valvoisin. And you got the impression that nothing new could ever happen here, nothing spectacular or dangerous, nothing that, judging from the conversations in these bars or in the queue at the *boulangerie*, could not be swallowed, digested, and finally restored to its fitting banality.

At Cassale's an armchair was waiting for you. This was your time, you were paying someone, he was obliged to listen to you, and you experienced it as a gift, "a moment of being close to yourself", according to the therapist. In the beginning, however, you almost backed out. It was costing a lot of money, and there were days when you felt anxious on leaving his office. One time you heard yourself say "I don't like myself very much", when in fact the opposite was true. Not to mention the fact that you often spoke badly about your husband, and that put you in an

226

uncomfortable position when you got home. But more broadly, this *work on yourself* was doing you good. François encouraged you to carry on with it.

"I'm getting a lot out of it, even if it isn't always easy."

You confided to Chloé, with a conspiratorial look.

Dr Luc Cassale, in his wisdom, prescribed serotonin and Diazepam. You liked going to the pharmacy with his prescriptions, their undecipherable signature, and without them you would probably not have placed the same faith in his authority. When you saw him sitting in his armchair, unfathomable, you would think to yourself that, alas, Cassale must not find you very interesting. Other women must have come and sat across from him, hysterical young women who had been raped by their father and beaten by their mother, orphans or schizoid paranoid cases: you couldn't compete with them. Your parents, poor things, had been very kind. And so you exaggerated, you speculated about your mother's life; you wanted to move him to pity. Instead of digging deep inside yourself to try to eliminate the powerful darkness that had compelled you to come and sit on this armchair now at the onset of menopause, you deployed your intelligence in an attempt to make everything you said to him either spiritual or moving; one week you tried to make him feel sorry for you, another week to make him laugh, in such a way that as the sessions accumulated, rather than granting him access to your inner self (but is that even something we can do?) you were presenting Cassale with an embellished and eroded image of yourself; like those translators who, either in obedience to editorial fiat, or voluntarily, remove from the original text one, two, three, then all the difficult passages, thus eliminating the prickle from the punctuation – in short, plucking the spines from the literary cacti in order to present readers with a product that is merely digestible, pleasant, and harmless; in such a way that, confronted with this falsification of yourself, Cassale could not really help you.

One day when the psychotherapist told you to take long deep breaths whenever you had hot flushes, you asked him for his opinion of yoga.

"Yes, yoga, why not."

Said he.

His words gave you the courage to return to the Aquarius Club. The man with the ponytail recognised you and pointed to the little stairway. It led to a very bright room with foam mats piled by the door. Each participant had to take a mat and unroll it in front of her. They were almost all women, two of them seemed to be professionally active still, and none of them wore flowered dresses the way you had imagined.

First you did stretches. The teacher, whom you took an immediate liking to, was called Niréna. She explained that *yoga* means "union"; that conscious breathing, *inspir* and *expir*, brings mental clarity, balances the two sides of the brain, and generates a feeling of inner peace that contributes to greater self-confidence. When you heard the words *inner peace* you pricked up your ears. The body constituted a whole, what we accomplished inside ourselves would change our outer reality; as this was an initiatory session for newcomers, you would learn the Sun Salutation. Put your palms together, point to the sky, bring them down level with your ankles while breathing out, extend one leg behind you while holding your arms out in front of you as if to touch the horizon, raise your buttocks as if to shape your body into a circumflex accent, drop your chest down to the floor as if you wanted to become a root again, raise your upper body and take a very deep breath; then perform all the movements in the opposite direction.

Niréna spent some time next to you to correct your alignment. You liked her presence. She found you very flexible for your age. That was it, that was all for today.

"Those of you who would like to are invited to stay and have some tea together."

Niréna reminded everyone of the rules: you would all say *tu* and there was to be no talk about work. The tea, which tasted of cinnamon and cardamom, was called *yinyangtea*. Everyone said her name in turn, and all these ladies were very chatty. They asked you if you had ever gone hiking in the desert, it opens up your chakras, they talked to you about the Enelph method, family constellations, Kundalini energy and the liberation of the voice; one old woman with long hair offered to read your cards for you, and a woman called Caroline maintained that tarot cards could not compare with a good medium. You opened your eyes wide when Sylvie said that's all rubbish, you're going to terrify the newcomers. Everyone laughed. Then you talked about your acupuncturist, and the time you went to see a clairvoyant, and all in all you found your niche in the little group. Outside, Françoise told you that she ran a business, and Caroline that she had had four children. The following week you enrolled at the Aquarius Club, which also gave you access to the library.

Thomas, the boss, and his companion Sylvie were great

readers of books by Christophe André, Boris Cyrulnik, and Krishnamurti. Niréna also recommended books by Jocelyne Roy and Jacques Salomé. They were entitled *Moving Beyond Anxiety; Mid-Life Crisis; What is Happening to Me?; Going Through Analysis (for Women); Happiness is a Skill You Work At; Realise your Potential; Express Your Anger; Forgiving Yourself; Why Can't I Smile?; Get Yourself on the Right Path; The Ten Secrets of Optimism; Letting Go; Love That Stands the Test of Time; Let's Talk . . . Before It's Too Late; Simply Loving Each Other; Listening to One's Murmur; Yes, I'm Beautiful!* The authors narrated their own experience, or their patients', in long testimonials; dialogues were set next to alarming figures about the melting of the ice caps; diagrams were set out according to the two axes: powers of life / powers of death. The reader was instructed to follow virtuous circles, to work her way back to childhood wounds, because it was at that moment that the membrane of the self had hardened. A few pages further on, images of suns represented the "self in shadow" and the "self in light". It wasn't difficult reading. In *Learn to be Happy* you read, "Happiness is like a dandelion: its deep roots are planted at the very heart of the humus of life. With their somewhat astringent taste, dandelion leaves can be eaten, and they prepare our palate for other pleasures. Open yourself to this plant for, as everyone knows, its generous flower scatters to the four winds." You read a lot and drank a lot of tea.

But if truth be told: extending your ankle downwards in order to hollow out your solar plexus became rather tiresome over time. Particularly as your reading was arousing your interest in the esoteric. You would have liked to be initiated into Freemasonry, to call on spirits, or at the very least to make clocks run backwards, but you supposed you weren't *in the right circles*, because no-one suggested anything other than pottery workshops entitled "Healing with Clay".

At home you made the most of the status as a depressive which those around you, and you yourself, had eventually conferred upon you. It allowed you to say things like:

"It makes no difference, nothing makes any difference."

"Why don't we go and have ice cream for dinner?"

And they gave in to your every whim, more or less.

However, one day when François was doing the books with the help of a software program called Money (for P.C.), he pointed out that between your membership in the club, the yoga, the two monthly acupuncture appointments and your sessions with Cassale, the column "M.A. – Personal" had come to almost 350 euros for March alone. You asked, testily, whether he had a problem with that.

"Of course not, darling, I'm just letting you know."

Initially you thought François was being petty, confined in a narrow vision of his chakric self. But his comment came just as you were about to sign up for the Eastern yoga workshop. It would be held at a monastery in the Chartreuse. The thought of sleeping for three nights in an uncomfortable bed in the middle of the forest, without television, frightened you. You cancelled. At the club, the workshop led to a major fiasco. Thomas and Sylvie had not been informed of the presence of Michel Colombier, the grand master of Surya Yoga. Niréna had wanted to surprise the participants, and she would tell you later that his visit had been a triumph. All the participants had been delighted. But Thomas and Sylvie didn't like Colombier. They preferred Janisselle, who practised Iyengar Yoga, said Sylvie, and she described the same event to you as a putsch: Colombier had always viewed Janisselle as a charlatan because he was not a true vegan.

You could not understand the motives behind this conflict. But before long Thomas had taken down the posters for Niréna's class. The tea had not even had time to brew before everyone had got in their cars and driven away. Cassale, who seemed to disapprove of your increasing involvement with the Aquarius Club, laughed when you told him about it.

"You know, the decisions you make in life don't depend on some gymnastic stretching."

His comment made a very strong impression on you. You decided not to renew your membership of the club. Basically, you had already learned a great deal, in the morning you did your Sun Salutations, and when speaking about a certain friend you referred to the fact that she had not enhanced her resiliency. You even knew how to brew your own *yinyangtea* for your visits with Chloé, except that you put more cinnamon in yours.

"When you think, your friends over at the Aquarius Club, they didn't just smoke tea!"

You both laughed. With the help of the serotonin and the hormone replacement you were feeling better. You were no longer afraid of coming back to an empty house. Even though Juliette too had just left to go and study in Lyon.

"I mustn't let myself go, life isn't over."

"Ah! That's what I like to hear, my darling."

You went on seeing Cassale. There was something in his office that intrigued you. To the right of the big desk, on a small glass shelf, there were dozens of statuettes of tortoises: little ones and big ones, mischievous ones and dark ones, tortoises in wood, in cloth, in iron, in tortoiseshell, sleeping, laughing, meditating, solid gold or fake. They fascinated you: was the tortoise the psychiatrist's totem? You pictured Cassale hunting for unusual specimens in antique shops. Or maybe it was his patients who, before saying goodbye for good, gave him a figurine in gratitude for the work he had done. They had come into these rooms, suffering from claustrophobia and multiple trauma, now they would go back out feeling serene, those mysterious patients whom you never saw; and on the armchair, in memory of their passage, they would leave a tortoise symbolising their former illness. The animals listened to you in silence, their short-clawed feet clinging to a glass plate. He had certainly treated a lot of people, you thought, and you admired him all the more for it.

III

An enormous shopping mall called Le Grand Pont had been built at the entrance to Grenoble. It covered a surface of forty thousand square metres. Shopping at this mall became one of your weekend pleasures.

Shopping was a very common activity in that era. It consisted in approaching the entrance to one of the shops, where a sensor would detect your presence, and the two sides of a glass door would slide open to let you in. On rare occasions, in a low, calm voice, shop detectives would ask you to open your handbag, but these men (as a rule they were black, and muscular) most often remained silent, observing the customers' comings and goings. Once you were in the shop you would head for the area where you thought you would find the item you were looking for. You examined various products on display, and on an urge you might pick one up. You could try it on in a *fitting room* if it happened to be a piece of clothing. Once you had decided to buy it, you kept it with you, or you might put it into a shopping trolley. The act of purchase was conditioned by the budget at one's disposal, by how closely the actual product corresponded to the commentary one had heard about it, but also by its size, solidity, make and the time one could devote to such shopping trips. This act of purchase would be repeated several times over. In certain shops you would ask for help from the shop assistant whom you identified from his or her badge or waistcoat. It was always better to go up to this person and say "Hello" before asking any questions, but most of the time you could make up your own mind. When your trolley was full it was time to go to the checkout. The woman (in general it was a woman) would use a laser scanner to read the barcode on each product, a manoeuvre which gave off a characteristic little beep. If there was no beep, the checkout assistant would stop and call for a higher-ranking employee, to whom she would say something like: "I don't get it, it doesn't want to register." Then the electronic cash register would calculate the amount due. The woman would repeat the amount, using a polite formula. You paid with your bank card. The woman would say, "Thank you, bye now," you would pick up your plastic bag with the shop logo on it, and go back out through the same sliding glass door.

Once you'd finished your shopping you went back to your car in the nearby car park. After all this time spent in a vast and busy public space, when you sat behind the wheel a sweet feeling of cosiness came over you. Mentally you added up everything you had spent, it was often a bit too much, you exchanged a few words with the person at your side, comments on how late it was or about some items that one of you had not managed to find, but that was rare. You could find everything at Le Grand Pont.

Then you started the car. You drove off. New roundabouts had been built between Empan and Terneyre. It was true that the traffic was getting congested.

"All these cars . . . What's going on today? They're parked every which way."

"There must be a baptism. That always causes congestion."

"I should have gone via the cemetery."

You might go and fetch your mother so that she could come for dinner at your place. It was the weekend of May 8, or of Whitsun, and the children would be back for two days. You saw Xavier pull up in his car and it seemed like only yesterday you were buckling him in his car seat . . . Your face lit up whenever one of them sent you a text message to say that he or she was *coming down* for a visit on Friday evening. You would open up the rooms upstairs, and bake their favourite cake, François would set one, two, or three additional plates on the plastic tablecloth, you went to fetch them at the station. When you saw them alight from the train, so tall, so grown-up, you could not help but say:

"Aren't you cold?"

"You've lost weight!"

"What sort of rags are these? I'm ashamed to see you dressed like that, Nathalie."

And you hugged them, for the sake of that privileged moment when your lips touched their cheeks once again. They would tell you that this jumper was in fashion, that they were hungry, that they were "knackered", they told you about their first work placement or the latest film. After scarcely an hour, their gaze once again lowered to their phone, you would call out from the foot of the stairs:

"Dinner!"

You could not follow their conversation.

"I see you've got loads of friends on Facebook."

"One hundred and twenty, I think, and I haven't friended everyone who's asked . . ."

"And you've got a lot of activity on your wall."

"Oh, I'm mostly just adding tags to photos."

You and François tried to re-enter the conversation. He might express his concern about their future:

"And will that placement look good on your C.V.?"

They would answer that their C.V.s were already first-class, and what you needed these days was a network, they weren't children anymore, and you mustn't worry about them. Can we borrow the car next weekend, we're going to see some friends. In short, the main thing was that they ate well, during these meals, and said:

"Great dinner, Maman."

In the afternoon they would ask you to give them a recipe, to sew on a button, to fix a hem, and you gave to them, happy to be useful in the lives that they led far away from you. In the evening they went on their way. A brutal silence fell over the house, you changed the sheets and closed the doors to their rooms. At least the fact of having given birth to three children meant you had regular visits, particularly since your depression, they were careful to get in touch, and they advised you to get out more.

Get out more, said Cassale. Get out more, said the children. And the young people, raising their heads from their frenetic exchanges of text messages, brought out the ping-pong table. They began to move around it, laughing, evoking childhood memories as if they were already old. The meal was coming to an end. You felt sad thinking about when the time would come to take them to the station. François was already loading their suitcases in the boot, you left Juliette on the platform and waited for her train to pull away, then you took your mother back to Terneyre, you wrote her a cheque for the gas bill, tidied her kitchen, helped the old woman into bed, and you always felt that pang in your heart when you left her alone.

"Have you taken all your medicine?"

Now that the children were grown-up, you would be on your own again, and before long your invalid mother would take up all your time. Your car came home empty on Sunday evenings, and after the trip was over you left it in the garage at the clos des Narcisses. It came home empty and in conclusion to your festive weekend you would say:

"That's it then, everyone's gone."

Then you curled up next to François in front of the latest model plasma screen, as sad as a cat deprived of her kittens, motionless on the sofa; while the train sped heartless along the high-speed rails, taking your progeny from your embrace, their cases crammed with jam and nougat.

"Yes, sweetheart, I think I took everything the way I'm supposed to."

"But, Maman, there are still some left in the pill box."

You missed the days when you had to go and fetch one of the children from the childcare centre, and now at six o'clock in the evening, after a few roundabouts, you found yourself in Terneyre with your mother's instant coffee, and her little old telly turned to *her favourite quiz show*: she smiled at you with a tenderness that softened your heart, leaving inside you another sad sticky sensation, the visceral attachment you felt for this *maman* who would die soon. On Sunday evening you found yourself alone curled up in a blanket in front of the television, and you only got up to answer a final call from Juliette, who told you yes, "not to worry", they had got home fine.

Fortunately, it was a time when a tidal wave filled the television screen with images of brown-skinned victims turning to the microphones of reporters who had just flown in, to plead for charity from their white-skinned brothers.

You sent a cheque to the address on the screen. A few weeks later, the urgency was no longer to help those who were injured but to rebuild their flooded huts: you sent another cheque. You drove to the post office, but once you had dropped the envelope into the letterbox you still felt a pang of hunger. A worry persisted, like a whistling sound in your ears. These initial displays of generosity had aroused an impatient sympathy inside you, which you nourished every evening with the latest televised newsflashes. But the news was always the same; so many seas, so many faces; how big the world was, how small one felt. You realised that you had never made any gestures towards the poor, towards these countries without motorways where children died with insects round their mouths. And so you decided; with renewed enthusiasm, once you had made your decision, as if the whistling sound had stopped or as if it had become a music that was no longer irritating but triumphant; support, wings, a sense of empowerment not powerlessness – you would leave your little problems behind and *get involved.*

One morning in September, you went to the Humanitarian Forum in Chambéry. It was held in a huge covered hall with rows of stands. People put papers in your hand. You could do

239

everything: fight hunger, A.I.D.S., torture, cholera, but leprosy killed, too, every other day a woman was subjected to genital mutilation, you could sponsor a child so that he or she could go to school, you could send spiral notebooks to Mozambique, feed the homeless, contribute to the de-mining of valleys in Vietnam, you could volunteer to work with people who had been marginalised or wounded by life, you could pay for the construction of an infirmary, you could write to a former child soldier who needed crutches, you could purify the water in the forests, give prostitutes a second chance, get them off drugs or give them an education, there was a direct debit option to make things easier, share, support, join here, join there, and you drifted from one stand to the next, dazed.

You put the pile of brochures on the coffee table when you got home. After you had made a *yinyangtea* with the electric kettle, you started leafing through them. The names of provinces and diseases in Asia left you indifferent. You filled out a few cheques for Latin America, unenthusiastically. On the other hand, as soon as you read the leaflets about Africa, a charitable urge was born inside you, a deep, irrepressible pity, like a bite you could not help scratching. You felt a wave of tenderness as you looked at a black child smiling on recycled paper. Togo-L'Espoir was an association that sent educational and medical material to a village in the Plateaux Region. Their headquarters were located near François's agency. You jotted down the telephone number, because you might as well join a deserving little association that took concrete action rather than sign up with one of those huge machines with thousands of members. Your husband approved of your choice, obviously.

You were ever so pleased, after making your phone call, to know they would be expecting you at their next meeting.

There was a warm atmosphere. Several other "newcomers" were there as a result of the Humanitarian Forum, which had received very positive feedback. A few men with greying hair led the discussion, there were some pleasantries about the agenda, a few terms were explained, others were not. Two hours later you helped fold the chairs with a woman called Marguerite – or was it Marion? She lent you the association's photograph album. In your bed you gazed at the dirt huts. Your day had brought a complete change of scene, in every way.

Very soon a container filled with ballpoint pens and sticking plasters would be on a chartered flight bound for the indigent little Africans. The association raised money with the help of jumble sales, and every member of Togo-L'Espoir was duty-bound to sell some personal objects. For the sale you chose:

- a tea tray,
- a fondue set,
- some children's books,
- a candlestick,
- a terracotta vase.

But you quickly wearied of the association lifestyle. Obviously, it was not unpleasant to leave François at the house while you went to the meetings, and it was easy to park. But there was something unpleasant about the group, something that precluded all charm. You found them inelegant, these men with their union activist look, in their T-shirts and trainers, these women who made no effort to hide the hanging flesh of their upper arms. But above all you could not believe that this was what aid work involved: folding and unfolding chairs in a multi-purpose meeting hall. You would rather be elsewhere, in the field, in the action, in a Jeep next to a U.N. delegate wearing a reporter's waistcoat; you would have driven all day long, blinded by a cloud of sand, and when your car arrived at the camp, dozens of black hands would reach out to you; the car door banging in the wind. You were a doctor posted near the front, where fierce battles were being waged; your hands covered in blood, you saved a child with a bullet wound, you hadn't slept for forty-eight hours and you stared out at the rocky, windswept runway, your cigarette in your hand. They called you on a walkie-talkie, you were the pilot saving a family stranded on the roof after a tsunami; clinging to a winch, they rose to the helicopter numb with fear, you turned round to them from the cockpit, your thumb raised in a victory sign, and all their lives they would remember that sign; and you; as the first human being after the Catastrophe, the woman who had brought them back to life.

Why were you a woman, anyway? If you had been a man, you could have gone off to vaccinate African children rescued from famine. Maybe you had just happened upon poorly organised people. Maybe you ought to be more modest, and take care of the homeless in your own country. Winter had come, and you joined a major national association that distributed meals to those who were *most destitute*. No more chatty meetings, now once a week you scooped lukewarm ravioli into a bowl. In the beginning it made a big impression on you, and when you came back to François you told him some sordid anecdotes, you weren't used to seeing so much poverty. Then you got bored. The volunteers were women in their fifties like you, it was always the same thing: a big, draughty hall, your clothes impregnated with the smell of soup. You found it unhealthy, that sort of naïve joy you could see in the other volunteers' eyes.

In the spring the great campaign came to an end. You say goodbye without regret. You did, however, keep one friend from all those evenings, a cheerful woman, who always wore something different: Sidonie. You wrote down her telephone number before you went home, and it was a good job you did because, with the days getting longer, you wanted to put some fertiliser on your lawn. After all that time spent in dimly lit rooms, you needed some greenery.

Monsieur Pommier, your neighbour, died.

The last butcher's shop in Empan-sur-Nive closed down.

Nathalie got married.

You repainted the shutters at the front of the house.

"Oh! I stopped off at Renault."

"What did they say? Can they take the car?"

"They didn't seem in any hurry. I told them what the problem was, they said it would cost eight hundred euros."

"As much as that! To do what?"

"Everything. Distributor, oil, belt. But I don't like that garage, they don't seem reliable."

"I thought it might come to five hundred, but not twice that."

"Less than twice."

"If you don't think they're reliable, you shouldn't go there. At that price, it's worth a second thought."

"It's true they don't really seem reliable."

"Why don't you try the Citroën place? They must be able to do it too. You tell them all over again, and see how much they would charge."

"You're right, I'll go to the Citroën place. It's worth a try."

All these things you said so seriously, both of you very preoccupied, in the living room, very involved in your conversation; and it was the same thing when you were looking for the insurance certificate for the car, as you were very worried you had lost it. You were in life again. As you would be a few years later, waking your grandson from his nap, you were every bit as involved:

"Did you have a good little nap, Milo my sweet?"

But before that; you remember the day you went to Le Grand Pont to buy a Nespresso machine, the compact model that cost one hundred and fifty euros. Thrilled with your purchase, you decided to call Sidonie and invite her over for coffee. She replied in an original fashion:

"What a charming idea, I shall be sure to come!"

One thing leading to another, this former German teacher joined your Saturday gatherings among girls, a ritual that you and Chloé had almost never missed.

"So, how was your week?"

You all began by choosing your aluminium capsule: Brazil, Cuba, or Uruguay; you pressed it into the metal holder; you pressed a button. What a pleasure it was to see the red light come on, on the *designer model*, while the brewing started up with a hum. Each of you spoke in turn, unveiling her problems, it was a bit like being at Cassale's, you enumerated your little worries, except that here the audience displayed more warmth; there was laughter. The coffee from the machine was dark, satisfying, *with a powerful aroma*, and it made these moments between you all the more precious.

And when the cups were set on the tray with the pastries, when you had gone over the events of your week with a profusion of words, your shared anecdotes revealed an unexpected dimension; thanks to the advice one of you might proffer, you could all attribute great psychological wealth to even the tiniest event; you all looked forward to discovering the depth of that event, and anyone would have thought that by dissecting your women's lives so thoroughly like this – you were all past menopause, now – you were enjoying the benefit of some sort of flavour enhancer.

You could never talk for long about *clothes* with Sidonie. In no time this elegant woman would start talking about social issues. Sidonie endorsed some astonishing ideas, a bit too liberal, but initially you listened to her, the hot porcelain in your hand, as you looked at the thick, almost oily, beige cream that covered the liquid; this was the moment when you settled comfortably on a topic for discussion, a theme chosen from recent current events, or an anecdote Sidonie slipped into the conversation in order to inspire one of those debates she so enjoyed; there was a moment when you breathed in the bitter aroma of the coffee, *full-flavoured, lungo* or *dolce*, just before you would hunt for an argument to contradict her, you placed your lower lip against the edge of the cup, a gesture that was accompanied by a faint scalding of your tongue; then you could feel the liquid sliding into your mouth. That instant, you now knew, was total happiness.

Thanks to the website Copains d'avant, to your surprise you had found your old friend Catherine, with whom you used to correspond as an adolescent. After getting married in Saint-Étienne, Catherine had come back to settle in the region. She had turned into a quiet woman, and since the birth of her grandchildren she seemed to be enjoying the satisfaction of a mother who's been put to good use again. You had dinner just the two of you, to reminisce about your old schooldays, and were astonished to find you'd preserved the same jokes about teachers intact in your memory; you would sometimes pause to say, "He must be dead now, poor man," noticing all the while, with a secret satisfaction, that you were physically in better shape than she was. After this, Catherine joined your Saturday gang. You would talk about year-end balances, this or that company's latest restructuring programme, your concern regarding a husband who had a tendency to keep everything to himself.

"Oh! Thank you for the macaroons! You shouldn't have . . ."

As coffee was sipped and news was shared, a tumble of words spread all around you, whirling to Sidonie's soprano laughter, cloaked in the sort of vaguely erotic and relaxed manner you had always admired in Chloé, and you would add a detail before the buzz came to an end, initially launched by discussion of Catherine's extra kilos. A speck of foam lingered on the edge of the cup, a froth; you placed your finger against the curve of the pottery. Your group of friends had expanded, François even teased you about your "girls' club"; every week your discussions started up again, beginning with the events of the week gone by, then Sidonie would toss out one of her astonishing opinions. As she always acted – so you all told her – in a somewhat *extreme* manner, one of you might dare to confront her more openly; you would then try to find some common ground, and were very glad when Sidonie capitulated about something, for this enabled you to conclude with a more nuanced position, with everyone in agreement; halfway through the cup, the dark colour of the coffee turned slightly translucent, a circle of light appeared in the depths of the liquid, and the beige cream, homogenous to start with, fragmented into an archipelago of spots drifting towards the edge. You liked Sidonie a great deal. She'd been married several times and she impressed you with her culture. One Saturday when you were alone you told her about your affair with Philippe. You painted the picture of a turbulent passion, with numerous sensual escapades that finished in terrible misfortune. For the first time you felt Sidonie admired something about you. That was when it was good to have a real espresso, so that moments like these were more *intense*; you tilted your head to the right, to the left, replying then remaining silent to prolong the moment of intimacy; you hesitated before you finished your cup, at the bottom a small sprinkling of dark grounds had settled; finally you finished your story, you finished your coffee.

Sidonie's spirit began to work its way into you. She was a woman who loved to attend cultural events. Together you saw Tàpies, Turner, the Musée des Tissus, Alfred Brendel performing Mozart's "Piano Concerto No. 21", the exhibition *"Lumières!"* and the biennial of contemporary sacred art. She took you to the

theatre. As you drove back, she gave a running commentary, using words
you would never have dreamt of. She said:

"The stage designer is a great master of sensitive forms."

Or:

"The direction was completely non-existent."

Sidonie said "non-existent" almost angrily, which then made you afraid of saying something untoward. At the interval you said, tentatively:

"The pianist plays well."

Relief, when Sidonie approved:

"His touch is so precise, it's divine."

"Di-viiiine," she said, dragging out the "viiine", adding a triumphant certainty to the last syllable. "His virtuosity is implacable", "a certain roughness that is not altogether displeasing", "brilliant use of tempo", and you repeated her words, filled with wonder, turning them over in your mouth and causing them to ring out in turn; like earrings sparkling in a darkened concert hall, it was her brilliance you would have liked to capture.

One day Sidonie invited you over for lunch, a meal consisting of organic Lebanese dishes which you ate in a leafy little courtyard. She lived in a *maison de ville* with very old walls, a beautiful place of the sort you never imagined might exist in Grenoble, which struck you as a noisy, polluted town. She suggested you become a member of some of the subsidised cultural institutions. This elevated your standing in the Saturday group. You received concert tickets and wrote dates on your calendar. That was the point: "To be obliged to get out." The problems began when your new friend, following a serious hip operation,

248

could no longer go with you. Chloé was rather jealous of Sidonie, and did not want to fill in for her. It was François who, only just home from work, grabbed a sandwich and went with you. But the pleasure wasn't the same. The performances no longer led to informed discussions. Try as you might to make him share your recent passion for the long sighing of the violins, telling him that the "osmosis between the conductor and the soloist had reached an unparalleled level", François merely nodded, incapable of knowing what he had liked best on the programme. He was even frank enough to say, one evening:

"You know, what I like best of all is going out with you. Whatever we do I will always enjoy it."

You were hoping for grand disquisitions on art, and you were left with the words of a domestic animal.

IV

François was getting old. He jiggled his foot under the table, he cut himself while shaving, he chewed his meat slowly, he said, "I did three clients this week"; "I haven't done anyone in ten days"; "There have been a lot of accidents." In the morning before leaving he would fidget for a long time on the ground floor with his briefcase in his hand – "Do I have everything I need?" – and then he left at last.

The speed limit for all of La Garotte was lowered to thirty kilometres an hour.

His body had undergone a sort of gradual slackening. Once the debt was paid off, François seemed to relinquish his chronic insomnia. His three children were settled, in relationships and in good health, there had not been any *hidden vices* on the property, so he could breathe at last; the young man who'd been raised in the fear of not being *enough* (rich, serious, cautious enough), or of being *too much* of something (too nice, too naïve, too spend-thrift), had realised, on seeing the photograph of his sixtieth birthday: everything had gone smoothly. It was the arrival of the grandchildren that triggered the greatest relaxation, since there were no personal worries, no material anxiety, to trouble their arrival in the world.

"For Papy and Mamie, nothing but pleasure!"

Your husband smiled more often, was almost funny when he imitated the Big Bad Wolf. As a grandfather he allowed a certain lightness to surface, something he had hitherto kept in check, something simple: François feeling relieved. Because in the end they never occurred, those moments when the man in the family would be called on to prove his strength, to fight, alone in the arena, that evil power he found so terrifying – "the responsibility it represents", "a family to support", as his parents used to say; all his life François had dreaded the attack of the long-toothed beast that would come and take away his happiness, a power that could be incarnated by a tax collector or a rapacious C.E.O., that would vanish again just as arbitrarily when the beast was drawn, no doubt, to a meatier prey. Yes, it had all gone smoothly. To accomplish that mission which from the distant past of his youth had seemed to require heroism, François had discovered that the hardest part did not consist in serious gestures, like speaking with authority to his son caught with a cigarette, but rather in the tiny, wearing, everyday acts; leaving every morning with that fear in his stomach, that fear of failing, his anxiety hidden from his family all these years and paid for with an insomnia that gradually etched the wrinkles on his brow.

In any case, it was always François who installed the stereo or computer equipment. He would put on his glasses and read instruction manuals:

> To adjust timer start time
> (solely with remote control)

1. Press CLOCK/TIMER until ON XX: XX appears on the screen.
2. Press <<AND>> to adjust the hour.
3. Press PROG/SET/CLEAR to proceed with adjustment of minutes.
4. Press <<AND>> to adjust minutes.
5. Press PROG to confirm start time of timer.
6. Press <<OR>> to select source (CD/TUNER/TAP/REC TUN)
7. Press PROG/SET/CLEAR to confirm previous settings.

He was touching, this white-haired man fiddling with the remote control, you were no longer so irritated by his annoying habits, or the laziness he had always manifested around the house. Every morning you rinsed away the little hairs in the sink, you turned the blade of his razor downwards; every evening you noticed how his shirt collar was folded the wrong way, and you smiled to see how stubbornly he went on making the same mistakes. But no doubt you would have found yourself with a lot less to say if, through some improbable revolution in your domestic life, François had actually cleaned the sink after shaving.

In the winter he would join you by the fireplace where you were cracking nuts a neighbour had given you; on another evening you might be knitting. François sat down beside you, the flames sending a red glow to both your faces; an old couple tucked away by the warmth of the hearth, voicing their satisfaction at being able to stay by the fire when it was cold outside.

You had cut down on your cultural ambitions. A weekly trip

to the new multiplex was enough to replenish your stock of aesthetic emotions. You would leave after a quick dinner, François bought the tickets, you sat neither too close to the screen nor too far away. The advertisements were more vulgar than they used to be, you noticed. Then the lights went out. And your husband could not help – perhaps in memory of the first time you met – taking your hand, putting his arm round you; and what was love, if it was not a man taking your hand in the dark?

You still had your mother. It was sad to see her *decline* with each passing year.

"What do you expect? I'm all she's got."

You went to see her nearly every day, alternating with the nurse and the home help who was paid with service employment vouchers. You often thought about your mother. You had to take her her bread, her newspaper, her lotto, you often had to reassure her over the phone, because the old woman was afraid of everything. With your husband's comings and goings, and looking after the grandchildren, it was one of the many chores that filled your days, now that you were no longer working

You recall your departure from Coead as a painful episode. For months your manager had been implying, in private interviews, that you belonged to a *culture of complaint*, that you were one of those people who would never meet her targets; it was regrettable to notice the degree to which senior citizens in general in this country were incapable of adapting or displaying a positive attitude. In short, it was *time to go*. So you left the company – "voluntarily". As it was too soon to claim your pension, you had to sign up for the second time at the job centre, first by Internet, then at an office where they called you in for another type of private interview. The counsellor nodded her head.

"We're here to help you."

"You have to show that you are actively seeking employment."

"You fall into a category of people who are difficult to place."

You received compensation for two years, then you were pensioned off.

So, retirement at last, for M.A.

François found you more relaxed in the evening. You had almost missed him, your man, and he found a warmer welcome when he came to join you by the fireplace, and now your usual critical remarks – "What sort of tie is that supposed to be?" "Did you remember the bread?" – had become mere harmless teasing comments. You scolded him gently, and all the while you thought, poor man, still working, at his age . . .

You found it harder to put up with the heat in summer. You had air conditioning installed.

A technical college opened in Empan.

The market was moved five hundred metres because of urban construction.

"I felt really down for a while when I first retired."

Said a former colleague, as you bought tomatoes.

"You have to keep busy, otherwise you get nowhere fast."

*

Since the menopause, you had been keeping a journal which you used as an outlet between sessions with Cassale. Before long the mysterious notebook went everywhere with you. The month month of April that year was particularly lovely, the flowers were blooming, the air was pure, the birds nested in a joyful clamour. One morning while you were walking near the Aigue-belette lake with Chloé, a panorama of cliffs plunged you into an emotional enchantment. You jotted a few words down in your journal while your friend took some photographs (her arms outstretched, her upper body bent backwards in order to look simultaneously at what would be photographed on the screen; in a position that was almost the exact opposite of what a traditional camera had required, where your eyes were glued to the viewfinder, your shoulders were hunched, and your elbows together). Once you were back at chemin des Pins, you transformed those hastily noted words into pretty sentences. Without meaning to, you made them rhyme, a first time, then a second. To your great surprise, it wasn't difficult. You rewrote the entire passage. And that was how you took up poetry.

After studying for a few days, you decided you would mix rhyme and free verse, and this seemed exceptionally bold to you. You worked in the computer room, with a thesaurus and a rhyming dictionary you had bought at the Fnac within easy reach. At last it was finished, the first poem of your life. Which read as follows:

> On the track of the crows
> The path winding round
> As a green sun rose

Pine needles on the ground (you were proud of this association)
And a sad fall of trees
By the sheer cliff's breeze
Suddenly (you liked the break in the rhythm)
The fire of sky captures and frees
A landscape all of splendour
Vast drunken lake dancing in the rays of the sun
Here shall I call out the song
Touched to the bone
Today I will be the woman
Who will enter the cosmos.

You were very proud of the word "cosmos" in your composition: it sounded *epic*. You sent the poem to Sidonie; since her convalescence she'd been living on the Basque coast. Your old friend answered two weeks later with a letter describing how beneficial the ocean was for her health in every way, and she ended with these two sentences: "Thank you for your poem, I'm glad to see that you are still just as curious about everything. I think it's very good." And her signature.

"Very good": not great. You had expected Sidonie to comment on each verse, and say that to her stupefaction she had discovered writing the likes of which she had never seen, *et caetera*. Obviously, Sidonie was the pretentious sort, it would be better to share your art with more candid ears. Your husband heard it several times over. You repeated your recital to your daughter, and your son: *On the track of the crows / The path winding round* . . . The poem was short, retirement would be long; they encouraged you to continue.

And so; you remember going for walks more often. Because it was obvious to you that poems could only come about through contact with Nature, not to mention the fact that walking was good for your heart, "it would keep you fit". When you stood looking at the landscape you took out your notebook and waited, closing your eyes, searching for the appropriate word to sum up everything sublime about that moment; and a passing hiker would have seen a young pensioner leaning against a tree trunk, the grass tickling her calves, her face relaxed, and a furtive lizard raising its snake-like jaw to her, a flicker of its long narrow tongue as he warmed his skin in the sun; then the animal, moving fluidly, disappeared between two white stones.

When you got home, you re-read your notes, opened the dictionary and waited for the right association between the words to come. In the beginning it was exciting, to be on such familiar terms with Beauty. But after five poems, which you collected in a small booklet, you found that it was a paltry way to spend your newfound liberty, this sitting still at a desk for hours. It was late already. You went on the Internet to see the weather forecast. You downloaded your messages. Because that long-awaited word, that charming word, that precise word that would cause the music of your sentences to resonate while connecting to a new idea, that word never came. You saw in your Gallimard anthology how great writers attained that mysterious harmony, their sentences moving at a tranquil pace towards completion, eliciting a sure emotion without anything laborious creeping in. Whereas in your case, the poems limped along, were halting, did not come easily. Obviously, back in the days of all those suffering male artists, it was the absinthe that guided them, not the timetable of meals to prepare.

Not to mention:

       – calling the plumber

       – printing out bank statement

       – Casto – see about house paints for hall

       – apricots for jam

       – present for Véronique

To ward off the emptiness of your days, you made lists. Dipping into them meant you would fill your afternoons for sure. Because if retirement was going well overall, there was nevertheless a dangerous hour after naptime when the clock on the stereo on the buffet indicated "14:00" and you had to decide how to spend your afternoon. You had used up all your morning energy, and nothing had come to replace it yet, all around you the pieces of furniture in your bedroom crushed you with their presence. Everything seemed dead, it was as if the day would remain indefinitely submerged in this bog of despond. You knew this mood well. If you did not shake it off immediately, the hours that followed would be spent multiplying inefficient gestures, your anxiety would increase, you would pick up a book and then put it back down, you would start knitting, and put it aside, and so on until you said to François in the evening:

"Today I just wasted my time."

The lists worked as a remedy. Because in order to cross off "Casto – see about house paints for hall", you had to do one thing after another: take the car, drive to Le Grand Pont, compare the cans of paint, come back, have a long discussion with François in order to choose a colour. The next day, a sudden about-face: it would be wallpaper. Never mind, the week had been spent doing concrete things, modifying the aspect of a wall.

"Oh, I'm so pleased, it looks great."

"It makes the room look bigger."

But; there came the time came when Véronique's present had been bought, the wall had been papered, and the jam was waiting in a cupboard. The birth of Nathalie's twins and Xavier's son, a few months apart, provided a welcome resurgence of activity. You liked waking them up:

"So, did my little Milo have a nice nap?"

And Wednesdays were once again inhabited with children and dummies.

When François asked you in the morning what you had to do that day, you replied:

"For heaven's sake, it's Wednesday, I have the children!"

"What was I thinking . . ."

"Don't be late, so you can enjoy them little."

Just looking at them was a pleasure. When you kissed them it was as if you could feel cool, invigorating spring water. Because something inside you, too, was coming loose; a thrill of happiness swirled around you, you could cuddle them, all they asked was to love you, and their disinterested affection had a calming effect. A wave of joy washed over you, and the children felt its spray in the form of kisses. They would rub their eyes. Before long they would say, "Mamie, Mamie, read us a story." You tucked them in, little birds in their nest. Then you opened a book. Milo and Léa listened. It was the story about the mouse that had lost a tooth, or the story of the pancake rolling through the forest, or the one about the hen going for a stroll; stories where grown-ups, reassuring figures, were never very far away, stories that ended happily after a certain number of incredible adventures. You would read, adding the tone: "A blanket of thick snow has covered the entire forest. A young deer has lost his way . . . how frightened he looks!" The next day, when their mother put them in the car, they waved their little fists out the car window. You watched them drive away, and you were tired and happy.

Every Christmas, you made it a point of honour to invite everyone. Xavier, Nathalie, Juliette, their spouses, their children, everyone was invited to come and celebrate. It was good to have them all there together again, four generations around the Christmas tree for a photograph that would then serve as a screensaver on your P.C. Your old mother, as still as a ghost, was in the process of passing into another world. She no longer managed to make her traditional cake but as you had the recipe down pat, yours was a perfect reproduction. When it came time for dessert the family ritual was met with cheers and applause. Then the old woman smiled, brought back for a moment to the side of life.

This feast was prepared long in advance. You ordered the meat from the meat section at the hypermarket. Everything had to be perfect, and for a long time now your lists had detailed the importance of each gift, of choosing the right cheeses, of bringing the wine to room temperature . . . Once everyone was there, Juliette, Nathalie, and your daughter-in-law, Maya, enquired whether you needed help in the kitchen.

"Oh, no, don't worry, I'm used to it."

"It's a lot of work, but I enjoy it so much."

It was four o'clock in the afternoon by the time you had your coffee. On the table there were still dozens of little sweets set out to tempt appetites, a young father went to fetch a baby who had woken from his nap, the older children played in the garden; and thus one thing led to another, with just the right amount of technological change to indicate the evolution from one year to the next:

"What a great app. You can see the train departures in real time."

"Is it the S.N.C.F. app?"

"Yes, it only costs ninety-nine centimes a month."

"Show me? It's this one?"

"See, I can display both Avignon central and Avignon T.G.V."

"That'll be really convenient for when there are strikes."

"I use it every time."

At the far end of the table you were telling your son-in-law how Nathalie had caught the measles as a child, and he replied:

"Léa picks up absolutely every virus!"

As for François, the year you gave him a laptop computer he could be seen wandering around the garden saying, "I've got coverage here", or "No coverage", depending on the range of the Wi-Fi.

The hypermarket on the *route nationale* was replaced by a discount store.

The colour of the dustbins changed with the new intermunicipal links.

*

On the occasional Sunday Fabien from the cycling club would come by for an aperitif. When his wife was with him, you played a game of Coinche.

"After three months, the clutch started slipping again. It was constant, all the time, you can't imagine the amount I spent in repairs."

"Even the dealer agreed, he said as much: they do it so that people will spend to have regular services."

"If you ask me they're going too far, a good old saloon car, even a 207, you never got ripped off the way you do nowadays."

François scooped his hand into the bowl containing the olives.

"That radar thing is nothing but an organised racket."

"They are stuffing themselves, up there, just stuffing themselves."

You were sorry not to see Milo and Léa more often. Their presence kept that dangerous hour at bay. When they were there, you no longer thought about your lists, except to write a note of the sort "return baby bottle to Nathalie". You cleaned the house, lit the fire. François poked the logs. A smell of wood fire filled the living room; these were gentle moments; you would leaf through a magazine, he would listen to the radio, attention already distracted by the onset of sleepiness. You might suggest:

"It's going to be a fine weekend, we could go for a walk in the woods with the children."

"That way they won't get up to any mischief in the house."

"You say that as if you were the one who tidied up . . . They need to run, it's their age . . . Do you feel like coming with us or would you rather go out on your bike?"

"I'll come with you."

"But before I forget, we need both car seats. We don't have them."

"We don't?"

"Well, no, you know, we left Milo's in Nathalie's car for Justine."

"She has to get it back to us before she leaves."

"Give her a call."

"But wait, it's not that simple, because she needs the car for work, she'll be gone by then."

"She'll have to take it out this evening."

"It's a bother to ask her to take out the car seat, for all we know the car is already parked."

"You're right, I'd better ring them right away . . ."

Etc.

François had retired at last. He went to see friends who were ill, he was involved with his sports club, he looked after your life insurance. When he came back you sat for a moment by the fire. You had seen your mother, you had watched the children, you had done a little shopping, *if we want something to eat tonight.* You would chat while you did your knitting; just as your mother had during your pregnancy, while waiting for other lives to be engendered; a little blue bonnet.

V

In your memory the years, once full of contrasts which enabled you to distinguish them easily, were all about to fade into the same tonality. There were new births, there was Xavier's divorce, there were the times you bought a new car, but what you remember above all is that awful morning.

Still sleepy, you went down from the bedroom. You wanted to switch on the television, and started hunting for one of the three remotes that ordinarily stayed on the table, and there were none. You rubbed your eyes and looked over at the television console. A streak of dust marked the spot where the television normally stood. Failing to understand, you saw a cupboard door that was open, an object on the floor, then you looked again at the absent television. And your heart leapt: someone had been in the house during the night!

Your cry was instinctive:

"François!"

Your husband did not have time to get up.

"We've been burgled!"

As he told the story later, when you were describing the scene to your friends, François had imagined something far worse; fire, assault, that was how terrifying your cry from the hallway had been. But that was it; there was nothing to be done now other than to wander through the house in your pyjamas and take note of everything that had been stolen, and you said, "Oh please, not that!" when you saw your cameras had disappeared, along with the D.V.D. player, your cash, and your mobile phones, and François was silent to begin with, then said, his gaze circling the walls:

"We have theft insurance."

"We have to call the police."

"We have to block our credit cards."

How could the burglars have got into the house? A broken bolt set you on the track. The lock to the garage door had been picked, which gave access to the hall, then to the entire house.

"You see, it was the garage. Dear God, that door! I told you to fix it!"

The gendarmes came. They were two women, and they left again very quickly, without leaving you much hope regarding any eventual elucidation about the breaking and entering. To calm down you decided to go and see all the neighbours, something François had always advised his own clients to do after such an event. They listened from over the gate with sympathetic expressions.

"We're very glad you've warned us, we'll double-lock the doors."

"It happened to me, it's a nasty moment to get through, you feel quite naked."

"Of course the police couldn't do anything . . . And even if they catch them, I'll bet you they won't put them in jail . . ."

True to his habits, François saw the positive side of things.

The burglars had not gone upstairs and they had not taken any jewellery or the passports. But it wasn't the theft that disturbed you the most, you could buy everything again. What drove you mad was the thought that while you were asleep strangers had been walking around your house. And now the moment you closed your eyes, you could see them, those burglars, you imagined demonic individuals parking their van outside number 12, opening your poorly closed gate, going up to the garage, and with three precise gestures breaking the door. Was it a gang? Or was there just one intruder? The police officer thought there must have been two of them.

"It's not profitable for them to be more than two, with this type of crook."

You saw them break the ridiculous lock (for which you secretly cursed François), then take a torch out of their bag, and make off with your familiar belongings while you were naïvely sleeping; you pictured them, those thieves; they yanked out the stereo cables, they dirtied your interior with their congenital filth, their very breathing, slipping an agile hand into your handbag they entered hidden recesses and dug about, they stole your wallet; the most unbearable moment, your thoughts came to a halt, your stomach was in a knot. You woke up in the middle of your nap, and the woman gendarme's words came back to you:

"Those people are like a virus; the slightest weakness and they force their way in."

"And besides, with all those housing estates they built at the entrance to Empan . . ."

In spite of the reimbursement from the insurance, you could

not the erase the images from your mind. Your entire house seemed soiled.

And so you started cleaning the way others start drinking.

You could no longer stand the slightest speck of dirt on the floor. You would rather not see a single mote of dust drifting upon the sunbeams that came into the room from the French windows, to fracture against the side of the coffee table then rise again towards the sofa; the same yellow rays that caressed your face while you lay on the sofa for your nap.

When you saw infinitesimal molecules sparkling in the ray of light, it was like a provocation. You prepared to wash the floor, you had to upend the chairs, then sweep, then fill a bowl with hot water, add some detergent, soak the floorcloth; holding fast to your scrubbing brush you slid it over the entire surface of the room. It smelled good. The bleach would act, it would remove all the tiny germs. Then you ran sponges over the furniture, small sponges and big ones, with or without Scotch-Brite. They had come up with various sizes of scrubbing brushes and mops, and then there was the hand brush. You had noticed that without a wide hand brush and a good-quality dustpan – that is, one that had a little flexible plastic rim – you never got off to a truly good start with your housecleaning; what started badly finished badly. You could have used a vacuum cleaner, you'd had several different models, old ones with a long hose, right up to the bagless *special turbo*, but they were too heavy for you now. Often it was more convenient, to do the housecleaning, to stick with a good broom, a good hand brush and a floorcloth. Once the tiles gleamed with cleanliness, then you could have your nap. But now, with your eyes half closed, as you were trying to fall asleep, you happened to notice strange streaks in your eyes, filaments that would vanish when you tried to look at them. When you did manage to look at one, it reminded you of long-ago biology classes, the odd experience of examining a hair beneath a microscope, something translucent and fibrous moving across your field of vision, a wooden twig floating in one direction, then the other.

In the distance, as always, there were birds; a car alarm; winter, and then summer.

It was as if dirt had become a noise and every day you were struggling to restore silence to your house. In vain, because in just one day the floor would be dodgy again. It was as if an evil genie was hiding beneath a tile and secreting the dirt that went to infiltrate the space between the wall and the dresser; a spot which, even with a vacuum cleaner, was difficult to reach. And on the rare occasions when you had people round for dinner, when one of the guests reached casually for a cocktail biscuit and raised it to his lips, you saw a shower of crumbs fall along the way; only your desire to *be the perfect hostess* prevented you from sweeping the floor there and then; it would have been much simpler however, because afterwards it was so irritating to see the children crushing the crumbs then spreading them multiplied tenfold throughout the living room, exactly like an epidemic spreading, through negligence.

"Did you see that the sporting goods shop on the diversion has closed down?"

"Oh, really, and what's there now?"

"Nothing."

"Nothing at all?"

"You know, there are a lot of empty shops over that way. With the crisis . . ."

"Do you remember how in the old days there used to be a video club?"

"Oh, yes, we used to go there on Sunday evening with the children. They liked doing that. After that, François used to download films. Now they watch them on the computer."

"In any case, I think there are too many television channels. You get lost."

"I always watch the same ones. The same ones as before."

"That's true. Four or five, more than that and I can't keep up."

"And anyway, when you see the sort of programmes—"

"Oh, golly, it's dreadful."

"And so vulgar. When I think that Milo and Léa grew up with all that."

"What are they up to, have you had any news this week?"

François had never been talkative, and with age he spoke even less. These were conversations you had with Chloé, the two of you at her place. But, as was bound to happen one day, your oldest friend vanished from your life. After several episodes where she was bedridden with sciatica, then overwhelmed by rheumatism, Chloé finally agreed to move into a residence to be near her children. Her daughter came to fetch her with the car. Through the window, the two seventy-year-olds you had become waved to each other. You promised to visit, but from that day on it would be telephone calls that brought you together; even though it was no longer the same thing.

That same year your mother died of a pulmonary embolism. She had been in hospital for two weeks, you had been with her, holding her hand *right to the end*. Losing her was immensely painful.

"You can become an orphan at any age."

After you had dealt with all the paperwork for the inheritance, you got into the habit of going to replace the flowers on your parents' grave every Sunday. It got you out of the house. Near the cemetery there was an insalubrious little cottage where an old man with a beard lived. Every week as you walked along the wall, you felt sick on seeing that hovel of his. The man didn't seem sad, something almost consoling, almost attractive emanated from his person. Several times you were tempted to go up and speak to him but you didn't dare. You went over to row F. Once you'd filled the flower vase with water, you stood next to the marble, your arms hanging at your side as if you wished for a voice from on high to come and give you instructions for the week ahead. Nothing came, obviously, and you wrenched yourself away from the grave with a shudder. The cemetery extension had never been very far from the house.

To make sure that the rubbish chute did not overflow, you pulled out the bin liner before it was full. This always made you flinch with disgust because despite the care you took in throwing the rubbish right into the middle of the bin, the negligence of other people's hands meant the top of the bag always oozed with some dodgy liquid. You closed it then sent your husband to the container. He took the opportunity to smoke a cigarette. Rather unwise, at his age.

"If we listened to the doctors we wouldn't do anything anymore."

In the meanwhile, you checked to see whether any peels had stuck to the bottom of the bin.

"If they do, it leaves a smell and it is dis-gus-ting!"

You said, your voice catching on the high notes.

You unfolded a new bin liner, put some newspaper in the bottom: it helped to absorb the moisture from the waste, and prevented any liquid from accumulating and bursting the bag (so you explained to Milo, who teased you). You used to change the sheets every month, then every fortnight, now every week; you said it was unhealthy to keep the same bath towel for long, and you obliged your old husband to put his in the dirty laundry.

"But, Mamie, don't go doing so many loads of washing, you're wearing yourself out for nothing!"

"Mind your own business, I'm not senile yet."

Yet you enjoyed it when they worried about you. You could hear them talking behind your back when you went into the kitchen for the coffee.

"Just wait, a few more weeks and the trauma of the burglary will be behind her, you'll see . . ."

One day a black cat began stealing food from the patio. You felt sorry for the beast, and tamed it. François called him Moustache. At first the animal would pretend to stay in the kitchen, then sensing his adoptive masters' indulgence, he ventured into the living room and by evening he finished cosily in your lap. The children made fun of you, saying, "You have to put your foot down!" but they liked knowing the cat was there, a presence for their old parents, since they couldn't always go to see them.

Your lists got shorter. You no longer had the energy to do very much. On certain mornings in April, when the air was once again clear and mild and made you want to explore wild open spaces, you were caught between painful, contradictory urges. Because it is a mistake to believe that the years bring an amnesty; right to the end desire, imagination and anxiety continue to burrow into the foundations of our lives. How difficult it was for you, for example, to look in the mirror at the old woman you had become. You had once been so beautiful, and now your eyes were sunken in their sockets: they frightened you. Your skin marked with dark spots, sagging with wrinkles: when you looked close, it was terrifying.

Ironing was one activity that calmed you. You started with the laundry piled higgledy-piggledy to your left on the table. You unfolded an old blanket and took the garments one by one from the pile. The distilled water gave a clear gurgle as it went into the bowels of the iron up to the level indicated. Then you began. Ironing out the creases from each pair of trousers gave you a simple feeling of contentment. The ten-thirty soap was on the television, you set the iron upright on its base. An hour later, the clothing was neatly piled to your right. The morning was nearly over. The time it would take to fill out a few forms and you'd be ready for lunch.

In summer you ate out of doors. When you replaced your old plastic garden table with a teak one, you realised that you had risen on the social ladder. Thirty years ago you would have looked only at the lowest prices at the garden centre; now you chose items from the top of the range, highly resistant rot-proof wood. In the winter you ate in the kitchen.

And yet there were some things that were impossible to clean, the hob in particular. Around the gas burners or, worse yet, around the electric hot plate, there was always a ring of black grease that grew darker whenever the milk overflowed or the oil splattered. Over time these marks had formed a sort of crust that was impossible to get rid of, you would have had to change the appliance, but you refused: you were *used to things*. In that fine black magma around the hob, never annihilated despite your efforts, you saw time. You saw your entire past accumulated there, all those meals you'd eaten together, all those hours spent in the kitchen, as a couple, with the children, the grandchildren, then again the two of you, and soon enough, alone: as if your entire life had been precipitated into these traces of dirt.

After the meal you drank your coffee and read the newspaper. On days when the postman brought you a postcard, with thick eyeglasses you deciphered what your grandchildren had written; didn't they get around! Then you went and put the card on the fridge door. And sat back down. It was a quiet hour, conducive to melancholy. For a long time your mind was still; when you awoke from these miniature naps (outside, a shutter banged), you felt the contact of your hands against the plastic tablecloth. These hands had drawn flowers, dived into the sea, taken rice from boiling water, separated the egg white from the yolk, mixed flour and sugar, typed up management accounts, consoled children, touched men; and they preserved the trace of everything they had handled in this kitchen, everything that had been raw and which they had cooked, everything that had been whole and which they had sliced, everything that had been hard and which they had turned to porridge or soup by means of a knife; by means of effort.

Today these hands are holding a cardboard container of individual compotes, a green wrapper decorated with a computer-enhanced photograph – an apple and a chestnut against the leaf of a tree. You read: ANDROS FRUIT DESSERT, APPLE CHESTNUT FLAVOUR, and further down: PUT SOME FRUIT IN YOUR LIFE. The Andros company talks about the great care it has taken in preparing this dessert so that it will bring you all the benefits of a portion of fruit, and they recommend you eat at least five portions of fruit and vegetables a day; in accordance with regulations, these compotes contain neither food colouring nor preservatives nor artificial flavours, and if you want to play with us you can cut out the loyalty points to receive presents with the company logo on them.

And in the silence of the early afternoon, the refrigerator compressor begins to hum.

Only late in life, following certain events, do we become aware of what has been slowly changing day by day in our bodies and in our societies; overwhelmed by this discovery, it hits us like an explosion.

A fall in the street in Empan-sur-Nive was that event. So, we were well and truly old and, shaken by an abundance of fears, sensitive to the cold, what we sought more than anything was comfort.

When you emerged from *Les Urgences* you wondered where your life had gone, that vibrant rush of adventure that had been waiting for you outside your young girl's bedroom. Fortunately, a pedestrian had been there to help you, he called the fire department, "an elderly woman has fallen on her back", he had waited until they arrived and he reassured you. You had not spoken with a stranger for a very long time, "he must have been around twenty, a charming young man". On the stretcher you passed out. So that's all there is to it, to life, you thought on waking: family lunches on the patio; that day you'd gone swooping down the big dipper at the Luna park; a wedding bouquet; a swim in the sea; but then here they came, already, the crowd of your grandchildren's faces, and the profusion of images drowned the older memories in an immense sea from which nothing precise could surface anymore, other than a dreadful feeling of frustration.

The firemen took you home. Later, you took out the shoebox in which you had stacked your photographs. You found a thousand examples that were proof of family happiness. Simple scenes, which; you now realise; had been moments of plenitude. There was nothing else to expect, they were all there, François, Xavier, Nathalie, Juliette, all smiling on a Sunday spent skiing or an afternoon in the park. These photographs would never be glued into an album: there comes a day where one can no longer say, I'll have plenty of time.

Thus, you decided against further reminiscence, sometimes you mixed up their names, calling Léa Juliette, you were alone at home, your heart relented, even a short strain of music, a tiny flower, moved you. All you had to do was look at that almond tree, or even that cracked egg cup from Baux-de-Provence – which would still have its place in the kitchen after you died, convinced of its usefulness – for your pride to soften. You found life so moving that it was painful. They had carried you on a stretcher in the emergency vehicle, proof that you had to "be careful", "at your age . . .", "additional tests" . . . Because for M.A. old age had begun.

But before you declined further, you *got organised*. Nathalie ran errands for you, while for a long time you would go on ordering water, milk, and wine over the Internet, and have it delivered. This system was a relief to everyone.

"It's so convenient."

A number of gestures had become difficult for you, like getting tins down from the top of the cupboard; some of the shelves had been emptied, or their objects were moved to the edge. The lawn, like you, had grown tired, and in places the earth was bumpy.

When he was still alive, François had been in the habit of switching on the electric barbecue and putting the meat on the grill. You would eat together in silence. Salad, a glass of wine, a cigarette. Then he said:

"Isn't this the life, then?"

These are perhaps the words you will remember longest after his death – "Isn't this the life"; "Ah, tell me, this is the life" – to define what your husband was. He liked to tinker around the house, too. Back in the days, François had bought six solar-powered outdoor lights fitted with a sensor, and at night they lit up the flagstone path. On the rare occasions when your children brought you home after a celebratory meal, these cold pale lights would switch off automatically once you were through the door. Even when he was sick your husband had gone on tinkering about, "to be of some use". He didn't like going to the doctor's.

"That was his undoing."

"What's the point," he would say. "We're old, don't even try to understand."

When you got into bed at night, side by side, each of you reading a book, you always thought of the same image: your father and mother lying in bed when you went into the room for a goodnight kiss; he would be reading the newspaper, and she would be leafing through a novel; and there was something about that repetition, which would have made you shudder twenty years earlier, something which now, on the contrary, was reassuring; you switched off the light. You fell asleep holding each other closely.

But one day François would no longer be there. It was a very gentle death, while he was taking his nap.

"You seem very tired, you ought to go and have a rest."

"You're right, I'm going to lie down. Come and wake me before Nathalie gets here."

"See you later, my darling."

"See you later."

And thus one day; you become a widow.

All of a sudden François is projected far away, into a cemetery, into a conversation, into a picture frame. And at the same time, he becomes the person closest to you, the most intimate, the man in your life, the one who opens the way for you to death. In your sorrow, you cloaked him with qualities you had not often noticed when he was alive, François was funny, surprising, generous, tender, he was brave, he was jolly. During the funeral they sat you in Milo's car, the one that was right behind the hearse (you were, he recalls, on the motorway), and the young man heard you say these words:

"Oh, my François, how I'm going to miss him."

The saddest thing was eating alone, and the empty bed. Your husband had been the armour between the world and yourself, and now the slightest sound startled you. There was nothing surprising about the fact that several years later you would collapse in the street in Empan.

After dreaming sadly over these photographs for an entire

afternoon, you lacked the strength to put the shoebox away.

Someone was knocking at the door, it was Nathalie.

Everyone had been very frightened when they had got the call from *Les Urgences*. For a while your children stopped by more often. Your daughter commented on the photographs, laughed too loudly, took the shopping out of the bag, walked around the house, opened the refrigerator, put the dishes away, checked your supplies of medication. You let her scold you. On seeing her so restless, you would have liked to stop her and take her in your arms, tell her I love you, tell her thank you, but you didn't dare.

Entire afternoons were spent in nostalgia. You remembered the evening at the casino; in those days, you desired everything so strongly, you were so vibrant, so fulfilled, François put his hands on your hips, you were so intensely alive, both of you. Now when night fell, you struggled up the steps to the bedroom. For a long time you thought you could see your husband there, motionless, just as he had been after dying peacefully in his sleep. You sat on the edge of the bed, looking at the hollow left on the mattress by the imprint of his body. Frequently you cried, because it is a considerable loss when you no longer feel a warm body against your own, when you no longer hear the voice that called you by your name night and day.

In the morning Nathalie found you drowsing in the kitchen, sitting by the convector with Moustache and the humming of the fridge for sole companions. After the death of your husband, old age pushes you down several steps all of a sudden. White hairs sprout on your chin. You lose teeth. Your lips grow thinner. Through a phenomenon of atrophying tissue, the lower half of your face gets shorter, your nose gets longer. With age, the brain uses less oxygen, and your lungs lose some of their capacity; touch, taste, and smell are no longer as sharp, one loses one's balance more easily, then one day you will celebrate your eightieth birthday. Still fairly lucid, you will be surprised that this is you, this very old woman sitting in front of a round cake, and you will also be surprised by this sense of having another self.

"Oh, my darlings, how happy I am to see you all!"

During the week, the only cars to park outside number 12 chemin des Pins will be those of the private nurses from Valvoisin. They were helping you up the two steps from the patio to the kitchen. You were asking for your daughter.

"But she came by yesterday, madame, don't you remember?"

You will cling to what is unchanging: the baccalaureate results in the local paper, the fire station siren every first Wednesday of the month at noon, a cat miaowing by its plate.

And your son, so kind, comes to mow the lawn every month.

"But that's Milo your grandson, madame, not your son. You're mixing them up."

"What did you say?"

You will no longer go to the market without someone to help you. They will bring you your shopping. Before long, a stranger will be cooking for you.

You will say "I knew that" without remembering.

They will put a chair in the shower for you.

"Who are you? I won't open!"

The telealarm necklace is on the night table, Nathalie will scold you as she puts it back around your neck.

They wanted to *put you in a home*. Locked in a room, you cried out, enraged, "Help, I've been kidnapped!" They'd had to take you home, quickly. Since you knew you had been playacting, you will let them say, in your presence: "She's not really all there . . ." and that will be your last victory: to stay at home.

They will colour the OFF button on the remote control for the television.

The calendar in the hall will display the same springtime photograph all year long.

Nathalie will ask you to sign papers and cheques, you will let them dispossess you of all your worries.

You will find it difficult to eat.

You will fall a first time. A few days in hospital. A fog.

Once you are back at home, you will water your geraniums slowly, using the little watering can that Léa filled at the tap when she came to see you.

People will stop by. No-one has stopped by. Everyone has abandoned me.

You will lose the use of your voice.

One morning, you will have a fatal fall while getting out of bed. No-one will be there to pick you up, and two tears will remain hidden beneath the folds of your eyelids. The home help, as she taps you on the cheek – "Madame? Can you hear me, madame?" – is the one who will see those tears slip out and fall to the ground.

The funeral will follow; Xavier, Nathalie and Juliette will gather at the solicitor's. After setting aside the possibility of joint ownership, they will reluctantly opt for a sale; estate agents will come, potential buyers will visit, a bank account will be debited, a tree will be cut down, another pregnant woman will come to live under this roof, and everything will go on; won't it.

SOPHIE DIVRY lives in Lyon, France. Her novel *The Library of Unrequited Love*, a bestseller in France, was published in English translation by MacLehose Press in 2013. She was named one of Literature Across Frontiers' ten New Voices from Europe for 2017.

ALISON ANDERSON is a writer and translator. Her previous translations include works by Muriel Barbery, J. M. G. Le Clézio and Amélie Northomb.